BIBLIOGRAPHY

The Dash Hammond Series:

The Price of Being Neighborly
The Cost of Kindness
The Expense of Family
A Wealth of Women
A Reasonable Amount of Trouble
A Haunting at Marianwood
Old Sins

Short Stories:

Murder Under Sun
Anthology: *Derby Rotten Scoundrels*

If the Horseshoe Fits
Anthology: *Low Down and Derby*

The Long and Shorter of It
Anthology: *Mystery with a Splash of Bourbon*

OLD SINS

Old sins cast long shadows.

by

E.M. Munsch

Mystery and Horror, LLC
Clearwater, FL

OLD SINS
Trade Paperback Edition
E.M. Munsch, Author
Sarah E. Glenn, Editor
Copyright © 2022 by Mystery and Horror, LLC
Published by Mystery and Horror, LLC

ISBN: 978-1-949281-28-6

This is a work of fiction. Any resemblance to any actual person living or dead, or to any current location is the invention of the author's creative mind. Historical events and persons are entirely fictionalized within the bounds of what can be imagined without contradiction to known facts.

OLD SINS

Old sins cast long shadows.

Dedication

For Lawrence Block, Master storyteller whose books have brought me much joy and entertainment. Thank you for creating the bookselling burglar, Bernie Rhodenbarr, a very 'stalkable' man.

CHAPTER ONE

"Again, Owen, tell me why I'm driving you to Cleveland." Dash Hammond said to his father. "I'm not sure I remember this lady. You said she is some sort of cousin."

"She's a cousin to your mother; second, third, fourth or fifth however many times removed," Owen said.

"Was she removed from the family or just Ireland?" Dash asked laughing. He glanced at his father and caught him rolling his eyes.

"Both, if my memory serves me. The story goes she was such a pain in the ass her family bought her a one-way ticket to Cleveland. I bet there was quite a send-off at the dock when they loaded her on the ship." Owen shook his head. "A black day for the United States when she arrived. Bet she stepped off the boat complaining about the trip, the food, and even her new country. Never met a more mean-spirited woman. And she latched on to your mother who, as you remember, was the sweetest woman around."

Dash glanced at the side mirror as he changed lanes. He checked the GPS. They were almost there. Exiting the freeway at West 41st Street, Dash turned left heading toward Lake Erie. The address of this Cousin Maud was off Bridge Avenue. He negotiated the side streets and found her house.

If he remembered his history correctly, this part of Cleveland had been a destination for many of the Irish immigrants. As he glanced around, he realized the neighborhood was part of Historic Ohio City, the revitalization of the near west side. The housing was a mix of high-end refurbished homes and original houses now needing TLC. Even the value of the old untouched homes had risen considerably.

Dash pulled his truck to the curb.

"Okay, Owen, you never answered my question. What are we doing here? And more specifically, why am I here?"

Owen squirmed in his seat. He nodded. "Well, my son, we are both retired and have plenty of free time, so no really good excuse *not* to help Maud. And I'm guessing you don't remember this, but she adores you. You and your dimples."

"Oh shit, she's the lady who always pinched my face when she came to visit, which thankfully, wasn't often." Dash's head fell forward in dismay. "Okay, now, why are we here *today*? Give me some idea or I'm not getting out."

"You were always a difficult child and now you're a difficult adult." Owen turned to face Dash. "Maud called me Saturday afternoon to say something odd was going on. As a former sheriff, she thought I should at least check this out. I told her I couldn't get here until today since I had medical tests scheduled with prep work involved. Anyway, I brought you along for company and laughs. You always have a peculiar take on things." He sighed. "Don't worry. Maud won't be pinching your dimples. She is ninety now, and shrunk by a foot, so I doubt she'll be able to reach your face." Owen sighed, "She's been shrinking and dying since the day I met her at my wedding. Always something wrong with her, something that surely would prove fatal. Hate to be mean, but unfortunately it never was!"

They exited the car and stood on the tree lawn looking at Maud's house. Dash stared at it, wrinkling his brow. "I have the weirdest feeling I've been here before, like a million years ago. Stupid head injury, always reminding me that I can't remember anything clearly." He surveyed the house. It needed a fresh coat of paint; the lawn needed mowing; the roof probably leaked.

Dash turned to his father. "If she has a mower, I'll take care of the lawn. I don't suppose we could move her into a home or condo where she wouldn't have to worry about maintenance."

"If you do mow the lawn, be ready for a critique. Maud's always ready to tell you or anyone what they've done wrong. After each of your Ohio State football games, she would call and tell your mother all the things you missed. Your mother bore up well, though I could see smoke coming out of her ears. We never bothered to pass her comments on to you, figuring you might not appreciate them."

This had Dash laughing out loud. "Hell, I got enough critique from the coaches and my roomie, good ole Billy Mac." Now it was Dash's turn to shake his head. "Well, we'd better go in. I'd hate to disappoint Cousin Maud. I can only imagine what my sainted mother would say if we didn't help her cousin, no matter how many times removed from the family tree."

The men walked cautiously up the steps to the front door. The stairs and porch had several rotten boards. Dash made a mental note to see if there was a place nearby to buy lumber. He had the proper tools to do the repairs in his truck. Always prepared, and eager, to fix this, that, and the other thing.

He straightened his Ohio State sweatshirt. He wouldn't want Maud to think he didn't wear it proudly. He knocked on the door. No answer. He tried opening it, but not even a slight budge to it.

"Owen, wait here, and I'll go around back. Maybe that door is open. She does know we're coming, right?"

His father walked over to the front room window and peered in but the tightly pulled curtains offered no help.

"Yes, told her Saturday that we'd be here this morning. I'll keep knocking and calling her name; you do the same at the back. Stone deaf, for sure."

Moving cautiously, Dash stepped off the porch. As he walked, he shook his head at the state of the driveway where weeds poked through the asphalt. Being six-four, he looked into the windows on the side of the house. Unlike the front window which had heavy curtains, the ubiquitous Irish lace curtains covered these. Even so he couldn't see much other than stacks of papers and what could be plastic containers. He continued until he reached the back door. He turned the knob, surprised when it opened. He took one step inside and backed out. He knew that smell. Something or someone was dead.

He put his sleeve over his nose and entered. Flipping the light switch, he looked around. Nothing in the kitchen except rotting food. Flies were having a banner day. Mice and other critters scurried away. He rushed through the house not looking left or right, making for the front door. He walked into a table, knocking it over and then tripped over something on the floor but he didn't stop.

Flinging the door open, he pushed at his dad. "Owen, step back. I need fresh air. Hate to say it but Maud's 'dying since the day you met her,' well, she got her wish. Haven't found her but the stench is telling, though it might just be coming from the rotting food in the kitchen."

Owen shook his head. "Damn, I should have come right after she called instead of waiting." He exhaled loudly. "Well, let's see what's going on."

"Dad, what's done is done. She was over ninety, so death is likely." Dash took a deep breath and reentered the house with Owen on his heels. He left the door open for fresh air. He pulled the cords to open the heavy drapes. Dust motes flew through the air as the curtains parted. The window, very dirty, allowed just enough light to see the mess surrounding the men's feet.

"Holy guacamole!" Owen exclaimed. "She was never the neatest person, but this is insane." He slowly walked toward the staircase. "Maud's room is upstairs. I'll check."

"Stop, Dad," Dash yelled. "Look down, under the table. Unless I'm mistaken that is Maud's outstretched arm."

Both men crossed to the base of the stairs where they found her.

Dash turned the table upright and then joined his father squatting down beside Maud. He shook his head as he studied the almost skeletal woman on the floor. She wore a black sweatshirt with 'Eire' written across it. Irish to the end. His father had been right about how small Maud had become. She didn't appear to be much bigger than his four- year-old son.

His father reached for Maud's arm to check for a pulse, a matter of routine as there was no doubt Cousin Maud had crossed over to the other side.

Dash said a silent prayer, hoping she stayed there.

"Dead." Owen said as he studied her. "At least a day. Damn, wonder if she died right after we talked."

Dash motioned for his father to follow him outside. Owen pulled out his phone to dial 9-1-1.

Patting all the pockets on his vest and cargo pants, Dash pulled out a lighter but kept searching.

"What are you looking for?" His father asked.

"Old cigarette or cigar. Something to cover the stench. It's at moments like this I'm sorry I stopped smoking." He started down the steps. "Going to check the truck. If nothing else, I'll see what cleaning supplies I have. Not going to be able to stand being in the house unless I can get rid of the rotting meat. I'm sure I can talk the cops into that."

Owen nodded toward the street. "We're about to find out."

Dash turned to watch a black and blue pull up. Two uniformed officers stepped out. The taller cop, a huge Black man who looked fit enough to play any number of positions on the Cleveland Browns, nodded at Dash. The nametag said Rainbeaux, but Dash didn't see a bit of bright color on the man, around the man, anywhere.

"Sir, care to tell us what's going on? You called that there is a body inside. Is it Miss Grealis?" Rainbeaux asked Dash.

Dash extended his hand. "I'm Dash Hammond." He pointed to his father. "That's retired Sheriff Owen Hammond. And yes, the deceased is Maud Grealis, a distant cousin to my mother."

The cop looked from son to father. After a minute, he shook Dash's hand and said, "You're the military dude in the photo, aren't you?"

Dash did a double-take. "Say again?"

"Miss Grealis has your photo, dress blues and all, hanging on the wall in the living room. It's right between the

Pope and the Kennedy brothers. She always pointed at you and would explain how you single-handedly won the war."

Dash snorted. "You mean the one still going on. Poor Cousin Maud. Well, it's better than if she told you I was a bastard or son of a bitch. I'd have to object to sullying my mother's reputation."

The cop nodded toward his partner. "That's Lachman. We cover this area and usually stop once a week to see how Miss Maud is doing." He shook his head. "Nice old lady. Such a shame."

Owen arrived just as Lachman said, 'nice old lady.' Dash and Owen exchanged looks. Raising his eyebrows to his father, he thought they should check again to see if the body was Maud. 'Nice old lady' wasn't what she was called by those nearest, hardly dearest, to her.

More handshakes as Owen formally introduced himself to the officers.

"Gentlemen, shall we? I heard you tell my son that you stopped in to check on Maud. When was the last time you saw her?" Owen asked.

Lachman stepped forward to answer. "We were over here a week ago Saturday. She seemed a bit distracted but was happy for the goodies we brought." Seeing the look on Owen's face, he explained. "My wife is a terrific baker so, when she knows we're going to stop to see Maud, she makes a little extra. Saturday we brought sticky buns, as Maud called them." He chuckled. "For a woman with just a few teeth, she sure could devour food in a hurry."

Even though the front door was open, Dash prepared the cops for the stench. They gathered around the body staring at it. No question it was Maud.

Owen pointed out her crooked neck. "I think she fell down the stairs. That would also account for the bruising."

Dash moved back to stand in front of the window. He examined the staircase from afar, noting the undisturbed dust pattern on the steps. He was about to make a comment when Sarge Rainbeaux spoke up.

"It was my understanding that Miss Maud didn't go upstairs anymore. Remember her telling me how her knees gave out when she hit eighty. Had someone help move her essentials downstairs. Told me anything up there wasn't important and, after she was gone, they could throw it all out."

Dash motioned to the men. "Gentlemen, step back over here. Look at the stairs. I don't see any dust disturbed so unless Maud used her broomstick to go up and then fell off when she came down …"

Lachman became indignant. "Sir, mind your manners. Don't speak ill of the dead. You may not have liked her, but she always spoke highly of you. She was a good woman. Always helping out at the church. And, I say again, she always spoke highly of you."

Before he could continue, Owen spoke up more loudly than he intended. "Oh Lord, the church. We need to have her blessed. How could I have forgotten that?"

Dash held up a finger indicating 'wait a second' and he strode into the kitchen. He pulled off an old church bulletin taped to the doorjamb next to the wall phone. He hurried back to the other room. "This is from St. Patrick's; probably her parish, as it's in the neighborhood."

Lachman nodded, so Dash phoned the rectory. He explained the situation and announced that a priest would be here shortly.

They moved outside to get away from the stench. The officers conferred with Owen and called Homicide. Not necessarily a suspicious death but better to make sure nothing was overlooked.

Dash pulled Owen aside. "I'm texting Mae to say we will be later than I thought. We might even spend the night in Cleveland." The quick visit he anticipated faded, thinking it might take all night to clean up the kitchen. He shivered just thinking of that mess. Cousin Maud wasn't the only one with a quirk or two. Cleanliness was one of Dash's.

"Officer Rainbeaux, would it be okay if I did a little cleanup in the kitchen? No ransacking like what happened in the living room. Just want to remove the rotting food, open a window. Promise not to disturb anything pertinent. Was Maud just a messy housekeeper? Maybe she had a heart attack trying to clean the place."

"Give it a minute. Detective Kraft will be here shortly. It's his call. Don't need him chewing my ass off. Had enough of that in a different life."

Dash smiled. "Read you loud and clear. Marines or Army? You have a military look about you. I should know after almost thirty in the Army." Dash smiled.

"Eight years, Army. Most spent as an M.P. so this seemed like a good fit post-career. This will sound stupid, but I fell in love with a woman who wouldn't leave Cleveland. Go figure."

Dash wondered whether the falling in love was the question or the woman not wanting to leave Cleveland. He decided not to pursue it as an unmarked car pulled up and Detective Kraft, he assumed, exited the car.

Kraft tripped immediately, causing Dash to study the cop. He was a lean man with unkempt hair. He wore black-rimmed glasses which magnified his eyes. His Cleveland Browns tie was askew and spotted with remnants of previous lunches. The overall effect would make Columbo look like he belonged on the cover of *GQ*. Kraft's step was lively, like he was happy to have a body to examine.

"Don't let appearances fool you. He's one sharp dude. Puts all his effort into solving the case, not looking good," Rainbeaux whispered.

"Disarming, I'm sure."

Introductions were made. The men moved back inside the house. The smell, still noxious, had dissipated a bit with the open door.

Dash leaned against the wall. His head knocked against something. Turning, he saw the infamous picture of himself taken when he received his commission as a major. He shook his head wondering why his mother, and it could only have been her, sent this to Maud. He shrugged as Kraft glanced his way saying, "Nice photo."

He joined Owen and Kraft as they discussed the reason for the visit to Maud and whether her death was suspicious or just sad.

A knock on the door jamb turned everyone's head. A priest stood there, waiting for permission to enter.

"Oh my God," Dash shouted as he crossed the room.

"Only His servant, not the Man himself."

Dash enveloped the priest in his arms, patting him on the back. "Damn, Pat, good to see you."

They turned to see the police staring at them.

"Gentlemen, may I introduce Father Patrick McCafferty? He's an old neighbor and a cousin."

The reverend nodded to all. "Where is Maud? I would like to take care of business if I may."

"You may if you can stand the stench. Please don't touch the body, Father." Kraft motioned to follow.

"Understood," Father Pat said as he pulled out his stole and stood over Maud beginning the prayers for the deceased.

Owen and Dash moved to his side, bowing their heads. The police officers stayed back but stood respectfully.

Prayers completed, Father Pat glanced around at the living room. "Anyone want to tell me what happened here? Maud wasn't the best housekeeper in Cleveland or the world for that matter, but this mess is as unholy as it gets."

CHAPTER TWO

Dash motioned for Owen and Father Pat to join him on the porch. "Let Kraft get on with his work so maybe we can get on with ours." Before leaving the room, he turned to the detective asking, "Sure I can't have just ten minutes to clean up the kitchen? The only crime committed there is one of slovenly housekeeping."

Kraft slowly shook his head. "Hold your horses, Hammond. This won't take long. Why don't you and your relatives get a cup of coffee? There's a nice little café at the West Side Market. Start your day off right. I'll call when we leave."

Dash scowled but made his way down the steps to join his dad and the priest. He yelled to the detective, "Hey Kraft, just make sure you don't leave a bigger mess than there already is."

Kraft's response was a one-finger salute which left Dash laughing.

As the men walked to Dash's truck, a boy of eleven or twelve accosted them. After wiping his nose on his sleeve, he asked, "Is the old lady dead? I figured she was too mean to die, but my ma says everybody dies no matter what."

Dash addressed the boy. "Listen here, Oliver, my boy. Show some respect for your elders, mean or not. Yes, you can report back to your ma that Miss Grealis has indeed passed. And why aren't you in school?"

The boy sneezed and again wiped his nose on his sleeve. "Got a cold. My room is up there and I watch everything that happens on the street. Saw you pull up in that shiny truck of yours and then the police. Got nosy, that's all."

Handing the boy a handkerchief, Dash said, "Use this to wipe your nosy nose and return to your bed, but keep watching. If anyone comes to the house after the police leave, give me a call. You do know how to work a phone, right?" He gave the boy his card and a five-dollar bill. "Back to bed with you, Oliver."

"Hey mister, my name ain't Oliver, it's Leon."

"Really! You sure look like Oliver Twist to me."

After finding a parking spot close to the bustling West Side Market, the men repaired to the recommended café.

The shoppers hurried around to the various stalls. Dash thought back to the European markets he visited while stationed abroad. "Man, it has been forever since I've been here. Hasn't changed much though. Still an incredible building. I understand it's on the historical register or something."

Owen inhaled deeply. "Your mother always stopped here after visiting Maud. She would bring home the most delectable baked goods. I'm going to wander around a bit. Just coffee for me. Be back in a bit."

"Take your time, Dad. You know cops. 'Hurry up' isn't in their vocabulary."

He studied his cousin and long-ago playmate, Father Pat McCafferty. "Okay, Padre Pat, spill the beans on Maud."

Father Pat leaned back in his chair. "St. Patrick's was my first posting after ordination, so I saw Maud often at church. Now, the current pastor is my best friend which is why I stopped there before the planned visit to Maud. You know the Irish: even though my mother wasn't fond of Maud, she always insisted I stop to visit. Frankly, I think she was just being nosy."

"I hadn't seen Maud in forever. She was at my mother's funeral, but I don't remember much. Still reeling from the brain trauma. Would you say what we saw at Maud's was usual?"

"Hell, no. She wasn't the tidiest of women. In fact several years ago, I hired a cleaning crew to help her. She ran them off her porch waving a broom. Next time I visited she almost parted my hair with the same broom. Decided it was best not to interfere. She was who she was."

Dash leaned in. "Between us, what do you think happened to Maud?"

"Heart attack or stroke. Don't think anyone broke in to steal anything. Even at first glance you could see there's nothing there." He added cream to his coffee. "Don't suppose she has any relatives back in Ireland, or maybe even here in the States, who should be notified?"

Dash shook his head. "You would know better than me, but I'll check. You're right. Someone somewhere cares and needs to know."

They sipped their coffee. Owen rejoined them, carrying several bags of goodies.

Dash jumped when a set of keys dropped onto the table.

"There you go, Mr. Clean. The house is officially NOT a crime scene," Kraft said, pulling out a chair to join them.

"We found her heart pills. The prescription is two months old, but only a few taken." Kraft shrugged and continued, "I decided it was easier to let you clean the place than have my men do it. But I do have to ask, what's with the cleanliness crap?"

"A defective gene, for sure. Add a helping of OCD and a shitload of PTSD. The Army was a perfect fit for me. I can give you the name of my therapist if you want," Dash said.

Kraft stood. "No, no. But, if by some odd chance, you find something that suggests a crime, promise me you'll give me a shout." He threw his card onto the table.

Dash raised his right hand. "I promise. And thank you." He turned to his father and the priest. "Gentlemen, I think that's our cue to get busy."

After a quick, but necessary, stop to gather cleaning supplies, especially air fresheners and garbage bags and cans, they pulled into Maud's driveway.

Dash glanced at Leon who sat on his porch rather than on his bed. The boy gave a thumbs up.

The men started the unloading process when a black Mercedes pulled next to the curb.

Dash smiled broadly, thinking of its occupants. "Owen, Pat, we have visitors."

The car doors opened. Out stepped wife Mae, son T.J., and niece Kathleen.

"Daddy, Grandpa, surprise, surprise!" T.J. shouted as he waved.

After making a big deal about looking both ways, Mae, T.J., and niece Kathleen crossed the street.

Dash bent down to scoop up his four-year-old son, giving him a big hug.

"Are you surprised, Daddy? We decided to come and help you. Mommy said we could go swimming tonight at the hotel. Won't that be fun?"

"Hotel? So we're spending the night," he said to Mae in mock surprise. He knew how she loved hotels with spas and shopping.

"Kathleen, why aren't you in school?"

Before she could answer, T.J. said, "Daddy, they can't use the bathrooms, so all the kids got sent home. Kablooie, the pipes exploded, and water went everywhere. Isn't that right, Kathleen?"

T.J. threw his arms open wide in a gesture demonstrating the explosion and caught his father's chin. Dash promptly set the child down.

"Whoa, take it easy, little butt."

He looked at his niece. "Is that right? Kablooie?"

Kathleen laughed. "Yes, sir. School is cancelled but we have those stupid online assignments, of course," she said with a shrug. "I offered to come along since Mae said it sounded like you and Gramps could use extra hands."

T.J., Kathleen, and Mae all held up their hands.

Dash kissed his wife's cheek and reached around to pat her backside. "I guess a night in a hotel is payment for all the hard work you'll be doing. And this was quick. What'd you do?

Leap into the car when we hung up? And don't tell me, our good neighbor Annie gets the dogs for the night."

Mae nodded to her husband, then winked at Father Pat. "I heard there was a good-looking man here so of course I jumped in the car. These two tagalongs are just for fun." She stepped over to peck the priest's cheek.

Dash clapped his hands. "Everyone, thrilled you're here, but this ain't getting nothing done."

Owen joined his son. "As the colonel would say, let's get on it."

Dash frowned and asked his wife. "Do I say that?"

Mae shook her head. "No, but let's get on it anyway."

Dash passed out cleaning supplies. When they approached the door, he said, "Be forewarned. The stench is overpowering. And the mess incredible."

"The body is gone, right?" Mae asked. She opened the door and jumped back. After covering her nose, she turned to Dash. "Sure two days is going to help? Thinking I might decide to go shopping instead."

"What a wuss, Doctor Summers. Get your act together. Dead body, rotting meat, you'd never make it in the Army."

"Dead body? Daddy, can I see it?" T.J. asked. His eyes grew wide with anticipation.

"Gross, T.J. Why do you want to do that?" Kathleen cringed. "Think I'll wait in the car."

Dash held up his hand. "Sorry, T.J., the body is gone. The police took Cousin Maud away. Don't worry, we'll find another one someday."

Mae's mouth opened in shock. Knowing his wife well, he added, "What I meant to say is we'll probably find a dead animal someday, and we can study that." He nodded toward his wife. "When your mommy was little, she always investigated dead things; said it would help her when she became a doctor. Isn't that right, Mommy?" he said with a smirk.

Owen stopped the nonsense with a quick command. "Dashiell, Maevis, behave yourselves."

Dash resumed his mission. "Yes, sir. Right. Pat and I will do the heavy cleaning in the kitchen. That okay with you, Father? Mae, you and Kathleen take Maud's bedroom over there. T.J., you'll be Grandpa's sidekick."

Owen raised his hand. "If I may interject: we are looking for any type of legal paper, even if it's just a scrap. Maud asked me to be the executor of her estate after Helene-Marie died, a passing of the torch. Help me out, please."

Assignments assigned, the crew started working.

Dash and Father Pat donned masks and gloves. "Padre, you start in the pantry. Check expiration dates. If anything is still good, you can take it to whatever food bank you like."

Dash looked at the putrefying food. "Guess I'd better get going after all the grousing I did."

Working silently, the men accomplished a lot in a short time. The countertop was cleared of rotting food and mice droppings. Bleach liberally poured over everything in sight.

"Dash, do you have any bags or boxes for all this? Surprisingly not much was out of date. St. Patrick's food bank will be pleased with this donation." Father Pat had filled the small kitchen table with cans and boxed food.

"Check the truck. I usually have a few. I'll start on the refrigerator. Going to toss everything in it and the freezer as well."

After cleaning out the refrigerator, Dash emptied the freezer, studying each packet of meat. Someone had taken a lot of effort to label each piece with date purchased. He noted the writing was not that of an old lady. Wonder who the good Samaritan was?

When Father Pat returned with the bags, Dash pointed to all the meat on the table. "Check out the writing. Pretty sure it's not Maud's. Would your buddies at the rectory eat this? This is an awful lot for one little old lady. A lot of chicken and beef and some of the obligatory Irish mutton."

After inspecting the cache, Father Pat said, "I bet one of the church ladies did that. Several of them would stop over to see what they could do. Strangely, Maud never got upset with them. Probably because she could boss them around." He picked up a package labeled "Pot Roast." "Think I'll walk next door to the Bradys'. They have a bunch of mouths to feed so I'm sure …" He didn't have a chance to finish before Dash broke out in laughter.

"Seriously? The Brady Bunch lives next door. Wait 'til Mae hears that. She loved those reruns." He chuckled again and started singing the theme song.

After Father Pat left, Dash inspected a plastic bag he had pulled from the freezer. No label. Definitely not meat. He pried it open to find cash, very cold cash. Not a fortune, but several hundred dollars in small bills. He shook his head. Poor Maud, stashing money in one of the first places a burglar would look. He tucked the money into his back pocket. Might pay for dinner tonight though he knew he shouldn't just abscond with the money.

T.J. walked into the kitchen, sagging as low as he could and still move forward. "Daddy, I'm tuckered out. Grandpa is working me to the bone. Can't we just go swimming?"

Dash picked up his son, pecking his cheek. He carried him to the staircase. After brushing off one of the steps, he set the exhausted child down. "Sit here and I'll see if Mommy has a snack you can munch on until we head out." He glanced at his father who also looked bone tired. "Don't think we'll be here much longer. You're not the only one who is tuckered out. Hey Gramps, join T.J. in taking a break. I'll find snacks and water. Thinking we should call it quits soon, especially if we're coming back tomorrow. Agreed, old man?"

Owen nodded as he sat down next to T.J. "Maybe just another hour at the most, that okay, Dash?"

As he stretched his back, he said, "Fine with me. I could use a dip in the pool."

Calling for Mae, he walked to the bedroom.

His niece met him, sighing deeply and repeating, "Boring, boring, and even more boring. You owe me big time, Dasher." She held up those hands she waved earlier. "Ruined. Not made for manual labor. A mani-pedi on your dime."

"Poor St. Kathleen. Find snacks and water for your grandfather and T.J. Take a break."

"Maevis, our team is, and I quote, 'tuckered out.' Owen thinks he'll last another hour but I'm thinking we call it now and start again tomorrow."

"Before you go, take a look in the wardrobe and tell me what you see."

Dash stood before the cabinet, thinking he'd like to say a few smart things to his wife but wisely held his tongue.

"I'm a bit tired, my love. Why don't you *tell* me what I'm seeing before I lose patience with the love of my life?"

Mae chuckled, "Men, no stamina. Before you are six black dresses. If you were to examine the label, you will find that Maud, or someone, put the day of the week in each one. Still on hangers are dresses for Sunday through Friday. So have that detective check the dress Maud was wearing when she died. If it was the one for Saturday, that should give him, and you, a good clue as to the day she died. What do you think of that, Sherlock?"

"Brilliant," Dash said as he inspected the dresses. "Is this all there is? A few sweaters and one coat? Not much even for an old woman who never went out." He turned to see a small dresser across the room. Nodding toward it, he asked, "What's over there?"

"A few undies, though not labelled for the days of the week. And a collection of prayer books and rosaries. Haven't found her purse yet. Have you?"

"No, but I wasn't looking. Nothing unexpected in the pantry or refrigerator. Did find a bit of cold cash in the freezer but haven't looked in all the cupboards." He sat down on the bed to study the books on Maud's bedstand: Yeats, Joyce, and Heaney. The oddity was the poetry of Emily Dickinson, one page bookmarked.

Dash opened it and read aloud:
I'm nobody! Who are you?
Are you—nobody—too?

Then there's a pair of us!

Mae joined him on the bed, taking the book from his hand. "Good Lord, what do you make of this? Never would I have pegged her for thinking of herself as 'nobody.' Oh, if only your mother were alive to help with the mystery that is Maud."

Dash stood, holding his hand out to Mae. "Let's table that discussion for now. A meal and a swim sound better every minute. Let's help Owen pack up whatever he wants to take with him."

Back on the stairs, Owen, T.J., and Kathleen were falling asleep. Dash clapped his hands.

"Wake up. We're leaving now. First, Owen, do you want to take anything to the hotel? If yes, direct Kathleen. Mae, you're on windows. I'll lock up the kitchen and then secure the front door. I have caution tape I'll string over the steps."

Everyone turned when Father Pat knocked on the door. "Hey, just got a call from my parish, an emergency only I can fix. Good seeing all of you. Let me know if there is anything I can do to help with the funeral. Don't work too hard. See you soon."

"Thanks for all your help, Pat. Will be talking to you soon," Dash said. "And, hey, don't forget to see about relatives for Maud, other than us."

While Owen and Kathleen packed up scraps of paper which ostensibly could be the family history, Dash did one last walk-about. Everyone loaded into the vehicles to head to the Renaissance Hotel in downtown Cleveland.

CHAPTER THREE

The next day an almost rejuvenated crew arrived early to tackle the house once again.

Dash had on his work vest, pockets full with measuring tapes, pencils, and a small recorder. T.J. wore a similar pocketed vest, though he filled his with little cars and snacks. Mae and Kathleen wore tired expressions while Owen tried to look enthusiastic about another day of searching. The house still smelled but not as bad as yesterday.

"Kathleen, follow me. Let's head upstairs and see what's there." Dash said as he bounded up the steps. He waved to T.J. to join them.

The upstairs had two bedrooms and a bath. The dust fairy being the only visitor to these rooms.

"Daddy, can I play with my cars in this empty room. I'll be careful not to scratch anything."

"Have at it, kiddo. Try not to get *all* the dust on you." Dash turned to Kathleen. "And you, my pretty, look in the drawers, the closet and under the bed. Shout if you find anything. Maud's purse would be nice."

His niece nodded as she inserted earbuds and began swaying to the music.

Downstairs, Dash smiled at Owen and Mae, who sat sorting boxes overflowing with unopened mail.

"Heading for the porch to see what needs to be repaired for safety's sake."

Outside he pulled out his tape measure. He made notes on which steps needed replacing as well as any porch slats. Ah, tomorrow's job it is. And now for the kitchen cabinets and whatever they might hold.

Back inside, he asked, "How goes the search?"

"Nothing, not a bank statement or credit card statement among all this." Shoving the mound of envelopes aside, Owen asked, "You don't think she did online banking, do you? I mean she was older than me by a decade. If I hadn't had Helene-Marie, I wouldn't know whether I had a dollar or a million dollars."

Dash wandered the room. "Never understood that, Dad. I know you were busy but to not know how much money you had coming in, going out. Very uncharacteristic of such a detail man as yourself."

"Ah, but your mother was a wonderful house manager and accountant. Since I had to watch all the pennies spent by the sheriff's department, she volunteered to watch all our nickels and dimes. Did a damn good job of it too. And, sonny boy, it's not as if you keep a checkbook. Tommy Mac does all your accounting, pays your bills, and watches your investments, so don't start on me."

Mae sighed. "Gentlemen, it's unimportant. The bills get paid, end of story."

Dash leaned against the staircase, then moved again to Maud's first floor bedroom. "Now if I was a cranky old lady, slightly paranoid, where would I hide my important papers?"

Owen laughed. "You, a cranky middle-aged man, slightly paranoid, are the perfect person for that job. Have at it, Colonel Hammond."

"Love you too, dad."

His son walked over to Maud's exhibit of family photos.

"Did you or Kathleen think to take these down and examine them?"

"No, we were too busy cleaning and doing loads of laundry."

Dash picked a photo of the Hammond family, taken in the mid-Seventies from the size of him and his siblings. He turned it over to find scratchy handwriting naming the family and recording the ages. Running his hand over the back, he determined there was nothing tucked inside.

Another copy of the photo of the newly promoted Major Hammond, all decked out with his medals, hung in the bedroom. He wondered why she felt the need to have two, but on this one Maud had taped a small American flag. Flipping it over, he again saw the scratchy writing proclaiming his name, rank, and year. This time when he ran his hand over the back, he felt a lump, small but there. He slowly worked the backing off to find a key.

He walked back into the living room. "What do you think? Lock box at a bank or locker somewhere else?"

Owen fingered the key, "Bet it belongs to a jewelry box or a keepsake box hidden somewhere here in the house."

Mae took the key from Owen. "No, lock box at the bank. Just last week I got into ours at the bank and the key was slim and long like this."

Dash pursed his lips wondering what Mae had been doing at the bank. Pocketing the key, he decided to keep on message: find Maud's legal papers.

"Okay, gang, I'm going back into the kitchen and tear apart the cabinets. I glanced inside them but concentrated on cleaning up the food and stuff."

As he dried the last of the dishes, he felt a tug on his pant leg.

"Daddy, is this real money?" T.J. held out an Irish pound note for his dad's inspection.

Dash smiled. "I do believe it is real, at least for the time being. It's Irish money, T.J. Where did you find it?"

"In the floor of the almost empty room. Can I keep it, Daddy? It's pretty looking."

"Sure, finders keepers. Bet Cousin Maud just forgot to pick it up. Go ahead, buddy. Keep at it and one day you'll be rich."

Waving the pound note, he started up the stairs, T.J. stopped long enough to shout, "Look, Mommy, I'm going to be rich."

Owen and Mae smiled as they continued sorting mail. They worked in silence.

Dash joined them tearing up the cast-offs. He turned when he heard his son's footsteps on the stairs.

Glancing over he saw his son poke his hand through the railing.

"Daddy, is this a real gun?"

CHAPTER FOUR

"Don't move! Don't even breathe!" Dash shouted as he leapt toward the gun dangling from T.J.'s hand. He took the weapon from his son's hand and looked into the child's brown eyes, now filled with fear.

"You can breathe now," Dash instructed as he moved back across the room. He leaned his head against the door frame while he emptied the revolver. He muttered to himself, "Fuck! Damn, damn, damn. Hammond, you idiot. First rule. Recon before sending in the troops. You didn't even look past the dust. Somebody up there is watching out for T.J." He tucked the gun into his belt, the bullets into his pocket and willed himself to breathe slowly. Calm, calm, calm.

On the stairs, Mae cradled T.J. in her arms. The little boy's body trembled while he sobbed.

Dash wanted to wrap both of them in his arms, take them away from all this. But that ship had sailed.

"Owen, are you okay? You look a little pale." Dash asked his father.

"All our lives flashed before me. Where the hell did he get a gun?"

Father and son moved to the staircase. Dash knelt down so he was eye-to-eye with his little boy.

"T.J., you know I love you. We all love you, more than anyone or anything on this earth. I couldn't take it if something happened to you." He swallowed hard. "Having said that, what are you supposed to do when you see a gun?" he asked as calmly as possible.

The boy buried his head in his mother's shoulder.

"Thomas, answer your father. And I'm sure you know what you're supposed to do, so take your fingers out of your mouth, young man," Mae said firmly but gently.

Dash watched his son decide what to do. Finally, after taking a deep breath, the child faced his father.

"I'm supposed to call for a grown-up and not touch the gun." Building up steam, he said emphatically, "Daddy, I thought the gun was a toy. Are you mad at me?"

His father shrugged. "No, not mad at you. Very angry with myself. But I am *disappointed* in you. You may only be four, but you understand what you're told to do. I'm mad at myself for not checking in on you after you came down with the Irish money." He reached over to T.J.'s fishing vest, the one which, that morning, had toy cars and snacks in each pocket. Now currency, both Irish and U.S., spilled out of them.

Dash pulled out some of the money. "Was this on the floor? Where?"

Exasperated, T.J. said, "Daddy, I *told* you it was *in* the floor. Under the bed. My car rolled into this hole and when I crawled to get it, I found the money. After I showed it to you, I tried again to reach my car but found the gun."

All three adults asked simultaneously "*In* the floor?"

T.J. took his father's face into his hands, staring into Dash's blue eyes. "*In the floor*, Daddy!"

Owen frowned. "God … bless America. What the devil was Maud up to?" He sat down on a step. "Shit, shit, shit!"

"Grandpa! That's a bad word."

Dash pulled his son into his arms. "You haven't heard anything yet, my boy. Now show us this hole in the floor." He looked at Owen. "Lock the doors, please." To his son, "And just where was your cousin Kathleen all this time?"

"She's singing and dancing in the other room. She looks really pretty too," T.J. reported.

Mae tugged on Dash's shirt. "We're not very good at this parenting stuff, are we? Sweet Mother Mary, I could use a good cry about now. When we get home, you're throwing out all your guns, got that?"

"Not now, Maevis. And as you know, my weapons are secured, far from four-year-old hands."

He wrapped his arms around her. "They say girls are easier than boys so maybe we have a chance with this new babe coming. If they're wrong, we are so screwed and so are our children." He crossed his fingers behind his back, hoping girls were easier.

They climbed the stairs and walked into the not-so-empty room.

T.J. pointed to the bed. "I'm not strong enough to move it so I hafta crawl under it." Before he could continue, Kathleen drifted into the room wearing a fringed mini skirt and white go-go boots. She took the earbuds out and asked, "What's going on? Isn't this the coolest outfit ever?" She twirled around to let her audience get the full effect.

Dash shook his head. "Have you been changing clothes this whole time? Ever think to see what the little guy was doing?" He looked again at her outfit. "Must have been Maud's Halloween costume one year."

"Oops. What did I miss?" Kathleen grimaced. "Please don't say he got hurt."

Owen spoke up. "No, something worse. He found a gun and you can imagine the bad things that might have happened. Young lady, straighten up."

"Yes, sir, Gramps, sir."

"We'll fill you in later. Dash, move that bed and let's see this mouse hole," Owen said.

"Mice!" screeched Kathleen. "You never said anything about mice up here."

"Figurative, not literal. At least that's my hope," Mae said to her niece.

Dash shoved the bed aside to uncover a sizeable cavity. A very nice hidey hole cut into the floor; the lid had fallen into it. Dropping to his knees, he fished around, pulling out a more bundles of money. He tossed these over to Mae. He found more loose bills as the rubber bands had dried and fallen to pieces. Eventually he found the missing car which started all this.

Mae and Kathleen sat on the bed. They counted the bundles, including those taken from T.J.'s vest. The young boy knelt before them; his eyes widening as his fortune grew. "Daddy, can I buy a pony?"

Dash sat back on his haunches, stunned by the amount of bills on the bed.

Kathleen announced, "By my reckoning, each bundle contains $5000. With the loose bills tossed in, we have approximately a hundred grand. Cousin Maud obviously didn't trust banks. I've heard of putting money under your mattress, but in the floor!"

Owen picked up one of the bundles and shuffled through it. "Fifties and hundreds. Non-consecutive numbers." He rifled through the loose bills. "The printing dates on these are all over the place. Wonder how Maud managed to save all this. *If* it was Maud who put these bills in there."

Rubbing the back of his neck, Dash paced the room. "We've been looking in all the wrong places." He stopped. "New plan. Let's move the furniture and look for more hiding places. Don't forget the closets. Check for any loose floorboards and give the walls a good pat-down."

He muttered, "Wonder who took the boards up so the car could tumble in?" He glanced at his father. "Any ideas, Owen?"

Mae walked up to her husband. "I know that look and no, you are not staying here overnight to guard the place or keep searching, or whatever you think you might do. No, you are coming home with us. No further discussion needed." She folded her arms across her chest. "You are not responsible for this mess so don't think you have to clean it up, uncover whatever there is to uncover, got it?"

Husband faced wife and wife faced husband. A standoff.

"I am not ..." Dash said but his father stopped him.

"Son, hate to say it, but she's right. We'll need your help to get this home safely. Whatever else is in the house has been undisturbed this long; one more night won't matter. Tomorrow Sam is off and the three of us can come back and tear this place down if that's what you think needs doing."

Dash moved to perch on the bed. He let out a deep breath. "You're right about securing the money and the gun. And I should collect additional tools and supplies if we want to do the job right." Then he sneezed. "For now, let's get busy so we can head home at a reasonable time. We can't go out for lunch so, Maevis, dear heart, do that thing with your phone and find a place to deliver food and drink." He turned to Kathleen. "First, get out of that ridiculous outfit. If you want to take it, set it aside. In fact, set aside whatever else you want, and we'll inventory it at home." He narrowed his eyes. "Please tell me you did some proper searching before the fashion show."

"I did but all I found were tons of shoe boxes filled with receipts, bank statements and stuff like that. Very organized by year, but there must be a million of them. Well, almost ninety since she was ninety years old. Found a few purses but they're empty, or so they seem."

"Put the purses in the bag and we'll investigate those later." He turned to his father. "Owen, shoe boxes. Do we need to take them with us?"

Kathleen raised her hand. "Dasher, I did find one thing that seemed out of place."

Dash glanced at her outfit and almost questioned her 'one thing.' "Well …"

"There is an old suitcase full of clothes, but they can't be Maud's. Much larger, breath and width. And a pair of ghastly shoes. If I had to guess, I'd say they were your size. The luggage tag says Moira McGreevy. Know who that is?"

"Hell no. Right now, I'm not sure who I am. Take it downstairs. Might take that with us. Okay, gang, let's get on it." After uttering that phrase, he looked at Mae, who chuckled.

Dash felt a tug on his pants. T.J., with his lower lip protruding, "What do I do, Daddy?"

"You're my number two man. You're going to help me inspect the floors. Let's start in here. First, we'll need to replace the lid to the hidey hole, so the next person won't see it." He looked around, clapped his hands. "You all can start moving anytime now."

Mae smiled. "I just love it when you're so bossy." She pecked his cheek and patted T.J.'s head.

They finally took a break after searching high and low for any more hidey holes. Nothing, nowhere. The absence of more goodies made the cache more of a puzzle.

Over lunch, Dash and his father speculated about the origins of the money and what Maud intended to do with it.

"I can't believe she 'forgot' about it when she moved all her stuff downstairs. Do you think these are ill-gotten gains, planted by person or persons unknown without Maud's knowledge? But that again begs the question: how do you forget about a hundred grand and a gun? Why not retrieve it?" Owen asked.

"What about I.R.A. money? Damn, wonder if Maud had those leanings." Dash here turned to his father. "Remember that summer Billy and I went to visit Mom's family in Galway? Uncle Mick, the one I'm said to resemble, nearly put me through a wall when I offhandedly asked if he was a member of the I.R.A. The look on his face scared me shitless. Wasn't that frightened when facing ISIS or the Taliban." Shivering, he continued, "I still have nightmares about it. Uncle Jimmy pulled us apart and whispered to me that there was a late train leaving for Dublin. Billy and I were on it in a flash."

Owen rubbed his hand over his head. "Wish to God I knew the answers. Looking around, you can tell she lived frugally, and I do remember your mother saying Maud was working two jobs, which is why she didn't visit more often. After thanking God for whoever gave her the second job, I nodded sympathetically. Doubt that fooled your mother." He shrugged. "Maybe Maud just saved all her earnings from the second job. Still seems like a lot of money. And why the need for it."

"Well, we'll have to sort this out before T.J. spends it all. If it is ill-gotten, restitution needs to happen. If it's I.R.A.

money, we run like hell," Dash said as he crumbled up the remains of his lunch. "Don't know who inherits all this mess, but I pity the poor sod."

A knock at the front door stopped all conversation. Dash glanced around to make sure there was no money in sight. He opened the door. A woman stood before him, average height, brown hair, brown eyes. She wore the wrinkled face of a woman who worked hard, worried harder and found no relief doing either.

"Excuse me, I'm Cindy Brady, Maud's next-door neighbor. Are you—but of course you are." She pointed toward the wall and the infamous photo.

"Please come in, Mrs. Brady. Yes, I'm Dash Hammond, former soldier now reduced to cleaning out freezers. Let me introduce my father, Owen Hammond, and my wife, Maevis, son T.J. and niece, Kathleen." He looked around and pulled a chair over. "Please have a seat. We have a million questions for you if you don't mind."

Owen scrambled to clear off the chair. "Can we offer you something to drink? We're just finishing up our lunch."

She smiled and her face brightened. "Thanks, but no. You're Maud's cousins, right? She talked about you all the time when she was in the talking mood. More often she just complained about you, the neighbors, the city, the state, and the government."

Mae chuckled. "I had heard she was a bit of a misanthrope. I only encountered her a few times over the years. The last being at Helene-Marie's funeral six years ago. She always looked me up and down. I constantly waited to hear what I did wrong, was doing wrong, but she never complied. She was very good at telling you with her eyes you were wanting in some measure, but she never vocalized it."

At that, Cindy Brady threw her head back and laughed. "Well, you should have been here when she got home from one of her do's. She'd sit on the porch waiting for the unsuspected to pass by. Calling them up to sit with her, she then wailed on and on about all that was wrong with the world at that particular moment. Grumpy doesn't begin to describe her." She glanced at the Hammond family. "She was lonely. Sad but true. And it was all her own fault. Every time someone tried to get friendly, to offer to help her, her back would bristle and a frown would appear on her face. You knew it was time to retreat and let her sulk."

Dash took a seat across from her. "Did you visit often? Any idea where she banked if she did? We're at a loss trying to find her will and any other important papers. And would you say she was a lousy housekeeper? When we arrived, this place was a disaster. When did you last see or talk to her? The coroner hasn't ruled on her death but is leaning toward a stroke or heart attack."

Mae muttered, "Why don't you shine a light in her face while interrogating her?"

Dash frowned at his wife who then wrinkled her nose at him.

Cindy slumped back in the chair. "I should have checked on her. I haven't, hadn't, seen or talked to her since last Thursday. I helped her with the shopping for the last ten years or so. She decided she didn't want to go out anymore, not feeling well. I work at the West Side Market so she would give me her list for meat, cold cuts, etc. My daughter Ellie would get the other items when she shopped for our family. Maud even let me drive her car once after she gave up doing it herself. Though I'd have to listen to 'watch out, slow down, turn now.' A world-class backseat though seated up front driver."

"Not feeling well, how?" Dash asked.

Cindy glanced at her watch. "She was always complaining about headaches, upset stomach and generally getting old."

She stood to leave. "Sorry, I have to run, or I'll be late for work. Oh, her bank is the new one on West 25th Street. She hated it, preferring the old Cleveland Trust that used to be at Lorain and Fulton. It's something else now, but Maud never changed with the times."

Dash stood as well. "Can I give you a lift? Save a few steps."

"No, but thanks. And again, thank you for all the meat. My bunch of hooligans will appreciate it. I'll be home at six. Just pop next door if you need anything."

Owen stepped in. "We'll be heading home this afternoon and return tomorrow or the next day. Say, could I ask if you or one of your family can keep an eye on the place? I'd be happy to pay you." He pulled out his wallet. Taking out a fifty-dollar bill and one of his cards, he handed them to Cindy. He raised his hand when she objected to the money. "You will be doing us a big service."

Dash walked her down the steps though it was obvious she knew where to step so she didn't fall through the treads.

When he returned, Dash reminded Owen of Leon across the street.

"That's okay. Won't hurt to have more eyes on the place," his dad said. "Well, at least we have a clue where her bank might be. Another job for tomorrow."

Four hours later, they gathered in the dining room which was full of boxes and bags. Every piece of furniture moved. Every throw rug rolled up. Every picture taken down and carefully inspected. Nothing more found.

The Hammond family, tired and dusty, wanted to return home.

Dash and Owen made one final walk-thru making sure every lock was locked, every window closed. The place had a neatness about it. Anyone breaking in wouldn't guess there might be something to find if anything had been missed by the Hammond crew.

After he secured the backdoor, Dash nodded to his dad. "Let's start loading and head home. I'm going to stand under a hot shower for about an hour. And even then, I'm not sure I'll get all this dust off of me." He punctuated that statement with a mighty sneeze.

Owen laughed. "Well, at least tomorrow we won't face that since we're carrying all the dirt out with us now. I'm going to sleep forever."

Dash sighed. "Think I have some lumber I can cut so we can repair the steps, and I'll get new locks for the place. Hopefully, we will avoid any problems while the place sits empty. Don't need any lawsuits for negligence."

The drive back to Clover Pointe was quiet in both vehicles. Dash followed Mae. He and Owen tucked the money and gun under the front seat. The truck bed held all the shoe boxes, the old suitcase, and several boxes of vintage clothes.

"Drive carefully, son. If we are stopped or in an accident, I haven't the foggiest idea how to explain the cash and gun. The truth sounds too screwy." He leaned his head back. "So scary, Thomas finding the gun. By the way, have you told him about his little sister yet?"

"No, to telling T.J. I told you when we have a healthy baby in our arms, that's time enough. I don't want to listen to him complain about a baby sister when he ordered a baby brother. Surrogate Sue is doing just fine, but the waiting is killing me." He took a breath. "Have you decided what you're going to tell Sam, aka our favorite sheriff? And I'm a bit surprised you didn't call Kraft. I expected him to turn up, cigar in hand. 'Just one more thing.'"

When Owen didn't answer, Dash looked over to see his father sound asleep. He smiled, wondering if T.J. and Kathleen were asleep as well.

CHAPTER FIVE

The next morning Sam heard his brother's truck pull into the driveway. Grabbing his thermos of coffee and the bag of donuts he bought especially for the trip, he yelled to his wife, "Marie, I'm off. See you later, sweetie."

Full of energy, he jumped into the truck waving the bag. "Good morning, gentlemen. I have goodies!"

The only response was Dash putting the truck into reverse and backing out onto the street.

"Dash, Dad, Donuts! Fresh from Hevezi's."

He studied his brother's profile. Not an iota of interest. He turned to his father, a cop's cop; donuts were part of their DNA.

"Sam, please take this in the kindest way. Shut up!" Owen said.

"Jeez, somebody's got out of bed on the wrong side. What the hell's the matter with you two? If I wanted the silent treatment, I could have stayed home with the wife. So much for a day out, having fun."

Dash let loose with a mighty sneeze. Sam then saw the red nose and runny eyes.

"God, you look awful. Pretty sure there's medicine for that. Hey, aren't you the one married to the doctor?" Sam said sarcastically.

Dash glared at him. "One more word, and I'm going to cut your tongue out."

Sam stuffed a donut into his mouth. Didn't have to tell him twice.

From the backseat, his father asked, "You gonna eat all those yourself? Hand me a couple. Had a bad night. That fool brother of mine kept me awake going on and on about the family history Maud had been working on. I could use some sugar to jumpstart my day."

Sam passed the bag back to his dad. "Help yourself." He glanced again at his brother, wondering if he could use sugar to sweeten his personality.

"Can I ask a question? What went on these last two days that both of you look like you've been through the works? It can't be finding a dead body since Maud's wasn't the first for either of you. Do I need to know something, or do I get to walk blindly into the fire?"

"Sorry, bro. There was so much dust, dirt, critter feces and dead bugs to fill a dumpster. Even with a mask on, I breathed in too much crap. Told Mae I have the plague, but she dismissed it blithely. So much for the medical degree if you can't recognize the plague when it's staring you in the face." Dash punctuated that with another sneeze. Reaching for his water, he added, "You should be safe now. We carried all the dust out with us yesterday."

"Thanks, everything's settled. The plague. Good deal. Thanks for inviting me along." And he stuffed another donut into his mouth.

The men were silent for the rest of the trip. Sam licked his sticky fingers as quietly as he could so he wouldn't disturb anyone.

After Dash pulled the truck into Maud's driveway, Sam got out and studied the house. "So, this is where old Maudie lived. Marie came with Mom a few times, but she mainly visited the West Side Market. Never said much about the house though." He looked around. "Isn't this part of Ohio City? Didn't that used to be prime real estate? This street looks a bit shabby."

"Yes and yes. Today we are going to fix the steps and a part of the porch. It'll need painting, but not today. I also brought new locks for both front and back doors." Dash turned to his brother. "So, Sammy boy, that's what you'll be doing today.

Helping me accomplish those few tasks. Dad is going to supervise. At some point we're all going over to a bank where Maud had her account. We found a lock box key and hope we can gain access to her box." Again, he sneezed.

Sam said, "This is so much crap." He looked at his brother. "Might as well start before you collapse on me. I have a vague idea how to do what you're proposing but haven't done as many renovation jobs as you, Mr. Fix-it or should I say Mr. Fix-anything-even-if-no-one-asks-you-to-do-it."

With that, the men unloaded the tools and lumber Dash pre-cut the evening before. The work began in earnest.

The repairs were made. Sam took the front door key from Dash. A waft of stale, awful smelling air greeted him. He stepped back quickly, almost knocking his brother off his feet.

Owen jumped back. "I guess we should have left a window or two open, at least a crack. Don't remember it smelling this bad yesterday when we arrived."

Dash looked at Sam. "Trust me. It smelled worse yesterday, but not as bad as Tuesday." He walked over to the porch railing, leaned on it, then jumped away remembering how tentative it was. "Damn, do you think there's another body inside? Sam, would you do the honors?"

Sam studied his brother, then his father. "Never do I recall either of you being so squeamish. Stand back and let a real man do the job." He pulled open the door and stepped gingerly inside. He tried not to gag at the rancid smell since he professed to be the manly man of the group.

Without the curtains, the living room was well lit. Sam moved cautiously from one room to another. After clearing the front room and bedroom, he wandered into the kitchen where the stench originated. After opening the window, he propped the back door ajar.

Calling out, he said, "Didn't find anything or anyone. I'm thinking that the smell spread from the kitchen and wafted through the place. Little bro, you said you cleaned the kitchen. Well, get ready to clean it again."

Dash's shoulders slumped. "I am ready to burn the place down. By the time we fix it up to get it on the real estate market, we'll be as old as Maud was."

"Nah, did you guys look at the newer homes built in the neighborhood? But not on this street where time seems to have stopped. All around are new homes on old lots. I bet this one will fetch a good deal of moola. Wonder who Maud left this pile to."

Owen moved to the dining room table, the new center of operations. "Sam, give me a hand with these shoe boxes. They have what Maud considered to be financial records. We need to organize them according to year and look at every piece of paper for a clue as to where Maud might have put her will or any other important papers. These are the older boxes. We took some home last night. Kathleen and T.J. moved these down from the upstairs bedroom. These were in the closet. Important enough to keep, I guess."

Dash wandered around, finally announcing he was going to give the kitchen another go. If nothing else, he planned on spraying air freshener.

"Might I suggest you get a couple of fans and place them throughout the house? At least the air would circulate. Not sure if that would help but it can't hurt," Sam said.

"Spoken like a man without a headache. I'll be right back." Dash headed out the door, coughing and sneezing as he went.

As soon as his brother had left the building, Sam turned to his father. "Okay, Owen, fess up. Now that 'cheerful Charlie' is gone, what went on those two days you were here that Dash frankly looks like shit?"

"Other than finding Cousin Maud dead and the house smelling worse than this, not much. Oh, Thomas did find a gun. We almost had a heart attack. Don't know how many times that child has been told not to touch a one and still he comes down the stairs to ask, 'is this gun real?'"

"And when were you going to tell me about this gun? You're as bad as Dash. Mr. Secrets himself." Sam said very perturbed.

"Your brother is just very private. He shares when he's ready," Owen said in defense of his youngest.

"Yeah, I remember when he *shared* his plans for the Army. It was at his graduation party when old Mr. Morelli asked him what his plans were. I can still see the shock on your face when Dash answered, 'well, next week I'm off to basic training. Then in the fall I'll be at Ohio State playing football and hopefully learning something.' You and Mom didn't have a clue, did you?"

"No, but it was all my fault. Dash and I had one of our lengthy discussions, years earlier. I'd refused his request to go off with his buddies to a cabin in Canada to fish. That flaky kid, Johnny Meiser, arranged all that and I didn't think it was a good idea. I told Dash that, as long as he lived under my roof, he had to abide by my rules. Told him he could leave when he turned eighteen. And the day after his eighteenth birthday, he joined the Army. Didn't need my consent. I blame my brother Joe. His death in 'Nam turned him into a mythical hero to Dash."

Owen turned back to the piles of paper on the table. "All water under the bridge now."

Sam shook his head, realizing his brother wasn't the only stubborn one in the family. Subject closed, so he asked, "Where's the gun now?"

"Locked in Dash's safe. Was going to talk to you about it later today."

"So, Maudie had a loaded gun. Seeing the neighborhood, it wouldn't be a bad idea when she was younger, but at her age, and as frail as she looked at Mom's funeral five years ago, she should have sold it and bought an alarm system," Sam said. He began sorting through the shoebox in front of him, thinking the gun was probably just the tip of the iceberg here. He could read his father well enough to know the story was far from complete.

Dash returned with a half dozen fans, which he placed throughout the house.

"How's the head?" Owen asked.

"Better. A bit of coffee, couple of aspirins and some fresh air did the trick," Dash said. Then he sneezed. "Still stuffy, but I'm going back upstairs and have another look in the nooks and crannies. Thinking Kathleen might not have been as thorough once she found the go-go outfit."

"Go-go? Cousin Maud? Two things that should never be said in the same sentence. Wonder what else the old gal was up to," Sam laughed. He did catch the look that passed from his father to his brother, but no comment from either.

CHAPTER SIX

The Hammond men decided to break for lunch a little earlier than usual. Sam googled nearby diners. He found one a few blocks over on West 25th Street near the West Side Market. Dash teased him about always having to eat diner food.

"That is rich coming from the man who has tuna salad, apple pie and iced tea five days a week at our local diner," Sam shot back at him.

They walked over to Zara's Place. Obviously, this was *the* place where everyone in the area went to grab food for carry-out or, if time permitted, had a quick sit and chat while eating with their fellow employees.

Sam grabbed a table near the front window. "I like to watch the pedestrians walk by. Always find my fellow men and women interesting to study."

As they perused the menu, which offered the usual short order dishes, the waitress stood chewing on the eraser on her pencil. Her name badge said *Owner*. She smiled at Dash every time he looked up.

When Dash finally nodded at her, she winked at him, causing his brother and father to chuckle.

After taking their order, she retreated to the kitchen, but not before grinning at Dash one more time.

He leaned in to ask his brother and father. "Do you get the impression that she knows me or thinks I know her?" He looked over his shoulder at her as she took orders from the other tables.

"Now that you mention it, I did get the feeling she thought you were going to have an ah-ha moment, jump up and throw your arms around her, your long-lost something or other," Sam said. "Hey, another kid hanging around. A half-sibling for little Thomas."

"Well, son, does she ring any bells?"

"Hate to say it but sorta, kinda. I mean I have met a lot of women over the years. I don't recall any from this neck of the woods. But hell, she could have served in the Army, and we crossed paths there. She seems very young to me." Dash shook his head as if that would shake loose the memory. "And, Sam, as I've told you, there are no other kids out there. The time with Jamillah was a one off."

Sam threw his head back, laughing, "One off is all it takes, as you now know."

When their food arrived, all three men watched the 'Owner' carefully. She again smiled broadly at Dash when she placed his soup in front of him.

He stood up, throwing down his napkin. "I give up. Do I *know* you? Or do you want to know me? Have you seen a photo of me somewhere, and *think* you know me? Little lost on reading the signals, I guess."

The woman threw her head back and laughed loudly. "Know you, as in the biblical sense? That would be a no, even though we did spend a night together."

Dash sat down sharply as Sam broke out in laughter. "Okay, cut the crap. Just tell me or you'll be wearing this bowl of soup."

She walked around the table and plopped down next to Dash. Her shoulders were shaking. "Yes, yes, you're right. I shouldn't tease you, but Maud would approve." She tilted her head. "Twenty-five years ago, give or take a year, you were in Cleveland with another Army buddy. Forty-eight-hour pass or something like that. Your friend had a girl here and spent the weekend in a hotel with her. You ended up at a St. Paddy's Day shindig. Any of this ring a bell?"

"Of course, of course. Now I remember. St. Patrick's weekend. You were the very young girl with green hair. Ran into Maud, who introduced us, and we all ended up at her place, drinking and singing and drinking and laughing."

Dash stood up and pulled her out of the chair, giving her a big hug. "Now if I can only remember your name, I can eat lunch without getting indigestion."

Owen and Sam looked at each other, shaking their heads and rolling their eyes.

"Ma'am or miss, do you have a minute to join us and explain all this? Especially the connection to Maud Grealis," Owen said.

"Forgive me, I should have opened with my condolences to all of you. Cousins of hers, right?"

Owen shivered. "My late wife was some sort of cousin. You know the Irish; all are related one way or another. I just happened to outlive my wife and so inherited Maud. How well did you know her?"

The woman stood. "Give me a minute to turn the floor over to Betsy. She won't be happy, but who is? I'll call Henri and Willie for you. They are, excuse me, were Maud's lawyers. Quite sure they are searching for you now." She bolted from the table.

Dash watched as Sam dove into his lunch and Owen began to eat his sandwich. Thinking he should eat something, he started on his bowl of chicken soup, a panacea to all ills. His head pounded and he hoped food would help. At least now he knew why he had the feeling he'd been in Maud's house before, since he had. Now if he could just remember more about that night. He wondered whether it was the drinking that long-ago night or the brain injury that kept him from recalling the details.

As Dash finished his soup, Sam practically licked his plate. The 'Owner' returned, standing by the side of the table. "Henri and Willie will be right down. Their office is above the restaurant. They knew her better than I did and can answer any questions."

Dash asked, "Pardon me, but what the hell is *your* name? I can't keep thinking of you as the green-haired girl or 'Owner' as your nametag states. And are you the owner? Cool place if I may comment."

"Comment away. My name is Zara, as in Zara's Place. This used to be Al's Diner and before that, Stan's Restaurant. I figured I should change it to my name once I bought it, kinda keeping a tradition going. Henri and Willie own the building, so I finagled a very reasonable rent. Oh, here they come."

Two women made their way over to the table. Both wore ties but only one had a suit jacket on. The other had on a long-sleeved shirt, rolled up to the elbow. Their strides were confident and their miens, business-like.

The Hammond men rose as they approached the table. Dash studied them. He guessed they were in their late fifties or early sixties. The taller one had a no-nonsense hair style, gray streaks shining through. The smaller, more rotund lady had shoulder-length hair, chestnut brown. She wore tortoiseshell glasses, adding a hint of authority but just a hint. She was quite pleasant to look at, especially when she smiled broadly as she did at the men.

Zara stepped forward to make the introductions. "Gentlemen, may I present Henrietta Sloames and Wilma Wilson, Maud's lawyers and my mothers." The taller of the two women said, "Call me Henri, please. It's good to finally meet all of you." She looked at each man. "Owen, Sam, and of course, you're Dash. Look a lot like your photo. Good looking men."

Dash smiled. "Maybe I should check to see if there's a billboard with my picture on it. So far everyone I've met has seen that photo." He sneezed again.

A round of 'bless you' followed.

Henri turned to her partner. "This is Wilma Wilson; we call her Willie and so should you." She stuck out her hand. Owen and Sam shook her hand. Dash declined, citing his cold as an excuse not to join in.

Instead, he helped Zara move two chairs to the table so all could sit. The waitress started to clear the table and Sam jumped in to help.

"Shall I get a pot of coffee and some dessert, or is this strictly business?" Zara asked.

Everyone agreed that coffee and pie would be nice, so the waitress took orders as she piled the dishes onto her arm.

"Well, Mr. Hammond, or do you still use your title of sheriff?" Henri asked. "May we extend our sympathies on your loss. Just heard the news this morning when Officer Lachman collected his coffee. Foul play suspected?"

Owen answered, "No ruling on the foul play. More of a precaution calling in homicide. When we arrived Wednesday, the place was in shambles. Unless you are about to tell me Maud was the worst housekeeper in Cleveland, as a former lawman, I wanted to make sure we did everything by the book."

The coffee arrived hot and black. Pieces of apple pie were distributed, and Sam dove into his without waiting, causing Dash to wonder if his brother had eaten in days.

"If I may ask, how long have you known Maud? And do you know what this key opens?" Dash placed the key discovered behind his photo on the table.

"Ah," said Henri. "Her lockbox at the bank across the street. She gave us the other key when we co-signed for her box just in case something like this happened. Never was privy to what she kept in the box, just that she considered it important enough to pay to protect it."

That statement brought a smile to Willie's face. "In case you didn't know, Maud was extremely frugal. We joked with her about having the first dollar she ever made."

Sam chuckled, pointing his fork at his brother. "Guess you inherited that gene, brother. We used to say Dash still had his First Communion money tucked under his mattress."

Frowning, Dash turned to the lawyers. "Speaking of money, do you have her financial records? She told my father he was to be her executor, and we have scoured the house looking for any papers which would help him."

Owen snorted. "For a woman who was constantly dying, she never let on what I was to do when that happened. I figured she would outlive me and my sons."

Henri tapped a folder she had placed on the table. "We do indeed have all the necessary papers. We can even adjourn to our office and read her Last Will and Testament if you are so inclined. This is now your show."

Owen rubbed his face and then looked at his sons. Sam shrugged. Dash glanced at his watch and said, "It's only a little after twelve. Let's hear what Maud has to say. We can still get in a little hunting if all our questions go unanswered." With a sigh, he stood up ready to move.

The rest followed his lead.

He whispered to Zara. "I would like to talk to you sometime. Need to discover why we only talked, drank, and laughed. Seems to me I should have enticed you into a bit more."

"Take care of business first and then we can delve into the whys and wherefores."

"Spoken like the daughter of lawyers. You did call them your mothers, correct?"

"Spot on. Interesting story there." Zara nodded and then walked away.

The office of Sloames and Wilson, located above Zara's Place, was well-appointed. The chairs were leather, soft, and comfortable. Only one desk, large and well-polished, stood in the center of the private office.

Henri sat behind the desk, while Willie and Sam pushed chairs to the front. Sitting off to the side, Willie could survey the Hammond men.

"Shall we start with the will? Do you want the formal reading with all the wherefores and there-ins?" Henri asked.

Sam spoke up. "Cut to the chase. Who gets what? If she put her first dollar in the bank, it should be worth a good deal more after all these years."

"Geez Sam. A little respect. It's not like Maud would leave us anything. She barely knew us." Dash said shaking his head.

"Might I apologize for my sons? Ms. Sloames, please do what you think is best. It doesn't look like her will is very long.

I'd just like to know what she wants me to do. Happy to give it all to charity or the church if she wanted that." Owen leaned back in his chair.

Henri silently read over the document. "Okay, bottom line is this, with the exception of a few monetary bequeaths, the bulk of her estate goes to Dashiell Joseph Hammond." She nodded toward Dash whose mouth dropped open. She continued, "The bequeaths are these: a sum of five thousand dollars each to Samuel Owen Hammond and his sister, Bridget Marie Lovell. If Owen survives her, which he has, he receives ten thousand."

Sam straightened up. "So, the golden boy gets more gold."

Dash looked askance at his brother, then to Henri. "Don't suppose she said why I got all the goods. Seriously, not sure I can accept this without a good reason. As I said, we barely knew each other."

Henri looked down at the will. "Let me read what she wrote following the declaration that you were to inherit all. 'Dashiell is a good man, a reliable man. He will do the right thing. He is a seeker of truths and a finder of lost things.'"

Dash sighed again and held out his hands. "Bullshit. What truth? What am I supposed to find? That tells me exactly nothing. Are you sure she was of sound mind?"

Shuffling the papers, Henri added, "Maud changed her will every few years. As her siblings in Ireland passed on, she would call and re-work the will."

Willie spoke up at this point. "I have all the financial records of her savings and investments. You will see that, as is often the case, the quiet spinster accumulated a nice sum."

Dash sat tapping his foot. He glanced at his father and then asked quietly. "Two questions: First, do you have addresses or something for any relatives, no matter how distant, who might still be alive? And, off the top of your head, did she believe in bank accounts or was she more apt to squirrel money away in her mattress?"

"You ask this why?" Willie inquired.

"Just wondering, that's all." Dash said with his best smile.

Owen held up his hand. "Back to business. Did Maud give instructions as to her funeral, burial? Don't suppose she pre-planned anything?"

Henri slid a piece of paper over to Owen. "Here are her instructions. The O'Conner Funeral Home will oversee the wake and burial. She covered all the bases: hymns, pall bearers, wake and naturally her final resting spot. All paid in advance. You and your family just need to show up."

Stacking papers together, she added, "At one time she wanted to be cremated and her ashes returned to Ireland." She looked at Dash. "I believe she appointed you to do that but once you had that accident, she decided against 'all that fuss,' as she called it."

"Now, gentlemen, if you wish, we can proceed to the bank across the street and see what wonders Maud considered sacred enough to lock away." Willie stood, gathering her files. "This way, please." And she led them out of the office and across to the bank.

The Hammond men walked silently. Dash, lost in thought, wondered what Maud locked away. More secrets, more money, another gun? His head began to pound again. His shoulders unaccustomedly slouched as they traversed the street to the bank.

Dash looked at the bank, all sleek and modern. Mrs. Brady was right. This building didn't have the trappings of old money, no intricate marble work. He understood why Maud might not look favorably on it.

Immediately, the branch manager greeted Henri and Willie. He led everyone to the vault to the lock boxes. Dash and Sam wanted to wait outside, but the lawyers insisted everyone be present for the opening of the box. "The more witnesses, the better," Henri said.

"The box was 2111, chosen by Maud particularly," the bank official said.

"She never explained why that number, and I for one was not about to ask," Willie said.

Dash snorted. "Obvious. November 21, though the Irish would say 21 November. Bloody Sunday, 1920. A pivotal date in Irish history. My mom told stories of lost relatives. I'm sure Maud had similar experiences passed on to her. Talk about never forgetting ..." He stopped when he noticed the incredulous expressions on the faces of the others. He shrugged. "Just saying."

The keys inserted and turned. The long slim box removed. The bank official carried it to the room set aside for private viewing.

Owen and Henri stepped forward to open the lid. Both frowned.

"What's in it?" asked Sam, trying to peer over their shoulders.

Reaching in, Owen pulled out a sealed envelope. It had Dash's name scrawled across the front. His father handed it to him.

All eyes turned to Dash who fingered the envelope. The paper was crinkly, like the old onion skin his mother used when writing to her relatives back in Ireland. Less weight, less postage. Maud's missive was fairly thick with something small tucked into it. Nodding, Dash tucked it into his pocket.

"What? You're not going to open it! Aren't you curious? Even a little bit?" asked Sam.

Hand to his nose, Dash backed out of the room, letting loose another sneeze. After wiping his nose, he said, "Yes, I am curious, but to be honest, I want to read it in the quiet of my own office. Cousin Maud obviously wanted me, and only me, to know the contents. Since she thinks I'm a good man, I will act like one, sharing the contents on a need-to-know basis." He turned to leave. "Let's head back to the house, secure it and go home. My head feels like it's going to burst, and I would prefer to be there than here."

Owen and Henri reversed the process, handing the box back to the bank official. The group headed back to the lawyers' office to pick up all the pertinent papers.

"Ms. Sloames, Ms. Wilson, I'll review all this and get back to you in a day or two. And I'll let you know if we need further assistance. Dash will surely compensate you for your time and help. I will let you know about the funeral arrangements." Sticking out his hand for one last handshake, Owen bid the women goodbye.

Owen trotted to catch up to his sons. "Dash, Sam, wait up for your old man."

Dash stopped to stare at the ground. He turned to Sam, pitching the truck keys to him. "Would you drive? I need to get home."

Seeing how pale his brother had become, Sam asked, "Would you rather go to a hospital?"

Inhaling deeply, Dash shook his head. "No, Mae will know what to do. It's stress, I'm sure. Dad, would you lock the place up? Probably need to hire someone to look after it. Why me, Maud? Why? What did I ever do to you? Seeker of truth, finder of lost things. Again, bullshit with a capital B."

Owen and Sam looked at each other. Owen said, "Let's just go home. Give me a minute to lock up. You boys get in the truck."

Dash buckled himself into the back seat. He pulled out his phone and tried to text Mae, but the letters danced around on the screen. "Owen, Sam, would one of you tell Mae we're heading home, and I would appreciate it if she could be there. I can't see the screen."

"Roger that, bro. Consider it done," Sam said as he texted his sister-in-law.

CHAPTER SEVEN

Sam kept to the speed limit but made excellent time.

Mae and T.J. stood on the side porch when Sam parked the truck under the carport.

Dash crawled out of the backseat and sat down on the steps. Eyes closed, he said quietly, "Mae, I need a pill or two or three. Head is about to split open." T.J. moved to rub his father's back.

Sam helped his brother into the house and to the front bedroom usually reserved for Owen. He took off Dash's boots and belt. "Rest easy, bro. I'll hang around a bit to see if you need to head to the hospital."

"No hospital. I'll be …"

Mae appeared with a cold compress for his head and the requested pills. "Listen, you rest for a bit and then we'll take a look to see if we need to do something else. We'll be quiet."

"Turn on the classical station. That will relax me. Luv ya, Mae B girl."

She closed the bedroom door and pulled the pocket doors to the front room closed. Owen, Sam, T.J. and the two dogs waited in the kitchen.

"Well, gentlemen, what the H went on? He left here sneezing and comes home begging for pills."

Sam reached in the refrigerator, pulling out several beers and one apple juice. "Sit down and listen to the tale, the tale of a fateful trip …"

It was several hours later when Dash emerged from the bedroom. Owen and T.J. sat in the recliner watching a Disney movie on mute. Having seen it so many times, sound wasn't necessary.

"Daddy, you're alive!" said T.J. "I was afraid you were going to die on me and Mommy."

"Never, little one, never." He made his way to the sofa and sat down. "Where's Mae?"

As if on cue, the pocket doors slid open, and Mae stood there smiling. "Ah, I thought I heard my manly man's voice. How are you feeling, sweetheart?"

"Much better, still a little throbbing but so much better than when I arrived." He punctuated that with a giant sneeze.

"Hungry? Sam and Marie are about to head this way to return your truck. Would you want Marie to bring dinner?" Mae asked.

T.J. jumped up. "No, Mommy, I want pepperoni pizza and bread sticks from Papa's Pizza Parlor. Please, please."

Dash raised his hand. "I'm with T.J. A little pizza, salad, bread sticks and nice cold beer, sounds good but I think I'll stick to broth and water until my head stops pounding."

Mae nodded, pulling out her phone. She texted Marie about the pizza menu, then invited Dash's uncle, Father Tom, and Miss Ruthie, a long-time family friend and now Owen's companion. After counting heads, she ordered enough pizza and sides to be delivered.

She motioned Dash into the kitchen and told him to sit. Owen and T.J. followed.

Mae sat down and reached for his hand. "Want to tell me why you got so upset that your head went wacko? Sam and Owen gave me the highlights of today's events. Care to add your thoughts?"

"Hard to pinpoint it, Mae. Just got a horrible feeling about all this. They told you Maud's comment about me being a good man, will do the right thing, seek the truth, and find something lost. Spooked me, that's all. Got the feeling the letter would reveal Maud was my mother." Dash waved off Owen. "I know, I know I have always said I was adopted. Really just joked about it until earlier today. Sinking feeling in my stomach."

T.J. walked over to his father. "Daddy, it's okay to be adopted. It doesn't hurt like when the doctor gives you a shot. Mommy adopted me when we got married, 'member?"

"Yes, little man, I remember. And, yes, adoption is a good thing. I'm being a silly old man." He picked his son up and kissed him.

"Don't start with the adopting thing again. I would have told you," Owen said. "Your mother would have told you. Believe me when I say I tried to give you away and no one would take you. Now drop it." He patted his son's shoulder.

"Consider it done. Now what can we drink until the pizza arrives? Suddenly I'm thirsty and starving. Mae, please tell me we have some broth." He rummaged around the refrigerator until he decided on iced tea and found a non-sugary drink for T.J. "Let's sit outside and you can tell me all about your day and how you plan to spend all your money."

Mae pulled the broth out of the freezer and began heating it up.

That night, after all the relatives had departed for their own beds, Dash and Mae settled into theirs.

"Going to open the letter?" Mae asked.

"Guess I should or else I'll speculate myself into a sleepless night." He got out of bed and retrieved the letter. Grabbing his glasses, he switched on the table lamp next to his side of the bed.

"You can read it out loud if you like. Share the news, good or bad." Mae snuggled up next to him. "I promise not to tell anyone without your permission. We can hope she'll tell us about the money and the gun. Who knows? Her being Irish could mean any number of transgressions that make her feel guilty."

Dash worked his finger under the envelope flap, not wanting to tear everything apart. He pulled out several sheets of paper covered with Maud's scrawl. A slender gold ring slid out. Dash inspected it but learned nothing, so he put it on the nightstand. He squinted at the letter, reached for his glasses, and began to read the letter aloud:

Dear Dashiell, I realize this is a shock to you. This and the will but I really couldn't think of anyone else as reliable as you.

First, about the estate and all that entails. If your quest is unsuccessful, you decide if you want the money and property or feel free to give it all away, preferably to worthy individuals or charities. I'm dead so whatever you decide will have to do. If you want to give it away, please include children and animal charities. The most vulnerable need our help. Bet that surprises you. That I have a heart and a conscience.

Second, the quest. Please be discreet with this information especially if Owen is still alive. We were all young once …

Pulling off his glasses, he put the letter aside not wanting to read what might come next. He expelled a long breath and turned to Mae. "Don't think I can read this. Not ready to hear whatever she's about to say." He shoved the papers into Mae's hands. "You read it and tell me only the basics. Or better, don't tell me anything. I'll feel better in the morning, I'm sure."

Mae pulled herself up. "I promise not to reveal to a living soul what's in the letter." And she began to read silently.

"I can see why you stopped when you did. Thought she was going to say she and Owen got it on, didn't you? Admit it," Mae said poking her husband with her elbow.

"Yeah, of course you're right. I could almost understand my mother cheating on my father since there were times when I thought he was a right son of a gun. But my mother was too good to have him disrespect her that way. Owen and I have just mended fences and I don't want to get upset with him. Suddenly life seems very short."

Mae folded the sheets together and put them back into the envelope. "I'll only say this. Either Maud had an enormous gift for blarney, or this is one helluva story." She handed the letter back to Dash. "Put it aside for now. Tomorrow is another day, my love."

Dash turned off the lights but couldn't turn off his brain. Just what did Maud do?

CHAPTER EIGHT

The next morning Dash sent Mae and T.J. off with kisses and hugs. Dressed in sweats, covered by his Pappy's old woolen robe, and warm wooly socks to ward off any draughts, he moved to his office. He carried his coffee and the envelope from Maud. His mission: transcribe her scrawl.

The dogs, Charlie and Pansy, followed him into the office and collapsed at his feet. He liked having them around. When he was alone, he felt he could talk out loud, conversing with the dogs. Often they were the most intelligent beings in the room and Charlie Dog, for one, always seemed to understand him.

He squinted at the pages, then remembered that in the office he had a magnifying glass he used when studying his combat maps. It took him several minutes to locate it. T.J., who had a desk next to his, had borrowed it without returning it to its usual location.

He typed slowly. The first two paragraphs were easy since he and Mae read them last night. As he continued, his frown grew larger.

Maud wrote:

None more precious to me than Declan Rooney. No reason the name should mean anything to you. Many thought he was IRA, but he wasn't. Accused of several crimes, the worst being murder, but he didn't do it. I was there. I know what happened. Yes, I loved, still do, a wanted man. Also a married man. He's the reason I left my home and came to the United States. My family thought I traveled alone to a brave new world, but

Declan outsmarted them and the Garda disguising himself as a woman, one of many sneaking into your welcoming country.

Dash leaned back in his chair, rubbing his chin. "Well, that explains Moira McCreery. Judging from the shoes this Declan was a decent sized man. Must have made a really ugly woman." Sitting up straight, he realized what a pair of rogues Maud and Declan were. Taking a deep breath, he continued to read.

I couldn't let your parents know since Owen was a lawman and would feel obligated to take Declan into custody. They did meet, once, at an Irish festival that your mother assured me Owen would never attend, but he did, that's how much he loved her. I pleaded a headache and we escaped before your father could question him too thoroughly. Your father always could slice through lies like a hot knife through butter.

"Ah, Maud had Owen's number for sure. Lawman, human lie detector. Curiouser and curiouser, as many have said."

Declan and I didn't exactly live together at my house since Father Dwyer of St. Patrick's visited often, me being a daily churchgoer, repenting my sins. And, yes, I was quite the volunteer in my youth. Couldn't deny the good Father entrance or a Guinness or two.

Declan changed his name when he arrived here. We had some good years together. Himself posing as an old friend from across the pond, a widower who couldn't let go of the memory of his poor wife. But all the time we were looking over our shoulders, fearing gatherings of the Irish, certain someone would recognize him even with a beard and a change of hair coloring.

He stopped typing and decided to read the rest of the letter, parts blotted and smeared. For a moment he thought of Maud crying as she wrote. Wondered when she penned this, and was it the first and only time she put these events to paper?

As you grew older, I was sad that you and Declan never met. Oh, the laughing, singing, even a bit of a jig or two, that's how we would have spent the day.

My Declan and I had so few carefree days, always waiting for the knock on the door. Our past invading our present.

He leaned back again, this time sighing. The past always invaded the present. He knew extremely well how the ghosts of days gone by tap you on the shoulder when you least expected or would welcome them. He drew in several deep breaths and decided he needed to refresh his coffee or make a cup of Irish tea since he felt himself drawn back to his mother's beloved auld sod.

Instead of tea, he settled on orange juice and a cold pill since his head was filling up. Onto the next paragraph or two. When did the knock come, for he was sure it did.

It finally came; our own form of troubles landed on my doorstep. An Irishman, Callahan, said he knew Declan was here, near me, his lover. Said our Declan had killed his brother and he was here to deliver vengeance.

Bollocks, I knew the truth. I knew who killed his feckless brother. Lies, lies and more lies. Damned to hellfire for all eternity before I would allow this crooked vengeance.

Ah, here it comes. His quest would be for vengeance upon the Callahan clan. He rolled his shoulders and shuddered to think what Maud wanted him to do.

He grumbled, "Always bring in the soldier to do the dirty work, thanks dear distant and now departed cousin."

The Callahan clan was thick as bricks and this poor sod was the dumbest of the lot. I was surprised he found his way to my house, but I played the good Irish hostess, invited him in and plied him with fine whiskey until he was legless and would stop with the lies. Using my God-given Irish wits and wiles, I learned he was on his own; his feckless family had no knowledge of where he was or what he planned to do. I'm sure they didn't care.

I know it's a mortal sin to kill but sometimes a little cleansing of the clans is good. All I had to do was keep him in the house until Declan showed up. Together we could dispose of him.

Dash stood up so fast he knocked over the chair. Looking at Charlie Dog, he said, "What the?" He took a deep breath. "What the 'sometimes a little cleansing of the clans is good!'" He whispered, "Please God let this be a piece of fiction, a big chunk of blarney from good old Maud."

He reconsidered the little old lady, the one he vaguely recalled from his childhood, always seemed ancient and fragile. Boy, did he get that wrong. Then again all he needed was to recall that St. Paddy's Day drink-a-thon at her house. Not so fragile that night.

I had a good life here and a good bit of gold set aside for unexpected emergencies, such as ridding ourselves of a piece of shite like Callahan.

A bit of gold? Was she talking about the one hundred grand hidden in the floor?

By the time Declan showed, Callahan lay passed out on the kitchen floor. I had tied his hands and legs just in case he woke up.

Declan was none too pleased at what I had done. Said I should have sent him on his way, denied everything. It wasn't as if I had photos of us plastered throughout the house. See, there is a reason I have so many of your family—for a long time underneath your smiling faces were a remembrance of other more precious smiling faces.

You of all people realize how hard it is to dispose of a body over here.

Dash wrinkled his brow, "What the hell does that mean? Me of all people?"

No bogs, too many nosey people out at all hours of the night. And the police, too diligent about identifying bodies and apprehending murderers. We finally hit on a solution, and, no, I'm not saying anymore. If you're really interested, I'm sure you'll figure it out for yourself.

"Crap, crap, a thousand times crap. So my quest is to find where she put Callahan's body. And what happened to good old Declan? Did this send him on the run again? Maud, Maud, what did you do?" He shivered. "We have a cold-blooded murderer on the family tree."

Dash picked up his phone to call his father wondering if Owen was pouring over the genealogy notes Maud gathered. No, no, don't call, not yet. He'd wait until he got to the end of the letter. Who knew what else this little missive held?

But our lives changed. You can't trust a Callahan. He said no one knew, but what if one of his relatives finally remembered that he hadn't been to Sunday dinner in a long while? Of course, this Callahan was a worthless creature. Bet his family was happy he wasn't around. No reason to worry; what could this idjit get into?

Ah, but all this was too much for my poor Declan. He was such a decent God-fearing man. Two months later he died in my arms of a massive heart attack after partaking of my best Sunday roast. Fortunately, Father Dwyer was also there so Declan received the Last Rites, forgiven his sins.

Though his body was burned to ash, his soul resides with Our Lord.

There wasn't much more to read so Dash kept to it.

I wish I could say it ended there, but no, inside me was another babe, one who lived, not like the others. A baby girl with her father's gray-green eyes and dark brown hair.

And now, my dearest Dashiell, you have your quest. Find the babe and tell her of her parents' love for each other. I loved her so much I had to give her away.

You're a good man, Dashiell Hammond. Your reward will be in heaven; sorry I won't be there to thank you.

He got up and did a circle of the office. 'Declan? Decent? God-fearing?' Not how he would describe a man on the run, a man who deserted his family. Then he stopped. Do not judge, lest ye be judged. It wasn't as if he had led a blameless life. Who was he to cast the first stone? At least he didn't have a cold blooded 'cleansing of the clans' on his hands.

He returned to his desk and typed the rest of the letter into his laptop. He hit save and left the office with the dogs trailing him. When in doubt, his go-to place was the back porch. His meditative respite.

After the dogs had their break, Dash returned to his office to contemplate his mission: find a woman of indeterminate age, in an undisclosed location. He gathered the pages and the ring; these would go into his safe until he could decipher what everything meant. He said to himself, "And thank you, Maud, for providing dates and places and real names."

CHAPTER NINE

His phone rang. Father Tom. Best uncle ever, well, his only uncle now. Tom was Owen's older brother. The younger brother, Joe, was killed in Vietnam but not before becoming a hero in his young nephew's eyes. A career in the Army was in Dash's future since he was six, saluting his uncle's coffin before it was slowly lowered into the ground.

"Good morning, Tom. How you doing this good day?"

"Dashiell, Dashiell, I should be asking you that question. Feeling better, I hope?"

Leaning back in his chair, Dash nodded, then remembered Father Tom couldn't see him.

"Doing much better, thank you. Spending the day indoors, resting. Owen said he showed you the family tree Cousin Maud drew up. Just wondering how close a blood relative she really is." He cringed as he waited for the dreaded answer.

Tom laughed. "Well, Maud's box of scribbles is why I'm calling. I uncovered a manila envelope with news clippings from Ireland. All about a man called Declan Rooney. I'd call him a rascal, but his transgressions were rather more serious. And Maud had some relationship with him. Not sure what but enough that she kept these clippings, and it looks like a locket with a few strands of his hair inside."

Dash nearly fell off his chair. "Hallelujah, I don't suppose I could persuade you to bring all that to me. I have just read the most fantastic letter. I have to be careful sharing with you. Can't have my two favorite relatives dying of heart attacks in my living room." And to the dogs he added, "Like good old Declan."

Dash could almost see Tom rubbing his hands together and he definitely heard Owen ranting about the family tree and questioning why his wife called Maud her cousin.

"I can't wait to hear what you have to report. We are hot and heavy into this family tree. Should we bring it all over? We should do a white board."

It had been a while since the good priest had any excitement in his life, which wasn't necessarily a bad thing.

"Bring it all. Pretty sure I have plenty of fixings for a good lunch, snacks for energy and I might even find that whiteboard you need. See you soon," Dash said with renewed vigor.

He leaned back in the chair wondering how much he should tell Owen. Once a lawman, always a lawman, even if the possible murder was decades ago. How hard did he want to poke that hornet's nest? In the end, he decided to let his father and his uncle read the letter. Whatever will be will be.

CHAPTER TEN

The first thing Mae and T.J. noticed when they walked into the kitchen was the aroma of freshly baked bread. After setting down their things, they went into the front room, now a very active research area. The furniture moved to the walls; a four-by-eight table sat in the center, surrounded by three easels. One had a whiteboard and the other two were the old-fashioned cork boards which had been dragged down from the attic. Three smiling faces turned to greet the doctor and little student.

"Maevis, Maevis, Maevis. You're not going to believe the progress we've made," Dash said as he waved his hand around the room. "You want me to explain it to you?"

Mae pecked her husband's cheek. "Wow." She took a deep breath and motioned toward the kitchen. "What smells so good? Did Marie take pity and bring us dinner?"

"No, no. What you smell is the result of three Hammonds a'cooking! We made stew and sour dough bread for dinner. Been busy, my love."

Turning to her father-in-law, Mae said, "Owen, you were supposed to make sure he rested today. He was to stay still."

Owen shrugged. "Hard to stay still, Mae, when there are mysteries to uncover. Off you two go."

T.J. tugged at his daddy's pant leg. "What mystery? And do I get a snack or not?" Putting his hands on hips, he said, "This is not how we do things around here."

"Get crackin' kiddo. I'll have a snack on the table by the time you wash your face and hands."

A tad of dickering took place about whether touring the converted living room should be first or should they get dinner out of the way. Dinner it was. Before they ate, Mae pulled out her camera to get a shot of the three Hammond chefs, Dash in the middle with his arms draped across the shoulders of his father and uncle.

"This is one for the family picture wall. And this might be this year's Christmas card." Mae announced. T.J. didn't look pleased at this new side of his elders, but he shrugged, diving into his bowl of stew and warm bread.

Then the tour began. Father Tom explained the clippings, now posted on a board. The grainy picture of Declan Rooney featured front and center.

Owen had drawn up a provisional timeline on the whiteboard. It started with the date taken from the clippings which reported the story of the murder of one James aka 'Jimmy' Callahan. Rooney accused and then fled, leaving his wife and three children behind. Maud appeared in the clipping as a witness, now missing.

But the date she landed in the United States, July 9, 1956, was prominent as the starting point. She attends the wedding of her cousin, Helene-Marie Flynn, to Owen Samuel Hammond on August 3, 1957.

The rest of the timeline was blank until March 18, the day Maud died, found two days later by Owen and Dash.

Dash stood next to Mae and T.J. All three folded their arms across their chests.

"A lot missing, Maevis, if that letter is to believed. She deliberately left out dates which would help my particular cause significantly. I mean if she had just given me the date of her daughter's birth, I'd be way ahead."

Mae pointed to the third board. "The To-Do list is very long. Are these the unanswered questions? How can I help?"

Father Tom stepped forward. "We were about to divide the list up by subject. I'm taking this Declan Rooney and will see what I can learn online. I've got an account on the family search database. I've been working with the other folks at the home, piecing former lives together. And I guess I should see what we can learn about the feckless Callahan clan."

Dash stepped in. "I gave them the outline of what was in the letter—missing person and all."

Owen jumped in. "I'm going to run ballistics on the gun T.J. found. Very long shot that there is a cold case out there with the same bullet. And I will dive into missing persons. It's possible this Callahan had a family member who searched for him. In the olden days, the local newspapers published family queries asking if anyone had seen so-and-so. Tom shared some of these, very interesting reading. And we have the hair from the locket. Will run DNA on it to see what we can learn."

Mae turned to Dash. "Let me guess. You're going to interview the green-haired girl, probing her for information. You scoundrel you."

T.J. frowned. "I want to see the green-haired girl. I bet she's pretty."

"You'd be right, little man. She is pretty but she doesn't have the green hair anymore. But to your point, Mae, if the man Maud had with her that St. Paddy's Day was Declan Rooney, even if he used a different name, *especially* if he used another name, could shortcut a lot of research. Whatever this Zara knows about Maud and her gentlemen callers would help. Her mothers might know even more." Dash moved away from the research center to stretch back and forth. "Hate to say it, but I'm bushed."

"So, let me guess, no rest for any of you?" Mae asked.

Owen shook his head. "Not true. After we got some of this assembled, we ate lunch and then napped while one of his OSU football games was on. Can't believe he doesn't know all of them by heart, but they are useful as a sleeping tonic. Tom had the good sense to stretch out in the front bedroom while I slept in the recliner and himself over there on the sofa. We got an hour or so of rest, did more work. Then Tom got the idea to cook dinner and we had a ball. Glad you enjoyed it."

"Hate to break up the party but I have a poker game with the other priests at 6:30, so I need to run along. Are you coming, Owen?" Father Tom asked.

"Yes," Owen said as he turned to Dash. "Son, let us know what else we can do to help, okay?" Owen moved to kiss T.J. and Mae goodbye. "Talk to you in the morning."

Dash and Mae returned to the kitchen. The table needed clearing, and T.J. needed ice cream.

Mae leaned against the counter, watching Dash rinse the dishes.

"Would you kill for me?" wife asked husband.

Dash stopped to consider his answer. "Are you in imminent danger or is this just a whim?"

"No personal danger. But long-term unhappiness awaits. I'm thinking of Maud's mindset, *if* her story is true. She felt the need to dispatch this Callahan guy. That's cold blooded, yes?"

"Definite yes. For me, I've had enough experience that I wouldn't take anyone's life lightly. Now if you or T.J. were in danger, no question, no hesitation. Like when Kathleen was in trouble, didn't aim to kill but could have." He rinsed off his hands and dried them. "Would you? I mean, would you kill for me, *Doctor* Summers?"

"Only if danger was imminent and you were unconscious or disabled somehow. Otherwise, I think I would leave all that physical stuff up to you. Pretty certain I'd make a bad situation worse. Feel like I've done that in the past, you poor thing."

T.J. interrupted. "Can we read a book or watch TV? This is really boring."

CHAPTER ELEVEN

Dash woke up with a terrible sore throat and laryngitis. Any interviewing of people who might know more about Maud in the good old days was put on hold. He texted Father Tom who was tracking down Father Dwyer, former pastor of St. Patrick's. When Tom responded, the news wasn't good. Dwyer had died in 1995.

Texts flew back and forth between Dash and Brenda McCafferty, a cousin-in-law and owner of McCafferty Realty. Brenda had a meeting in Cleveland, so she volunteered to do a drive-by to scope out Maud's house. Eventually an evaluation would be needed for probate, but Dash wanted to do a bit of renovation before this took place. Brenda's recommendation was to tear down the house and sell the lot to an investor who would build one of the more modern houses that were springing up all over Ohio City.

Owen stopped by to pick up one of Maud's black dresses. The coroner had released her body saying no autopsy was necessary since her doctor confirmed her heart problem. The cause of death on the certificate listed heart failure due to advanced age; her broken neck caused by hitting the railing as she fell after her sudden death.

"General ill health and a bad attitude more likely," Owen commented. He handed Dash the folder of forms from Maud's attorneys. "Hoping this helps you in your search. I'm on my way to pick up Ruthie. I promised her an outing, just didn't tell her it was a trip to a funeral home. I'll text you with the final arrangements so you or Mae can alert the rest of the family. Tell them I expect a decent familial turnout. Can't have an empty church." As he exited the kitchen, he told his son to rest and get well soon.

Dash nodded and gave his father a quick salute. He settled down to look at the papers Owen had left. After a quick glance he decided they were duplicates of the papers given to him by Soames and Wilson. He hoped to find some dates that might be helpful in his quest to find the missing child, now very much an adult.

In exasperation, he turned to the many shoeboxes of bank records, old bills and who knew what else Maud decided to keep. He soon had the kitchen table filled with stacks of bank statements, cancelled checks, credit card bills, old utility bills and a miscellany of newspaper clippings.

He turned when he heard the door open to see Mae and T.J. coming in. Mae had her arms full of packages while his son carried two new books. He retrieved the packages and helped Mae store away the goodies.

"How's my main man feeling? Throat any better?" Mae asked.

Dash whispered. "Not really, but not any worse so I'm taking that as a good sign."

T.J. piped up immediately. "Daddy, you're not supposed to talk. Want to see my new books?" He then pointed to all the papers on the table and the shoe boxes on the floor. "What are you doing? Can I help?"

His father smiled. "Not a bad idea. I'm playing the matching game. I look at each piece of paper and put in the pile that it looks like. Let me show you." He demonstrated his method and T.J. jumped right in to help sort.

Dash glanced at Mae and gave her a thumbs up, his chest swelling with pride at T.J.'s ability to follow directions.

"How about soup for lunch and then we'll all pitch in? Many hands make light work or something like that," Mae said. "We'll move all this into the living room. Use one of those tables Owen and Tom set up for the 'research room.'"

So while Mae warmed up the soup, the Hammond guys carefully moved the stacks and boxes out of the kitchen. The adults were silent while eating but T.J. made up for both of them with his telling of his latest trip into town and the state of the family's bookstore.

They spent the next few hours sorting through all the shoe boxes. The bank statements were set aside for scrutiny, as were the newspaper clippings. These Dash intended to give to his uncle, hoping Tom might be able to learn more about Maud's life, her interests when she lived in Ireland.

For whatever reason, Maud also kept all the payroll receipts. Dash almost shredded these but decided to take another look. The money had to come from somewhere.

Dash sat at the table, his head resting on his hand. He opened his eyes when he heard Mae call a halt to the sorting, suggesting they head upstairs to bed to watch a movie so those who were tired but would not admit to it, could drift off to get much needed rest. He chuckled as T.J. started to protest until his mother, not so discreetly, pointed at his sleepy-eyed father.

Dash felt himself shaken and heard his name called several times. He slowly opened his eyes to find Mae's face a few inches from his.

"Is there a problem, Maevis? Why the scrutiny?" he croaked.

Mae pulled back. "It's just that you didn't want to wake up. Scares the crap out of me. Brings back too many bad memories."

Dash sighed and thought back to the horrible auto accident that changed his life.

"They shouldn't have called you."

"They didn't. Sam did. He felt as your ex-wife and dearest friend I would want to know that you were probably dying, if not dead, by the time we got to Kentucky."

"Well, I wasn't, and I didn't. And what could you have done? What did any of you do but hold my hand and pray?"

"I stroked your cheek and whispered into your ear about the wonderful life we would have if only you would wake up. And then you did, and, after a few bumps and bruises, we are having our wonderful life. See how that works."

She reached for his hand, kissed it, and set it back on the pillow. "Owen texted that he will be stopping with some information for you. That was a bit ago so he should be here shortly, and I wanted you awake and alert for whatever passes for breaking news."

Dash pulled himself up mumbling, "Why can't he just text the news? Always has to make a production of everything."

That comment sent Mae into a fit of laughing. "Talk about the kettle calling the pot black. You Hammonds have a real sense of drama about everything. It is quite amusing when you assemble all the usual and several unusual suspects for a great reveal." She started toward the door. "How about a cup of tea with honey in it for your throat? You sound much better, by the way, but don't overdo it."

He nodded and leaned back, hoping to drift off again. He barely had his eyes closed when he heard his father arrive with the appropriate fanfare.

"Dashiell, where are you? I've just broken the case wide open," Owen shouted from the kitchen. "Shall I come up?"

Dash jumped out of bed and headed for the stairs. Not wanting to waste his voice yelling, he pounded down the steps as fast as he could.

Owen danced around the kitchen waving papers about. Mae stood to one side, arms folded across her chest, slowly shaking her head. Ruthie waited in the doorway, a look on her face which said to all, 'I've had to listen to this nonsense for almost two hours now.'

T.J. came out of the front room. "What's with all the noise? I'm trying to put a puzzle together."

Owen ignored all the comments and motioned for everyone to take a seat at the table.

"The trip to the funeral home was enlightening to say the least. O'Conner, the director, pulled out Maud's file. He proceeded to go over all her arrangements, the usual stuff. Got that taken care of when he produced this little gem." Owen handed Dash one of the papers.

Dash read it and looked up at his father. "She bought two burial plots at St. Mary's. One used to bury Sean Kelly, a dear friend of hers. Since she had him cremated, she could have joined him in one grave. Wonder why she chose separate graves."

"Here is the death certificate for this fella Kelly and a copy of his driver's license. He look familiar?" Owen asked.

"It's Declan. Sean Kelly is Declan and he died September 10, 1967." Dash moved his mouth around. "So this daughter was born in 1968, three years after me. Turning fifty this year or just had a birthday." He studied the death certificate, "says Kelly died of a heart attack which jives with what Maud wrote. Wonder if the rest of the info, birth, occupation, are true or something Maud made up to fill in the blanks."

Ruthie raised her hand as if she were in class. "Another tidbit. O'Conner said Maud set up a fund for flowers to decorate Kelly's grave several times a year, one being St. Patrick's Day. The funeral home takes care of that for her. And, for what it's worth, I'm thinking she bought two graves so it wouldn't look like he was more than a dear friend. Cautious."

Dash nodded. "Makes sense. Still a grave short – for Callahan. But I'm sure we'll figure that out." He stood to cross the room to Owen and held out his hand. "Well done you. This *is* breaking news. I'll add the dates to the timeline. We can work back from Kelly's death date to an approximate one for their nemesis, Callahan. Then I guess I should concentrate on finding the child."

After a few more pats on his back, Owen led Ruthie out the door, saying that they had reservations at the Paprika Pot for dinner. Champagne on the menu to celebrate this latest find.

Mae's parting words to Ruthie were, "Call if you need a ride home, please, no drinking and driving."

Dash woke up to find himself alone in bed. He looked at his phone. It was 1:30 in the morning. Wondering where his wife was, he slid out of bed and peered down the hall. No lights on in T.J.'s room but a glow coming from downstairs.

Grabbing his robe and slippers, he headed down the stairs. As expected, he found Mae at the table. What surprised him was the number of papers she had strewn across the tabletop.

She glanced up at him as he pulled out a chair.

"That money had to come from somewhere. I'm checking to see if Maud was the source. We know she lived frugally ..."

"We do? How?" Dash asked.

Mae shook her head. "You did look around her place, right? See anything less than two decades old? And her wardrobe. She didn't spend money on clothes, jewelry, or books. So, what did she do with it? I'm cross-checking her paystubs with the bank statements. For example, in the month of September 1969, her earnings were $800 from her primary job as a bookkeeper—small manufacturing place close to her house, and approximately $100 from an overnight part-time job at the bank. If you compare the bank statement, you'll see she saved at least a hundred dollars a paycheck. Her cancelled checks show a mortgage payment, utility bills and a small payment to Fries and Schuele. Remember that was the department store at the corner of West 25th and Lorain? Landmark forever, or until 1979 when it closed."

Dash motioned for her to speed it up. "I'm growing old sitting here, my lovely. Can you cut to the chase?"

Mae stuck her tongue out at him. "Ungrateful sod. What I'm thinking is she banked a bit of money and hid some cash in the house. Why? Don't know. Those Irish notes are old issues, so my thought is that they were the getaway money she and Declan used to escape Ireland. They get here, stash the cash in the rented house with intention to buy. The stash just got bigger and bigger."

"You think she forgot about it? And the gun? I guess that's possible, given her age." He stood and took Mae's hand. "Leave it for now. I know you don't need your beauty sleep, but I do. Tomorrow, well, later this morning, I'll check some later months, years to see if you might be right."

"Might be! Might be! When have I been wrong?" Mae said as she followed her husband up the stairs. "Huh, huh, when have I been wrong?"

As Dash crawled back into bed, he asked, "When have I ever been right? That is the question, Red. Now go to sleep."

"It's auburn, you idjit. How many times to I have to tell you that?"

Dash sighed and rolled over.

The next day Dash cajoled Mae into making a call to Zara so he could set up a meeting with her after the funeral. Since his voice was still at the whisper only stage and he looked ever so mournful, she agreed, even offered to go along to take notes. He declined that offer since one of the questions burning inside him was just what they did that night at Maud's. And who was the man with Maud? He also needed time with her mothers to glean whatever information they could pass along.

Still feeling a bit under the weather, Dash was dozing in the recliner when Sam showed up with Owen in tow.

"What's up, bro?" Dash asked.

"This is going to be a little come-to-Jesus meeting for you and Dad. See I'm not as dense as you two think ..." Sam said before he was cut off by his brother.

"Dense. We don't think that!" Dash said. "You might not be the sharpest knife in the box but not dense, dumb, or even the dullest guy around."

Sam glared at his brother. "So how about the two of you tell me what's going on? Thomas finds a gun. Do you tell me? Not right away. And I bet neither of you thought of fingerprints, did you?"

"Sam, I did check to see if the gun had ever been fired. The answer is no." Owen said. "And what fingerprints would you compare them to? Think this Rooney fellow is on an international most wanted list, do you?"

The sheriff ignored all that and asked instead, "Where is the gun now? Any objection to taking it for testing?"

Dash said, "Not on my part. It's in the safe and I'll get it for you now." He walked to the office followed by Sam and his father.

Opening the safe, he pulled out the gun, handing it to his brother. "Here you go."

Before he could shut the safe door, Sam pushed him aside and reached in to pull out a wad of money.

"And this, dear brother, might be what? The reason you asked if Maud had lost trust in banks? Again, what's going on?"

Dash sat down on the floor. "T.J. was a very busy little boy. He was playing with his cars and one fell into a hole in the floor, upstairs bedroom. He reached in and first pulled out an Irish note and then these wads of good old U. S. of A. bills. A cool one hundred thousand, rolled in packs of five thousand. And, before you ask, we don't have the foggiest idea of how Maud accumulated this money, *if* indeed it was Maud. One of many things I guess I will be 'seeking or finding' an answer to."

Owen reached out to Sam, touching his arm. "Now you are up to speed. Bottom line, we know nothing. How, why, when. What was the money for if Maud was the one saving it? For all we know, someone in the neighborhood was taking advantage of her inability to get upstairs and stashed the gun and money. Doesn't explain the Irish money though."

Sam looked from his father to his brother. "Have you filed for probate? Did you include this money? You guys are up to your asses in trouble." He looked from one relative to the other, then sighed. "What can I do to help?"

By Monday, the day before the funeral, Dash had his voice back and he felt better. He decided to ask his construction partner, Danny Jeffries, to accompany him and Brenda on a quick trip to Maud's house. Inside again, Dash immediately felt uneasy. He cursed Maud, her house and all her dirty secrets.

After only a half hour, Dash turned to Brenda. "Well, kiddo, what do you think? Still voting for tearing it down?"

Brenda frowned. "Why wouldn't you? Do you really want to spend the money to fix it up? If you do sell it, the new owner will just tear it down. Any refurbishing would change the exterior as well as the interior so much so that this Maud person wouldn't recognize it." She put her hand on his arm. "Trust me, Dash. Sell it, get what you can and either donate the money or invest it and retire again."

He turned to Danny. "Want to weigh in on this? Your thoughts."

Danny sighed. "Can't totally agree or disagree with Brenda. Tear it down, easy money; fix it up, costly, but you'd preserve the neighborhood. Have you talked to the neighbors?"

Dash shrugged. "Not yet. Thought I'd do that if any of them show up for the funeral. Let's do another walk-through and tell me what needs doing if I decide to be really stupid and keep the place."

So they started another tour, ending in the kitchen. Dash reached for Danny's clipboard and read:

> *Coal chute – check old furnace and foundation.*
> *Flooring – remove all old vinyl or linoleum; asbestos ???*
> *Upstairs bathroom – save cast iron tub.*
> *Windows/doors – replace/update.*
> *Restore all rooms to original purpose.*

He handed the clipboard back to Danny. Instead of thinking about the cost to renovate the place, he shouted triumphantly to himself. A basement! Good place to hide a body; easy to roll Callahan into it. Put new flooring down and Paddy's your uncle, as the Irish might say.

As they locked up to head home, Dash asked Brenda. "Well, my dear, what do I owe you for all your advice? And don't think I won't pay you."

Brenda turned to him. "How about you put a bug in my hubby's ear that I deserve a week at a very fancy hotel complete with spa and shopping? You get Tommy to spring for a nice vacation and we're square. What say you, old soldier?"

"Pick a place and I'll make sure you get there, with or without that workaholic husband of yours. Danny, give me estimates on everything but the asbestos removal. I'll get a professional removal company to handle that. Better safe than sorry."

CHAPTER TWELVE

On the drive home, Dash received a call from Father Tom. Another excited relative.

"Dash, Dash, guess what I found?" Tom asked.

"The fountain of youth, Uncle, because I can see you smiling from here."

"Well, I formed a bond with a priest in Ireland while doing all this family tree stuff for the folks at Lakeview. Father Finn Flannery. Anyway, Finn is researching the newspapers for information on the infamous Callahan murder. He's found several things. When will you be home because you have to see all this?"

There goes my dream of crawling into bed for a quick nap, Dash thought.

"I'll be there in less than an hour or should I go to your place?"

"No, no, I need to post all this on the board. I'll head to the old homestead, and we can go over all this together," Tom said. Dash could almost see the priest rubbing his hands together.

"Roger that. Over and out."

Dash arrived home to find Tom sitting on the front steps, a large manila envelope at his side.

"Where's your dog collar? Incognito today? Out chasing the ladies?" he asked his uncle.

"Playing sleuth, like Father Brown but he wore his collar all the time. I've got one in the car if you insist."

"I don't. Come on in and let's see what your buddy Finn has discovered. Finn Flannery, good Irish name."

They sat at the kitchen table, which was always the central focus of the home. Spread before them were twenty or so news articles; most were from the *Meath Chronicle*, the weekly newspaper that would cover the small town in County Meath where Maud's family and the Callahan clan resided.

Dash picked up one of the earlier pieces dated June 6, 1956, and read it aloud:

"A tragedy took place Friday evening in Duleek. James Callahan, husband of Caitlin, cut down in his prime in a knife fight, died. No arrests at this time though Garda is looking for Declan Rooney. He resided at 21 Ruck Lane with his wife, Siobhan, and three children. Eyewitnesses report a nasty exchange between Callahan and Rooney who has since disappeared."

Tom jumped ahead five years with another short article: Still no arrests for the murder and Declan Rooney was still missing, along with his companion Maud Grealis. The reporter discovered Maud had emigrated to the United States shortly after the death of Callahan. No specific city named as her destination, nor could the reporter find anything verifying that Declan had accompanied her.

Each year on the anniversary of Jimmy's murder, this reporter, one Kevin O'Leary, would run a paragraph or two reminding the readers of the unsolved crime.

"I don't suppose this Kevin is still alive. Did Finn check?"

"No, no. I mean Finn hasn't found him yet. Not listed in the parish book as deceased so there is still hope," Tom said.

Dash reached over to his uncle. "Tom, you know I love you dearly. You're the father I always wanted, but I am exhausted. A real wuss in my middle age. Would you excuse me while I take a short nap? You can stay and do whatever you like. When Mae finishes her appointments and picks up T.J., we're going to JoJo's for dinner. You are welcome to come."

Tom gathered the papers. "Thanks, but no. Another poker game tonight. If you don't mind, I'll post these articles on the board and then sneak up to the attic. If I remember correctly, your mother had a box or two of Irish memorabilia. I'm wondering if she kept anything that might help us." He motioned shoo-shoo to Dash. "Off you go Dashy boy."

Dash slid under the covers hoping for a nap which should relieve him of his headache. The nap did not happen as every step Tom took sounded like a bowling ball dropped on the bedroom ceiling. Then he heard a crash.

Jumping up, Dash pulled on sweatpants and raced up the stairs to find Tom sitting on the floor with several boxes around him.

"Sorry, Dash, I slipped," Tom said apologetically. "But I found the box I was looking for. Here, let's see what your mother kept."

Dash sat down next to his uncle and began sorting the objects in the box. He stopped when he found a photograph of his mother on her wedding day. He handed it to his uncle.

Tom fingered the photo and smiled. "She was a beautiful woman. So delicate looking but tough as it comes. I remember when your father brought her to dinner so we could meet his new love. We listened *ad nauseum* about how pretty she was, how smart. My father, your Pappy, stood open-mouthed when Helene-Marie set foot on the doorstep with Owen. Then she joined us for dinner answering a ton of questions." Tom stopped and began chuckling at the memory. "She spoke with the thickest brogue ever. She was unintelligible but we were so polite we just nodded at her answers. After she and Owen left, Dad turned to me and Joe. He said, 'I can see why he wants to marry her, the prettiest little woman around. But, damn, he can't honestly understand what she says. For all we know she was making fun of us in Irish.'"

Again, Tom doubled over in laughter. Dash joined him, thinking his mother was mischievous enough to play the 'off the boat' Irish maiden.

They looked at every trinket and photo in the box. Nothing related to Maud.

"Help me up, Dash. I do believe I'm getting old."

Dash held out his hand and pulled his uncle up.

Tom said, "Well, I'm off to the 'restless' home. I do believe it is roast chicken night and it is the best. I always have two helpings."

Dash bid his uncle farewell. Deciding that he wouldn't be able to sleep now, he returned to the attic to hold his mother's private memory box. If only she hadn't died …

CHAPTER THIRTEEN

The day of the funeral dawned gray and somber with a light drizzle falling. Maud's instructions were simple: an open coffin viewing at the church, Mass, then a short ride to the crematorium. She made no mention of a 'spirited' Irish wake afterwards, but the Ladies' Society planned a fitting send-off.

The well-represented Hammond clan filled several pews. Missing was Father Tom who refused to attend and even went so far as to say uncharitable things about Maud. When asked, he told Dash, "She was a mean and spiteful old biddy. She hated my brother and was always filling Helene-Marie's ear with rubbish. She knew I didn't like her, and the feeling was mutual. No sense being a hypocrite at this point in my life. Old dogs don't change stripes." Since that last sentence made no sense to his nephew, Dash just nodded.

The church was packed with parishioners and neighbors. Some were even tearing up. Dash and Owen exchanged glances. Dash whispered to his father, "They must have heard about the spread of food I'm footing."

Once the Mass was over, everyone stood as the coffin rolled out of the church and into the waiting hearse for the final ride to the crematorium.

The mourners drifted over to the church hall for a bit to eat and a bit of neighborly gossiping. The Altar and Rosary Society matrons baked their hearts out, so the tables were heavy with casseroles, cakes, and cookies. Out of Maud's money, Dash paid a caterer to bring hot dishes and beverages. No one would leave hungry or thirsty as Dash also footed the bill for good Irish whisky and Guinness beer.

Dash watched as his father and brother made the rounds, thanking everyone for coming and encouraging them to take seconds and thirds, suggesting they take leftovers home for supper.

A tallish man approached Dash as he sat with Mae, Cousin Billy Mac and his wife, Elena. Extending his hand, the man introduced himself. "Colonel Hammond, I'm John Mullins. I live on the west side of Miss Maud. Would you join us, her neighbors, at the table over there? We'd like to ask you a few questions, please."

Dash shook the hand and said, "No problem. I was hoping to meet all of you, and this is as good a time as ever." Excusing himself, he followed Muldoon across the hall where the table of neighbors waited.

Muldoon began the introductions. "You know Mrs. Brady. Let me introduce the 'P' side of the street as Miss Maud called them. This here is Julius Potts; he lives across from the Bradys. Etta Ray Patton and her son Leon live in the middle house, and this here is Eddie Prusak. His place is opposite mine."

Dash shook hands with all. "I get the 'P' side now. Actually, sounds like one side is decidedly Irish and the other not. And please call me Dash or Hammond if you must. I dropped the colonel when I retired. So please, let's be informal here." He pulled out a chair and sat down. "I understand you have questions. I hope I have some answers."

Muldoon asked the big question. "Are you going to sell the house? Do you plan on tearing it down to build one of those designer homes?"

"Honestly, folks, I haven't made up my mind. Going to study all angles here. Your little block is a bit of an anomaly. All six homes are original to the neighborhood. Are you worried that if I don't sell and let the house sit there, your property values will go down? I imagine your places are worth a pretty penny with the development going on."

Julius Potts shook his head. "That might have been true, but there's a bit of a bust right now. The values are holding steady, much more than we paid or are paying for them. No, it's just that most of us have been on the street for at least ten years or more. Hate to say we don't want change, but we don't."

This time Eddie Prusak spoke up. 'You see, Mr. Hammond, if you sell there's no reason to believe the new owners won't tear it down and build a monstrosity. Now I'm for progress as much as the next man ..."

Dash looked around the table thinking none of them were for progress if it meant messing with their quiet street.

He held up his hand. "As I said, no decision. May I ask how you felt about Maud? I understood her to be a cranky old lady. Don't know if anyone's told you this but she called my father and said something funny was going on. Any ideas? I mean, was she just imagining things? Did she talk to any of you about this? My father and I are trying to settle in our minds what went on."

The neighbors looked at each other, most shaking their heads.

Lillian Prusak spoke up. "I can honestly say that Maud was the sharpest woman I ever met, even right to the end. If she thought something funny was going on, then probably something was. As for cranky, she might have had her moments, but I think of her as a wonderful neighbor. She always had her crock pot going with a soup or stew. If you stopped by, you had to sit and eat with her. And whatever she made would be good."

Several of the neighbors smiled and laughed as Dash made a mental note: sharpest woman, crock pot.

"Maud and her crock pot. She gave up using the stove a decade or so ago. Someone had given her a crock pot and a cookbook, and she never looked back. She said it was safer for a person her age. If she forgot to turn off the pot, it was unlikely to start a fire whereas the stove ..." Etta Ray said.

"Crock pot?" Dash asked. "There wasn't any crock pot when we showed up. All I saw in the kitchen was a lot of rotting food and rodents. If pressed, I'd say I might have seen a toaster and an electric tea pot. Big crock pot or little?" He leaned back in the chair. "Would you all mind a little round robin of questions? If someone was messing with Maud, I'd like to find out who and why."

He pulled out a notebook and turned to Muldoon. "When was the last time you saw or spoke with Maud?"

He asked that question of everyone at the table. "What did the crock pot look like? Did Maud usually carry a purse? How did she pay you when you brought her groceries? Did she have any workmen in the house recently?"

The answers came fast. Big black crock pot, 7-quart size. Old fashioned black patent purse with large handles. Very worn leather wallet, like a man's. A couple of hundred dollars, small bills and a single one-hundred-dollar bill. No work done on the house in a long time.

After a half hour of questioning the neighbors, Dash saw Billy heading his way. "Hey, Dash, are you bothering these folks? I see a notebook and that can only mean an interrogation. Shall I drag him away so you all can get seconds?"

Apologizing for taking up their time, Dash stood and said he would meet with them several times before making any decisions. Nodding to all, he and Billy walked across the room.

Dash spotted Zara sitting at a table tucked into a corner of the hall and raised his hand in greeting. He parted from Billy and made his way to her. Suddenly he felt Mae at his side.

"Is this your woman?" Zara asked, nodding toward Mae.

"Not only my woman but my wife. Zara, this is Maevis Summers. She's the one who called you about meeting." He pulled out chairs so they could join Zara.

"Sure you want your wife to hear what went on?" she asked.

Smiling, Mae answered for her husband. "Zara, unless you tell me he raped you and, I think that's highly unlikely, believe me when I say I've heard it all before. Nothing will shock me."

Dash shrugged. "So Miss Zara, reveal all. Let's start with the year this took place. Vague idea but nothing exact. Then I will have some specific questions, hoping the answers will help me on my new quest."

Zara ran her fingers through her hair, then reached into her pocket. She pulled out an envelope, handing it to Dash.

"It was 1993; recorded it in my diary. You left me this." She turned to Mae. "I'm not sure you've heard this before, but he was a huge disappointment to me."

Dash leaned in a bit. "Huge? I must say *I've* never heard that before. Wow! I must have been very drunk that night."

"No, you weren't. You were disappointing because you were the perfect gentleman. I was so hot to get into your pants and you were *so* not interested. Really was deflating to me, a young impressionable girl, hoping for a night of hot sex."

A broad smile broke over Dash's face. "Things are coming back to me. You were what, sixteen, seventeen at the time. You tried to convince me you were twenty-one but stupid I ain't. Very pretty, very willing but a career killer if not jailbait. I had at least a decade on you." He nodded. "Yes, little Zara, it's starting to come back to me."

Mae pulled the envelope from Dash's hand and slid out the letter. She read it then turned to Dash. "Shall I?"

He nodded, "Why not?"

Z. Here's hoping your hangover isn't hellacious this morning. I enjoyed talking and dancing with you. My advice is to avoid Maud and whatever machinations she has in mind for you. Get your education and follow your dreams. Remember that getting drunk is not as attractive as you think. Please take care and think fondly of this night. I will.

D.

Mae handed the letter and envelope back to Zara. "That's my guy. Education first and pleasure later."

"I remember Maud introducing us at the church hall when everyone was singing, dancing, and drinking. The bartender refused to serve you since he said you were a mere babe to him. I kept that in mind when you later tried to convince me you were old enough for a tumble in bed. Figured that guy knew your age," Dash said.

"Can't fault a girl for trying. Man, you were good looking, the best guy I'd ever seen. I couldn't believe it when Maud suggested we all go to her house so I could get a few belts of good Irish whiskey. She kept handing me glasses and you took quite a few away from me. You drank a lot but never got drunk. Maud and her companion were blotto. They made their way upstairs to her bedroom leaving us to whatever I could entice you into. Sadly, it was nothing."

Zara shook her head. "You tried to convince me to let you take me home, but I couldn't have my mothers see me like that and I had already told them I was staying at Maud's that night. You walked me upstairs to the spare bedroom, set a wastebasket next to the bed in case I got sick, told me to lock the door and bid me goodbye. Never saw you again until you guys sat down in my diner."

"After all this time, how did you recognize him? I mean, he has changed more than a bit," Mae asked and then added as her husband gave her a look, "Definitely for the better."

Dash held up his hand. "Maud and her photos, right?"

Zara nodded. "Oh, was she pissed at you. Not sure what you thought she was up to but that note you left her had her seeing red, through very bloodshot eyes."

"What did you say to her?" Mae asked her husband.

"Don't remember but I'm sure I called her a nasty name and insinuated she wanted me to do some bad deeds that night. I can imagine her seething. And now she leaves me everything. Go figure." Dash frowned. "Zara, I don't suppose you remember the name of the guy who spent the night with Maud."

Her shoulders started to shake as she broke into laughter. "Oh, him. His name was Alexander Bodnar. He was a butcher over at the West Side Market. He only had eyes for Maud."

Dash muttered, "So he was blind, was he? I hate to speak ill of the dead, but Maud wasn't anywhere near good looking when she was young, and she did not age well as my dear departed mother would say."

Mae reached over to touch her husband's arm. "Wait a minute. I looked at the pictures of Maud when she was young, and no Rita Hayworth for sure, but she had a definite look of mischief about her. I bet all the men wanted to find just what was behind that look. Mind your mouth, you ungrateful sod. She left you a nice pile, so say please and thank you."

Dash just rolled his eyes. "Zara, would your mothers have any more information about Maud's life since, and I am just assuming this, they were her lawyers and financial advisors. Hoping she confided a few secrets to them. I'm really struggling here to put together the timeline I so desperately need to help me with her last request."

"We honestly never talk about their clients, even the ones who are also my customers. Only if so-and-so is looking poorly do we comment. They like to help their clients out since many are right on the poverty-line."

"How does Sloames and Wilson stay in business?" Dash asked.

Zara shrugged. "Talk to them. I know Willie is a genius when it comes to investing. Have you studied the reports she gave you on Maud's finances? Let's just say this: my mothers aren't filthy rich, just extremely comfortable. And they've made sure my finances are heading that way. I mean they own several apartment buildings so I will always have a roof over my head. We work on a percentage deal – they get a percentage of my take at the restaurant for rent there and at the apartment. Nice deal for me, that's for sure."

Dash looked around the room and then asked Zara, "I thought I saw your mothers here. Could use a word with them today. Save myself a trip back."

"They had work to do so stayed the polite amount of time and then skedaddled. Hate to say it but they're not especially social," Zara said. "I'll give them a call and see if you, we, can stop by." She pulled out her phone, spoke into it, then turned to Dash. "They're fine with us coming now. Have a client in an hour."

"Excellent. Let's do it and then we can head home to our little guy, so he doesn't think we abandoned him."

"Don't worry," Mae replied. "He's in very good hands with Ruthie. She will take him to JoJo's for dinner if we're not home by six. He's having the time of his life."

With Zara in tow, Dash and Mae made the rounds at the reception, thanking everyone for coming. They let the Hammond clan in on their plans for the rest of the day before driving over to the law offices of Sloames and Wilson.

Henri and Willie met them at the door.

"We keep the place locked. Just super-cautious since a lot of our papers are confidential. No money in the house, but hard to convince the run-of-the-mill burglar. Come on up and let's see how we can help you today." Willie said as she ushered her daughter and the Hammonds in.

Once seated in the office, Dash said, "I'm hoping attorney-client privilege still applies."

Henri glanced at Willie, then spoke. "Of course it does. Death doesn't end our professional relationship with Maud, and now you, her heir."

Nodding, Dash said, "I'm not sure when Maud hired you to be her attorneys, so this may be moot. Here's the question: In the letter from Maud, the quest she set out for me was to find her daughter." Seeing the look on the attorneys' faces, he held up his hand. "Sorry, but she gave very little information other than that. No concrete dates, nothing about where she gave up the baby. I'm estimating the child might be fifty years old now."

"To be honest, Mr. Hammond, I for one am speechless. Maud donated money to several organizations that had child welfare at the core of their mission, but never did she indicate why." Willie got up and moved to a cabinet. She pulled out an overflowing file. After shuffling through it, she pulled out one sheet and slid it over to Dash.

"Don't know if this will help, but for years I summarized her donations by charity. As you can see, she spread her money around, not favoring one to a greater extent than the others."

Dash studied the sheet then handed it to Mae. "I can see that this little piece of news has surprised you." He glanced at his watch. "We need to get back to our son, but would you give this some thought? If any bells or whistles go off, give me a call, send a text. I will be going back and forth for a few weeks until I decide what to do with the house. Met with the neighbors for a short while after the funeral and they have concerns. Promised we'd have a sit-down to discuss all of this."

He stood and shook hands with the attorneys. Mae did likewise. Turning to Zara, he said, "Okay, green-haired girl, I'll be seeing you for lunch or dinner as the weeks go by. Can't promise I won't continue to disappoint you, but I'll try." He kissed her cheek.

"Ladies, until we meet again …"

As he pulled out of the tiny parking lot behind the attorneys' office, he glanced over at Mae. "Hey, what say you about a quickie at Maud's before we head home?" He turned his head so she couldn't see him smile.

"You're joking right? You want to make love to me in a house where at least one murder has taken place, not to mention the million germs from mice and rotting meat and stuff all over the place. If you even slow down as we go by that place, there might be another murder – and trust me, it would be justified." Mae crossed her arms and frowned deeply at her husband.

Dash broke out in laughter. "Can't blame a guy for trying!" He continued, "Honestly, after getting sick, I'm not looking forward to spending a lot of time there, and definitely not naked. Just jerking your chain, Mae B. Home it is!"

CHAPTER FOURTEEN

The next few days Dash and Mae tried to get the family back on schedule. Dash resumed T.J. duty, taking the little one to 'school' in the morning and picking him up in the afternoon. He checked in at the bookstore and was assured all was going well. He and Danny sat down to go over all the repairs and renovations needed at Maud's house. Danny found an asbestos removal company which wasn't cheap but more cost effective than buying the necessary equipment to do it themselves.

"And let's add lead paint into the mix. Maybe both contaminants can be removed at the same time." Dash said. Leaning back in his chair, he added, "Wonder if I should offer those services to the other families on the street. I doubt if those problems were on the inspection list back when these homes were last sold. All of these are post-World War II builds. I don't know if the hazards of asbestos or lead paint were known at that time. I'll check to see when Maud bought the house."

He shoved his tablet over to Danny. "Work your magic, my friend. After I get the figures, we can talk about bringing in our guys to do the remodeling. One or two things I need to check before we start."

"Got it. I'll have the figures by the end of next week. No rush, right?"

Dash nodded. "Right. Several items not related to the house need attention or Mae will have my head on a platter. And Owen, as executor, needs to file all this with probate before I start spending money left and right."

That night Dash and Mae sat in their bed, tired but unable to fall asleep. Dash wrapped his arms around his wife.

"You know I've been thinking about Maud and all this seeking and finding. Remember when Zara said Maud was very upset with me after the wild night of drinking that long ago St. Paddy's Day. Wonder if Maud hoped I would disgrace myself and my family by bedding that underaged but mighty delicious young Zara. I'm thinking this whole inheritance is Maud's idea of revenge. Dead body, missing child. A bunch of bullshit. She hoped I'd spend all my time and all her money running around looking and searching, not finding anything. A pretty good idea, toy with my battered mind, my morals."

When Mae didn't answer, he looked down to find she had fallen asleep. So much for her slant on his new theory. After kissing the top of her head, he gently slid down under the covers, wrapping his arms and the blankets around his beloved. He closed his eyes hoping to dream the dreams of the just and good.

CHAPTER FIFTEEN

Dash and Owen sat across the table watching Father Tom spread out the latest batch of news clippings from Ireland. The priest laid the articles out in chronological order. When he finished, he leaned back and smiled.

"Behold, before you is the conclusion of good old Finn's work. I've made notes about dates and personnel so I can walk you through it. This explains all, except why Maud thought it was necessary to kill the brother Callahan."

Dash reached over to pull an article over to him, but he got his hand slapped for his efforts.

"I told you I would explain all. Now, nephew, sit back and listen; take notes if you need."

Tom pointed to the first article. "This is the beginning, where one Seamus/James Callahan was killed in a knife fight. Here is where Declan Rooney is named as a suspect and Maud mentioned as a witness. Most of this has a 'rumor has it' flavor to it. Moving on are the clippings talking about the murder, the search for Rooney, and fresh evidence."

Tapping his finger on a rather long article, he continued, "This is a summation of all that is known. I told you the author, Kevin O'Leary, revisited the murder every anniversary. Well, as expected, O'Leary left the paper and disappeared." The priest reached into the deep pockets of his cassock and pulled out a slim volume, *A DEATH IN COUNTY MEATH*. He placed the book at the center of the table. "Gentlemen, O'Leary took that time to thoroughly research the Callahans, the Rooneys and Maud Grealis."

Dash reached for the book. He smiled. "So good old Kevin O'Leary, whose name I took in vain, has solved all our problems. Way to go, Kevin." He began to read, his smile growing larger with each page.

He looked at his uncle who was frowning. Dash was raining on his parade. "Tom, do you want to give us the summary?"

Tom, a little piqued, shook his head. "No, no, you do the honors. You're a much faster reader. Owen will lose patience waiting for me to muddle through."

"Well, son, you want to tell me what O'Leary says?" Owen asked.

Holding up a finger, Dash said, "Give me a bit to skim the book and I will give you the Cliff Notes version. From first blush, I'd say that County Meath was a hot bed of sexual antics and short tempers." He stood to move to the front room. "Gentlemen, get yourselves some refreshments. A beer for me wouldn't go amiss."

It was less than an hour when Dash returned to the kitchen table. Owen and Tom had decided to eat most of what was in the refrigerator, causing Dash to wonder about the food at Lakeview Retirement Home.

"Owen, Tom, are you ready for an Irish version of Peyton Place?"

"It took you long enough. Always thought you were a speed reader," Owen said.

Dash opened the book to a page with four photographs on it. "Here are the Callahan brothers, the center of all this. James, aka Seamus, was the oldest and now the deadest. Someone stuck a knife in him, more than once, not taking any chances. Liam and Conor are the middle brothers, with Sean aka John bringing up the rear. From what O'Leary writes, and it could be libelous though the Callahans didn't know what that meant, the I.Q. of the brothers went down with each new birth. So, Maud's 'cleansing of the clans' wasn't too far off the mark. Nothing in concrete, but I can believe Liam and Conor put Sean on a plane to get him out of the way."

The former sheriff asked, "Any motive for James' death?"

"O'Leary speculates the brothers were into wife-swapping and other decidedly nasty deeds. They were fine with passing their wives among themselves, but that rascal Declan Rooney invaded the cozy little arrangement. And Rooney's wife wasn't without sin, as they say. A regular round robin. Maud got in the middle of all this, more speculation that she was the cause of the killing, not the killer. Rooney fled with her to the states, leaving behind more wives than husbands."

Turning to another page of photographs, Dash continued, "These are the women in all this. O'Leary checked into their backgrounds and several had 'form' as the Brits or Irish would say. They were handy with the rolling pin and one, James' wife, was retained at one time for threatening another woman with a knife."

Tom asked, "Since I didn't get to the end of the book, what's O'Leary's conclusion? Did he think Declan or Maud did the deed?"

Dash shook his head. "His conclusion is based on speculation, using the information at hand. No fingerprints on the knife. No reliable witness statements. Everyone named a different person as the killer. Declan got two votes, so he was the one the Garda sought."

O'Leary's conclusion was that James' wife would have killed her husband over anything from forgetting to put the seat down to fondling Maud in public. Why she didn't go for Maud was obvious: Maud was slightly more dangerous, having IRA connections. Here, there, everywhere, you don't mess with the IRA. Owen, you're better equipped to determine if this speculation could be correct."

Dash slid the book over to his father. "Excellent work, Tom. You deserve a steak dinner with all the fixings. Anytime, on me." Turning to Owen, he said, "You're invited as well. Bring Ruthie and we'll make a night of it."

CHAPTER SIXTEEN

Dash spent the next week surveying the work at Maud's house. After receiving the report that no asbestos or lead was present, Dash and a few of Danny's crew pulled up all the linoleum in the house. He released the crew for the day not wanting company when he inspected the basement.

After taking a deep breath, he re-entered the house, trying to convince himself he was ready for anything. In the kitchen, he pulled the trap door ring to open the basement hatch. He lit his headlamp and stepped carefully down the stairs. The musky smell made him wrinkle his nose. What would he find down here in Maud's private dungeon?

Flashing the light around the ceiling, he looked for a ceiling light, something to illuminate this dark, dank space. The two small windows on the far wall only highlighted the cobwebs hanging from the ceiling.

He found the solo fixture with a thin string hanging down. When pulled, most of it came off in his hand, but the little bulb flickered and then lit. The circle of light was still small and dim, so Dash kept his headlamp on. He did a slow turn around the room. On one side he saw the furnace with a bit of coal around its base. He pulled the door open. For a second, he had the horrible thought he would find the remains of Callahan among the ashes but saw nothing of the kind. Thinking he needed to revisit this with a shovel or a rake, he closed the door.

In one of the corners was a stack of boxes. He walked over to inspect them. They were empty so he moved them aside, one after another.

On the ground behind the boxes, Dash saw three little mounds, a cross at one end of each. The remains of long-ago flowers lay scattered around the graves. He knelt down to read the writing on the crosses. He pulled his headlamp off and lit each cross. Lucy, Cora, Murphy. He fell back on his butt. The words from Maud's letter, *'one who lived, not like the others'* screamed at him. He stared at the crosses, asking himself if these were 'the others.' He swallowed hard and slowly shook his head. *Maud, Maud, what have you done?*

He reached out to the first mound but stopped himself. Instead, he pulled out his phone. Pictures of the untouched graves were what he wanted. Then he scrolled through his contacts until he found Dr. James Brooks, the coroner for Lakota County and a good friend.

"Brooksie, it's Dash. Say, you wouldn't be free for a long lunch, would you? I'm in Cleveland and have found what might be three little graves. Not sure if these are pets or babies. Can you help me out here?"

He heard Brooksie chuckle. "I'll say this, Dash, you never disappoint. It so happens I have a light day and I'd love to take a little trip. And, just to get this clear in my mind, why aren't you calling the coroner in Cuyahoga County? I do believe his office is located in Cleveland."

"Well, truth be told, if these are dogs or cats, I'd rather be embarrassed in front of you than a stranger. You will take this in stride, knowing this old soldier is a bit banged-up in the brain department." He stopped. "Listen, this whole thing is part of a very strange tale, entertaining for sure. I'll owe you a million favors."

"You had me at three little graves. I'll be there in under an hour; I'll put the sirens on, so I'm not hampered. Text me the address and I'll gather my things. See you soon." Before he rang off, he added, "You don't need to be reminded not to touch, disturb anything, right?"

Getting Dash's assurances he would be a model citizen, the call ended.

Dash used the time waiting for Brooksie's arrival to do a finger-tip inspection of the basement. He wondered if a larger grave, that of Mr. Callahan, would be down there. No such luck.

Moving upstairs, he sat at the dining room table staring out the window waiting for Brooksie. He wondered how much of the story he should tell him. A knock on the door disturbed his reverie. Leon.

"Why aren't you in school?" Dash asked the boy.

"I'm feeling a bit under the weather, so I begged off the rest of the day." Leon answered. "I saw your truck when I left this morning. Decided you might need help doing whatever you're doing."

"Ah, didn't think of that. Listen kiddo, I don't really have anything for you right now. Tomorrow is Saturday and I'm spending the night here." Seeing the look on the boy's face, he added, "No, not here but at a hotel downtown. I'll be back to do some work and you can help."

They both turned to see the Lakota Coroner County's car pull into the drive.

"Wow, that's a fancy car," Leon commented.

Dash stood saying, "I have business with that old friend of mine. Run along, preferably back to school. I'll check in with you before I head to the hotel, okay? Maybe get a burger, okay?"

He watched Leon as he slowly trudged across the street, all the time staring at the big black car.

The door to the car opened and Brooksie climbed out, wearing his usual dark suit. Dapper was the first word that came to mind. Brooksie was of decent height, pure white hair even though he was a few years younger than Dash, and the best crooked smile ever.

Dash walked over to the car. "James, I can't thank you enough for this. I'm hoping this is an exercise in madness on my part, because if it's not, it is a very sad story. Can I help you with your gear?"

The men gathered a few duffel bags from the car and headed indoors. Once inside, Brooksie turned to Dash and said, "Okay, now my good Colonel, what's going on?"

Dash relayed a part of the Maud Grealis story and how she wanted him to find her daughter given up years ago. "The reason I called you about the graves is she indicated she had several miscarriages or even a stillborn child before this live birth, the daughter she couldn't keep. Being of the old Irish mindset she felt her only recourse was to hand her daughter over to an agency or individual to provide a better life." He shrugged. "Brooksie, I'm terrified those graves are her lost children. If they are, I need to give them a decent resting place, not buried in a basement."

"Well then, I guess we should get started." Brooksie stood, rummaged through one of the duffel bags to pull out the standard issue coveralls for crime scene investigating. "Put this on. If nothing else, we'll keep our clothes clean." He gathered a small shovel and large evidence bags. "After you, Hammond."

Dash retrieved his ballcap and headlamp. He grabbed another flashlight from his go bag. He led Brooksie to the edge of the kitchen, stopping him there. He walked over to the hatch and hoisted up the trap door.

The men made their way cautiously down the steps.

"You take photos?" Brooksie asked Dash and acknowledged the affirmative nod. "From all sides?" Again, an affirmative nod. "Then get ready to document this step-by-step just in case these aren't tiny dogs or kittens."

The work began ever so meticulously. Dash knelt next to the coroner videotaping every move.

Murphy's grave was the first uncovered. Brooksie used his hands to wipe the loose dirt away. He then used the small shovel digging down about a foot. He reached in and touched something. Brushing away the dirt he pulled out the remnants of a pink blanket.

Dash moved in closer.

Brooksie slowly unwrapped the bundle. In his hands he held a small rubber baby doll, dressed in a now-dirty white dress. He looked over at Dash.

"Oh no. Poor Maud. I wonder if she thought this was her lost baby?" Dash asked himself. He fell back on his haunches, waving his hand about. "I'm sorry. You don't have to go on. So sorry. Maud ..." he stumbled over the words, "overcome with grief for sure." His thoughts turned to Mae remembering how devastated she was, well, they both were, when she miscarried.

Brooksie stood and reached for an evidence bag. "I agree but we're going to finish what we started." He knelt down. "Start filming again."

The second grave revealed another baby doll, again dressed in a long white dress. Again, bagged.

They moved to the final grave, that of Lucy. The clearing of the grave and digging went quicker since they were fairly sure of what they would find. This time the baby doll was wrapped in a baby blanket, and this blanket had dark brown stains on it.

Brooksie motioned to Dash. "See these stains. Pretty sure they're blood. Give me another bag." He held his hand out. When finished, he stood to stretch his back. He strolled around the basement. He said, "If I were to guess I'd say that Lucy was a later miscarriage than Cora and Murphy. Anything left of the baby disintegrated over time. Don't suppose you have DNA for this Maud, do you?"

Dash leaned against the wall. "Owen asked the coroner to collect hair and nail clippings after we learned that Maud had a child she wanted me to find. Our thinking is that I'd confirm anyone I find before turning over the estate. Err on the side of caution." He nodded toward the Lucy bundle in the bag. "Can you collect DNA from the dried blood after all these years?"

"Doubtful but I will try." Brushing the dirt from his knees, he added, "Let's pack this up. I do believe you promised me a good meal and the rest of the story."

Dash nodded. He picked up the bags reverently even though they contained only rubber dolls. His thoughts were on Maud and her emptiness—hope unfulfilled, a bassinet empty. He closed his eyes, slowed his breathing, reliving that feeling, that horrible feeling. Suddenly he felt immense sorrow for this enigmatic relative.

Before they climbed the steps, Dash pointed to the coal furnace. "One last question. Could that furnace burn an adult body to nothing, only ash remains?"

Brookie shook his head. "No, no, the heat needed to do the job impossible to reach in that home furnace. Oh, the flesh would burn off but the bones not so much. Want to look while we're down here?"

After digging around in the ash, they decided it was just that, ash.

After wiping his hands on his coverall, Brooksie asked, "Are you looking for another body? An adult?"

Dash shrugged. "Not sure. The dolls shriek 'out of her mind' to me so maybe she imagined killing an enemy. Lord, I just don't know. I'll have a migraine if I keep thinking about this. Let's go. I need food and at least one drink, more likely two."

After securing the trap door, Dash stripped out of his coveralls and helped Brooksie return the tools to the coroner's car. They placed the little bags in the back area of the van usually reserved for bodies.

Over dinner, and after a swear of secrecy, Dash filled Brooksie in on the now infamous, at least in his mind, letter from Maud.

Leaning back in his chair, Brooksie said, "Thank you for trusting me with all this. What are you going to do about this Callahan fellow? He's the one we were looking for in the coal furnace. You were thinking she used that to get rid of the body? I didn't see any mounds that would indicate she dug an adult-sized grave. That would have been much harder than burying these baby dolls. The poor woman. The dried-up flowers. She obviously visited them – her own private cemetery."

Dash said, "You ask a lot of questions there, my friend. Questions for which I don't have any answers. Again, thank you for indulging me in this madness. Let me get my thoughts organized about Callahan and where to look. And, as for searching for the daughter, I have been given a bit of advice on several agencies which might have handled the placement of the daughter. I'll keep you posted but would appreciate any thoughts you might have whenever you have them."

The men stood and Dash tossed down some bills for a tip. They moved silently to Dash's truck and drove back to the coroner's car.

"I'm spending the night in Cleveland and meeting with one of those agencies. Hopefully, they'll be able to help with the search for the daughter. Touch base when I get back to Clover Pointe. Obviously, none of this is a high priority being over fifty years old and not a crime. Again, thanks for coming and listening. Be careful heading home."

CHAPTER SEVENTEEN

Back on Maud's street, Dash looked up to see Leon sitting on his porch. He waved and the boy darted across.

"Did you go back to school or are you still under the weather?" Dash asked.

Wiping his sleeve across his nose, Leon responded, "Got a cold for sure so stayed home. Don't want to spread germs. Ain't that thoughtful?"

Dash pulled out his handkerchief, carrying one a habit ingrained in him by his mother. He offered it to Leon. "Here take this and use it rather than your sleeve." He put his hand on Leon's forehead checking for a temperature. Not warm at all.

Leon took Dash's suggestion and wiped his nose again this time with the handkerchief. "What are you doing now? Need any help?"

Figuring that he might as well engage Leon's assistance, Dash said, "I'm going to scour Maud's house looking for that oversized crock pot everyone talked about at the funeral. You know what it looks like, right? Any thoughts where she might have stashed it?"

They walked into the house together and stood in the living room surveying the room.

"Well, mister, the old lady always kept it on the stove like ma told you. We should start in the kitchen."

After opening every cabinet and appliance, they resigned themselves to the fact that no oversized crock pot was stashed in the kitchen.

Dash took a couple of soft drinks from the fridge. Handing one to Leon, he motioned for him to sit at the dining room table.

"Let's take a break and talk a bit. How well did you know the old lady as you called her?"

Leon took a swig from the pop bottle. "We moved here about five years ago, so I was too little to cross the street by myself. But if Maudie was sitting on her porch, she'd come over and take me across. Made a super big deal about looking both ways." Leon raised his eyebrows. "See, she had this little group of kids who would join her every afternoon and she'd tell us stories or have one of the older kids read a book to us." He shrugged. "I guess she wasn't so bad except she wanted us to read all the time. I mean what kid wants to read rather than play baseball? She did lend us her books, which was cool. A lot of times she let us keep them, which was cooler."

Dash nodded. "That is a side of Maud I wouldn't have imagined. I wondered about the lack of reading material around here. I mean newspapers are one thing, but nothing beats a good book." He finished his drink, beginning to revise his opinion of Maud from misanthropic old geezer to neighborhood teacher. "Do you have a favorite? I mean one Maud lent you."

"Oh yeah. It's by the guy with the bird, the big black bird. I think it's called a raven, like the Baltimore football team. Guy wrote a lot of creepy stories and Maud loved to tell them to us. She was a good storyteller."

"Ah, yes, well, she was Irish, and they are known for their creative gifts. Poe, that's your favorite? Edgar Allan Poe?"

Leon sat up a little straighter. "That's him. I bet he was the odd kid in his school, bullied a lot. Saw a picture of him on the back of the book and he even looked creepy. Have you read him?"

"A long time ago. We had to memorize a few of his poems. Lordy, Leon, I haven't thought of that in decades. Do you have a copy of his book? Because if you don't, I'll get one for you. I own a bookstore in Clover Pointe, and I love to help kids read."

Slamming his hand on the table, Leon said, "Well, I'll be a mother …" He stopped when he saw the look on Dash's face. "I meant to say hot damn! You have a whole bookstore to read on your own. I've never even been to one. We have a library at school and can take books out, but you have to return them. I'm on Sister Claudia's shit list since I've lost so many."

"Sister Claudia sounds like a very interesting nun. Shit list? Really? You sure that's what she calls it?"

Leon rolled his eyes.

Dash invited Leon to join him at Zara's place for a hamburger and fries. After texting Leon's mother, Etta Rae, they walked since the weather was pleasant. Leon kept up a constant conversation noting this and that about the neighborhood.

Having forgotten how much a growing boy could eat, Dash just kept the burgers and fries coming for Leon. Then he ordered a few take-out dishes so the kid would have something to warm up for dinner that night and lunch the next day.

After making sure Leon was home safely, Dash made one last tour of the house and locked it up tightly. He waved at Leon as he backed his truck out of the driveway.

Dash settled into his hotel room and stretched out on the bed. Rubbing his eyes, he thought about the findings in the basement. Unexpectedly his heart went out to Maud. His opinion of her revised from nasty old woman to very sad, lonely old woman.

He walked to the window to think about Leon and the other neighborhood kids Maud touched with her book readings and stories told with an Irishman's gift for drama. Now he wished he knew her better when he was a child. Maybe if she told him stories rather than pinched his dimples, he would have stayed connected while he was abroad. Maud and her pictures of him. Wonder who he reminded her of as he was sure she didn't just display his photo to please his mother. He gave up on all his fruitless musings and decided to swim away his memories of stories untold and babies lost. He headed for the pool and did laps until his arms ached. Back in his room, he raided the little fridge and ate all the snacks. He flipped through the television channels. Nothing to hold his interest.

Sighing deeply, he reached for his phone for a good old-fashioned dose of Mae and T.J.

"Hey babe, do you miss me? I sure do miss you and the little one. How about filling this lonely old soldier in on your very exciting day?"

He spent the next half hour listening to Mae and T.J. as they passed the phone back and forth, each topping the other with the exciting events of Clover Pointe. Soon Dash was laughing, shaking his head. "When I was overseas for long stretches of time and called home, Owen would tell me nothing happened. Now I'm gone one day, and it sounds like the whole town has changed. Love you two to the sun and back. Now, close those beautiful eyes, both of you, and dream sweet dreams."

He closed his eyes hoping for sweet dreams as well.

Whatever he was dreaming was interrupted by his phone ringing. He pulled it out from under his pillow. The screen read 'Etta Rae' which confused him for a few seconds before he remembered she was Maud's across-the-street neighbor, mother of one Leon.

He answered tentatively. "Hello."

A whispered voice asked, "Is that you mister?"

"Leon? What are you doing up at this hour much less calling me?" Dash asked.

Still whispering, Leon reported, "Mister, someone is prowling around in your house. I can see the flashlight beam moving about. Is it you?"

Now he had Dash's full attention. Sitting up, Dash answered, "No, Leon, I'm in a hotel in downtown Cleveland. I can be there in 10, 15 minutes tops. Where are you and please don't tell me you're on Maud's porch?" He started to pull on his jeans and reached for his sweatshirt.

"No sir, not that stupid. I'm in my bedroom but I have a clear view of the old lady's place from my window. Waiting for

Mom to come home from work. She's later than usual. You want me to wait outside for you?" he asked.

"No, Leon, I don't. You stay inside. If this person leaves and you can get a photo that would be good. Do *not* put yourself in danger. There's nothing valuable in that house. Gotta go. See you in a few." Dash finished dressing, grabbed his keys, and ran out of the room.

No traffic impeded his very rapid drive across the bridge and onto Maud's street. He cut the headlights. He quietly exited the truck since he could see the flashlight beams in the house. He stood for a minute watching when he felt a hand on his arm. About to pummel his assailant, he stopped when he realized it was Leon who definitely needed a lesson in following orders.

"Mister, I decided that I should help you. I've made a note of every license plate on the street, even the ones I know belong here. And I've got the cops on speed dial if you think we need them."

"Leon, there is no 'we' in this. If you want to help, sit on your porch. If you hear loud bangs, that'll be gunshots. Call the cops then, okay?"

Leon saluted. "Yes sir, you can count on me."

Dash crept up the steps to the front door. Last sighting of the flashlight was upstairs, so he hoped to get in before the culprit came down. He inserted the key and quietly opened the door. Once inside he could hear someone walking around, but no noise to indicate furniture was being moved. He moved to the doorway at the bottom of the steps, fading into the background. He stood next to the light switch and pulled his weapon.

He waited for the intruder to come down the steps. When he reached the bottom step, Dash flipped on the lights and stepped in front of the man.

A youngish man, barely out of his teens, stood there, mouth open in surprise. He dropped the flashlight and raised his hands. "Shit man, you scared the life out of me. You don't need no gun. I didn't take nuffin."

Dash shook his head at 'nuffin.' He waved his gun, motioning for the kid to sit down at the dining room table.

"You must be that military dude Maudie went on about. Said you were a right prig. Guess she was right."

"That's me alright. The priggish military dude, nice summary of most of my life. Now that we know who I am, how about your name, rank, and serial number. Your driver's license will do." Dash held out his hand while the kid dug out his wallet and slid it across the table.

Dash tucked the gun into his belt. Pulling out the license, he read: Zeke Lemmich. He compared the photo to the young man seated across from him. Brown hair, brown eyes, five-nine, no weight given but bantam for sure. His pale complexion was even paler now. Almost eighteen and now looking very, very young *and* scared. The jeans and jacket the kid wore had seen better days.

"Okay, Zeke, old boy. What were you doing in my house? I think I saw you at the funeral, though you didn't introduce yourself. Friend of Maud's, were you?"

The kid shrugged. "Sort of, more like an acquaintance. I'm a friend of Cal Brady's, you know, lives next door. Years ago him and me did some fence painting for the old gal. She paid us fine and then said to stop by whenever we wanted. So I did."

"Out of the kindness of your heart, was it?"

"Was what?" the kid asked.

Dash shook his head. "Let's skip all that. Why were you in the house now?"

"You ain't calling the cops, are you? Cause I didn't take nuffin. You did a good job clearing out the place, you did."

"Why thank you, makes all the effort worthwhile. Again, why were you in the house?"

The kid squirmed in his seat. "If I tell you the truth, you going to hit me?"

"More likely if you don't tell me, I'll whack you upside the head to clear the cobwebs." Dash told him. "Again, explain."

"Well you sees, old Maudie used to leave money sitting around. Nothing big, a ten or a twenty. Enough for beer and a pizza. I would stop by to visit and then step into the house and usually her purse was wide open on this table. Always had money just lying there. Never took all of it, but she was always a little confused."

Dash nodded. "So you would steal money not from just an old lady, but one who was confused and might not miss it OR if she did, would think she spent it or dropped it. Did I get that right?" He cocked his head. "Does your mother know you're such a sterling individual?"

Zeke sat up straight. "You gonna tell my stepma, cause if you are going to do that, it would be better for me if you called the cops. She has a mean right hook. As you can see, I'm not a big guy, not like you. I bet she'd give you a run for your money. Don't bet against her, ever."

A smile formed on Dash's lips. "Thanks for the tip. Back to the essentials here. After all this time, were you expecting to find a few bucks just sitting somewhere begging for you to pocket them?"

The kid shook his head. "What's it going to be: the cops or Godzilla?"

"Neither. Listen, Zeke, my boy. I'm tired and have a very important meeting early in the morning. Calling the cops would turn this into a lengthy interrogation and calling Godzilla would only upset both of us. Here's what's going to happen. I'm going to ask you simple, direct questions. You're going to answer them. And then we're both going home to our beds. Got that?"

"You're weird, just like Maud." Zeke pronounced.

Dash chuckled. "Well, that made my day. Not the worst thing I've even been called. First question, what were you looking for tonight, correction, this morning?"

"I told you money. There was a rumor that Maudie had tons of it stashed around the house. I was hoping you didn't find it."

Dash frowned, adjusting his next question. "Rumor? Know where it came from?"

"Nah, just a story tossed around the neighborhood. She was a strange old lady. One minute nice and sweet and then next slapping you around for no good reason. If she were on the porch which seemed like always, even in winter, she'd call you up to visit. Sometimes she'd invite you in for soup or stew and always served that Irish beer, Guinness, is it, with it. Quite the treat for me, to be sure."

"When was the last time you saw or spoke to her?"

"The night before they said she died. I was coming home from gaming at another guy's house. She was out on the porch in her nighty pulling that sofa out there apart, like she was looking for something. Now it was damn cold so I stopped, asking her if I could help her look. She didn't seem to be right in the head, mumbling crazy shit, like dead people who were coming to get her. I figured it was because her brain was freezing in the cold that she was talking such nonsense. Felt sorry for the old lady."

"What did you do?"

Zeke smiled. "I got her into the house and put her to bed, piling blankets on her. She had a pot of soup going, so I gave her a cup to sip. She kinda cried a bit and then told me to take some money from her purse, as a way of saying thanks." He shrugged. "So I did." He saw the look on Dash's face. "Hey man, it was only about forty bucks; I left the hundred-dollar bill in her purse."

Dash leaned back in the chair. "This was the Friday before she died. You didn't think to come back and check on her?"

"I told my stepma about it, and she came over here on next day. Told me Maudie was fine."

Dash glanced at his watch, almost three. "Okay, Zeke, this session is over, but I still have a lot of questions for you, but I'll end on this one: When you left Maud was her house neat, straightened?"

Again, Zeke shrugged. "Yeah, I mean she always had a lot of papers around, but they were in piles on the table here. And the kitchen had dishes piled in the sink but that wasn't unusual. Maudie always waited until every dish she owned was dirty before she conned someone into washing them." He smiled. "You know I think I'm going to miss her."

Dash stood. He pulled out one of his cards. "If you think of anything else I might need to know, I'd appreciate a call. Give me your number. Next time I'm here I want another sit down. Are you sure the crock pot was here that Friday?"

"Yeah. Why? Is it gone?" Zeke asked.

"Afraid so, which means Maud's death maybe not so natural after-all." Dash said as he escorted Zeke out the front door. He locked it and then waved to Leon who waved back from the top floor window.

Zeke turned to Dash, "Hey, military dude, thanks for not calling the cops or Godzilla."

"No problem. Need a ride home?"

"Thanks, but no. I just live around the corner." He waved as he walked away.

Dash returned to his hotel room but gave up on the idea of going back to sleep. Instead, he sat staring out the window. His thoughts jumbled: rubber baby dolls, rolls of money, a loaded gun, and a missing crock pot. He wondered aloud if Maud had been murdered. Wouldn't take much, her being so frail. Rumors that she had money in the house would be enough for someone to try to find it. There was the money in the freezer, not much but more than many of the kids around here would have and the money in the floorboard was more than even he had ever seen in one place.

CHAPTER EIGHTEEN

Suddenly, or so it seemed, it was seven in the morning. Dash showered and shaved, dressing in his second-best blue suit. He pulled his briefcase out from under the bed, examined his notes and research material. He packed up his stuff and checked out of the hotel.

After a quick breakfast he walked to the Key Building, now Cleveland's tallest building. Dash scanned the directory near the elevator and pushed thirteen, hoping it wasn't a bad omen for his mission.

The reception area for 'Find Me Inc.' was almost miniscule. Dash glanced down the halls to what looked like a rabbit warren of cubicles. He introduced himself to the young lady manning the phone and guarding the sign-in book. Miss Rembrandt verified he was who he said he was and that he did indeed have an appointment with Miss Elrod.

Rather than just point him in the proper direction, Miss Rembrandt stepped out from behind her desk and said, "If you'll follow me, please?"

And so Dash did.

Miss Eldrod's desk within her cubicle was piled with files and stray papers reaching at least a foot and a half all the way around. A very tiny space was clear, holding only a notebook and a pencil.

"Please take a seat and I'll let her know you're here," Miss Rembrandt said, pointing to chair. "I'm sure she's just getting coffee. She'll be with you shortly."

Dash nodded, about to ask if he too could get some coffee, but Miss Rembrandt strode away before he could.

Miss Elrod was an attractive woman in her mid-thirties if Dash guessed correctly. She had sparkling brown eyes and long brown hair. A smile tugged at her mouth as she handed Dash a cup of coffee.

"Figured if I needed one, you did as well. Have a seat, Colonel Hammond. My father was a lifer, so I figured you'd take it strong and black." She gestured for him to sit.

He took the coffee and sipped it watching the young woman as she puttered around her desk, clearing more space to set her coffee.

She turned and smiled very broadly this time. "Good to see you take it black. My father's contention was that real men and women drank it that way. Do you agree?"

Dash shrugged. "I knew a sergeant who was the meanest S.O.B. most of the time. He drank a frou-frou concoction with a million ingredients and always topped with whipped cream." He shrugged again. "Go figure."

"So, Colonel Hammond, I understand you are on a mission to find a baby who was given up for adoption almost fifty years ago. Can I ask why?"

Dash leaned forward in his chair. "For starters, let's drop the 'colonel' title. Dash or just Hammond is fine with me. The colonel coin doesn't go far in the civilian world, so I'll keep that in my pocket." He took a deep breath. "Sit back, Miss Elrod, and listen to this tale."

He then explained about the tenuous connection between his mother and Maud. He moved on to his inheriting her estate and related bits and pieces of the letter she left him.

Shrugging, he said, "I'm sure it's my duty to give a good faith effort to locate her child. Even though Maud didn't explicitly spell out that she wanted this child to inherit, I have to believe that's what she desired. I haven't set a time limit on all of this, but, as you can see, I'm not a youngster nor is this lost babe."

Miss Elrod's pencil hovered over her pad. "Before coming to us, what have you done?"

Dash flipped open his notebook. "I began by trying to determine an approximate date of birth using the father's date of death as taking place maybe when Maud was two months pregnant, three at the most. That date is September 10, 1967. I'm thinking the baby was born in April or May of 1968.

"I have a friend who is big into internet research, and she's been combing birth records for Cuyahoga County in those months. One of the problems is, I'm not entirely sure Maud used her own name or that of the father when giving information for the birth certificate."

He reached into his briefcase to pull out a single sheet of paper. He handed this to Miss Elrod. "Here is what I consider to be the pertinent information as best as I can determine. Maud's birthdate, and this Declan Rooney's, aka Sean Kelly's, information. It's my gut feeling that Maud didn't go too far from Cleveland to have or place the baby, but that's all it is: a gut feeling. Frankly, I'm very surprised she didn't look for and find the child before she died." He threw his hands up. "Unfortunately, I didn't know her that well. Maud didn't like my father so she wouldn't have confided in him. And if she confided in my mother, well, the sainted Helene-Marie took it to her grave."

Miss Elrod smiled at him. "I admire your wanting to get this right. I'm not sure how much money is involved, but the easiest thing would be to just keep it. I applaud you for your effort."

Tilting his head, Dash said, "If I knew the woman didn't need the money, I would just give it away. But if I don't find her, I'd be haunted by thoughts of her homeless or her children suffering from poverty. If I do find her and she's very wealthy, well just maybe, I'll go the charitable route and donate it all in her name."

"Can I assume money isn't a problem for you?"

"No, ma'am, it's not. Not that I'm overflowing with it but, what I've been through, I know that money isn't as important as family and friends. Of course, I'm lucky enough to have a roof over my head and food on my plate." He winked as he said, "Somebody up there has been looking out for me."

Laughing, she said, "Good to know. I'll start on this with some basic searches. I have your phone and email here somewhere." She swept her hand over the piles. Then laughed again. "Don't be fooled by all this. I know what every piece of paper says and where it is. I just like to *see* things rather than *file* things." She stood and extended her hand. "I'll be in touch. Anything else, no matter how trivial, send it along. One never knows what the key to solving the problem might be."

Taking her hand, Dash thanked her. "Hope to hear from you sooner rather than later." He started to leave but turned back to her. "Hey, thanks for the coffee. Give my best to your father."

She just nodded and smiled.

Dash worried himself all the way back to Clover Pointe, trying to decide if he should tell Mae about the three little graves. He was none the wiser when he walked into his kitchen, stopping short.

Looking at his wife he asked, "Where's my little man? And where's my old man, for that matter?" He set his briefcase down on the table and dropped his suitcase next to it.

"Welcome home, honey."

Immediately Dash wondered what went wrong or what he did wrong or was this wrong house.

"Honey? Give over. What's up Doc?"

"Have a seat, sweetheart," Mae pulled out a chair.

Okay, now I know I'm in the wrong house, Dash thought as he cautiously lowered his butt into the chair.

"Am I going to need a bit of Jameson's before I hear what I did when I wasn't here to do it?" He looked over to the kitchen cabinet holding the nectar of the Irish gods.

Mae shivered and laughed. "I can't wait. You bought Mrs. G's house. She decided to stay with Michael in Illinois and knew you wanted the property next door, so you gave her a good price. I called Tommy and Brenda Mac who are, as we sit, arranging for the financing and the paperwork needed. See, I knew you would be happy. And Mrs. G. is throwing in the secret recipe for her apple pies. All's well that ends well, a guy once said."

Dash smiled. "My, but I have been busy. And very efficient if I must say so. Accomplished a lot and I wasn't even here."

"When you focus, I have to say you are unbeatable." Mae leaned over to kiss his cheek.

"So where are T.J. and Owen? Please tell me we have the house to ourselves, because if we do, I'll march you upstairs and show you how unbeatable I can be." He stood and took her hand. On the way upstairs, he remembered the three graves but decided those could wait until another day. This afternoon belonged to the champion, him!

CHAPTER NINETEEN

The next morning Dash gathered nephew Mike and his best bud, Ryan. Their project for the day was to clean out Maud's garage. The possibility of finding a body in the car, under the car, behind the car was not mentioned to the young men.

When they arrived, they found Danny and his crew already working. Dash had decided to strip the house of all furniture and fittings hoping this would dissuade vandals from breaking in.

Dash and Danny met briefly and then onto their separate projects. Dash tackled the yardwork. He mowed the lawn, such as it was, and was now tidying the edge garden.

Two hours into their day, Mike called Dash over. "Dasher, we're almost done with clearing out the stuff. Most of it is garbage so we are rapidly filling up the dumpster out front. There are a few things you might want to look at to see if you can use them."

Before looking at the segregated items, he toured the garage. "Nice, good job. Now let's see what's left over."

He walked over to inspect what they had set aside. An old push mower, several garden tools, old window screens and an interior door were outside of the garage.

After looking over the stuff, he asked the guys, "Would you want to keep the garden tools, in case you decide to do landscaping as your summer job? I'd be happy to store them at my place. You already know my riding mower can be yours with proper maintenance. I'll even give you the names of some prospective clients. Spring, summer, fall income, gentlemen."

Mike and Ryan exchanged glances before Mike said, "We'll take you up on the offer and any help you can give us. Now, what should we do?"

"The screening can go into the dumpster; load the tools into the truck and carry the door inside. Danny might have a use for it." He pulled keys out of his pocket and handed them to Mike. "Once the driveway is clear, see if Maud's car starts and if it does, run it over to the garage at the corner of Lorain and 41ˢᵗ. I talked to a Roger Hickman over there and he's willing to inspect the car, make it right for selling. You'll have to move the truck but be careful where you park it. Okay?"

"Roger that, Colonel," Mike said with a smile.

They carried the door inside and leaned it against the kitchen cabinets. Yelling 'we're off,' they left the house.

Dash went in search of Danny and found him in the upstairs bedroom discussing what to do with the very old-fashioned bathtub.

"Here you are. Can I get a minute, Danny? I want you to look at a door the kids found in the garage. Never know if you can use it or not."

Danny followed Dash into the kitchen to examine the door.

"Looks like the old lady took this out, but where? All the rooms have all the doors they would need. Having said that, I'll keep it just in case we need a replacement here or on another project," Danny said. "Any thoughts on the old tub? If you don't want it, I'll take it in case I find a client who wants a claw foot tub."

Dash waved his hand. "Take what you want. If I keep the place, I'm going to update the bathroom and the kitchen. Time for a water break. You making sure the guys are getting theirs, right?"

"Yes, sir, I've been at this a bit and so have they. Everyone knows what to do and when to do it. Have a seat, old man."

After grabbing a bottle of water, Dash went to sit in the dining/living room. He checked his phone messages and sent a few while guzzling the water. He got up to get another bottle when he bumped into the hat stand which was next to the door to the kitchen.

Dash stopped after he grabbed the falling stand. He wondered aloud. "Hat stand. Why? The other homes have a closet under the staircase so they don't need a coat rack."

He backed up and returned to the other room to gaze at the paneling under the staircase. The door. He needed the door.

After placing it against the paneling approximately where it would have fit, if indeed this was the door replaced by paneling. He yelled up the stairs.

"Danny, can you come here? Bring a crowbar or chisel and hammer, please."

Danny stomped down the stairs. "I hate to be an old lady but how am I to get anything done if you're going to bounce me around? What bee is in your bonnet now?"

Dash nodded toward the door against the paneling. "Possible that the door would have gone there?"

"Yeah. But why remove it? Close off the closet, why?"

"How would I know? Maud was a strange old lady. Maybe she had nightmares about monsters in closets," Dash said. He thought *'wonder if that nightmare has the name Callahan.'*

Danny shook his head. "Well, let's see if she was right and there's a monster inside."

Danny knelt down, chisel in hand, and began tapping at the floor molding. "I'm going to do this gently so we can reconstruct without too much work if we have to." He handed Dash the crowbar. "Start on the top molding, gently, my man, gently."

They inspected the paneling to find the end of one panel and the start of the next. Very carefully they shimmied the center panel loose, opening the space under the stairs.

Peering into the darkness, all they could see were blankets and pillows.

"See no monsters. Well, start pulling them out or do I have to do everything?" Danny asked. He studied his friend's face. "Hate to say it but you look disappointed."

Dash scowled as he began to pull the bedding out, then flashed his light into the recesses. At the very back was a bundle, tied numerous times.

He glanced at Danny who said, "Don't look at me, bro. This is your house and the contents within are yours. You're the one to get that out." He nodded toward the bundle.

Dash pulled out his phone and began snapping pictures. He crouched down to enter the cubby and slowly dragged out the wrapped object. Dash faced his friend. "I'm going to tell you something you're probably not going to believe, and this is one helluva longshot. If I'm wrong, please don't think less of me or my skills."

"I'd say you're scaring me, but you do that all the time. You're going to tell me that's a body, right?"

"Why do you say that?"

"Because you have a sickly 'I think I found a body' look. And I know your record for stepping into shit. All along I've known there is something strange about this place and the old lady who lived here. Am I right? No fooling around, okay?"

Dash folded his arms across his chest. "I have a 'I think I found a body' look? But, sadly, yes, that's what I think this is."

Dash pulled out his knife and began to sever the ropes. He pulled back the plastic sheet and stared at the skeletal remains of Callahan, very lately of Ireland.

Danny stood with arms folded. "Know who he is? I mean he or she. Were we looking for a body all along on our many trips here? And you didn't think to tell me in the off chance I pulled up a floorboard and there was a smiling skull? I'm going to rethink our partnership in all this." He shook his head. "Now what do we do? And I'll tell you I'm not burying him. You're on your own, pally boy."

Dash slumped down in a chair. "Well, first, have the guys break for lunch. Ask them to exit via the kitchen. I'm going to call Cleveland homicide. Even if this is a very old one."

"Why are you sure this is a homicide?"

"Because, Danny, he didn't tie himself up, did he? Sorry, but this is just another thorn plunged in my side by good old Cousin Maud," he said more harshly than he intended.

He pulled Detective Kraft's card from his wallet and dialed the number. He put it on speaker phone so Danny would know what he was doing.

"Kraft, this is Dash Hammond over at Maud Grealis' house. I need your expertise, sir."

"Good morning, Colonel. You do realize that I'm not a home renovation expert but a homicide detective, right?"

"Only too well. Might as well call forensics and the coroner and your wife and anyone else. I've got a tale to tell you, sir."

"Be right there."

CHAPTER TWENTY

Dash and Danny sprawled across the front steps waiting for Detective Kraft. They basked in the sunlight and wondered at the quiet of the street, only a few blocks from the bubbling West 25th Street. The crew had been sent on lunch break with instructions to pack up just in case the house was sealed as a crime scene. *Highly unlikely* was Dash's take, but he wasn't a member of Cleveland's Homicide Division.

A car pulled up to the front of the house. Out stepped the rumpled detective carrying several bags.

"Gentlemen, have you had lunch?" Kraft asked. "Hot dogs and condiments in this bag; liquid refreshments in this one." He handed one bag to Dash and the other to Danny.

"Thanks, Kraft. I take it I interrupted your lunch. Sorry, I tried to tell you this was no emergency." He opened the bag and inhaled the aroma of stadium hot dogs. He handed one to Danny and another to Kraft. "Dig in. Looks like there's plenty, and here are some mustard packets, ketchup, chopped onion and sauerkraut."

Danny reached into the bag and pulled out a bit of everything.

"Ah, man, you're going to ruin the basic great taste of the dog. A bit of stadium mustard only enhances it," Dash said as he spread the premium mustard on his dog.

Kraft pulled out two beers and handed one to each man. He reserved the can of root beer for himself. "On duty. No alcohol."

The men took places on the steps, chowing down on the dogs and chips.

"Okay, Hammond, tell me how you're going to ruin this gourmet meal? What did you find that reverses the decision on Maud Grealis?"

Swallowing quickly, Dash said, "Nothing. As far as I know, her death is probably just old age and crabbiness. No, this has to do with something that happened half a century ago. See, good old Maud killed a man named Callahan. She hid his body in the house, and we just uncovered it."

Kraft started to choke on his food. "Seriously? Fifty years ago? You just found it."

Danny looked over to Dash. "You did say he was sharp, but not how sharp."

Before Kraft could reply, Dash jumped in. "Listen Kraft, this is a strange tale and I didn't call you about it earlier since I was pretty sure Maud was yanking my chain. See, she left everything to me. Yes, the hero on the wall. Didn't expect it, didn't want it. But here I am." He bit off another huge hunk of hot dog and chewed away. "Let's finish the dogs and beer, then we can go inside."

So they did. Standing they brushed the crumbs off, wiping their hands on pants. Might as well all be crumpled and stained.

Dash led the way in, Kraft on his heels. He pointed to the half-unwrapped bundle on the floor.

"Detective, I believe that to be a man named Callahan. Pretty sure Maud killed him and hid his body. And before you do anymore grousing about just finding him, I just *started looking* for him."

"Why don't you tell me how you know the little bit you know?"

"As I said, Maud, in her infinite wisdom, left all her earthly belongings to me. One item was a letter in which she confesses to this crime. I wasn't sure what to believe. In the letter was more information and a request for me to find someone."

Kraft bent over the bundle, using his pen to prod here and there. He pointed to the open space under the stairs.

"What made you look here, if I may ask?"

"My nephew and his friend were cleaning out the garage and found that door over there. Conferring with Danny, we decided it could have come from the closet that would have been in the house. Each house on the street has the same floor plan and each has a closet in that spot. Took me a bit to put it all together. Sorry."

Danny stepped up. "Can I ask a stupid question and, trying hard not to be insensitive, but will you be sealing this place off as a crime scene or can me and my crew continue working upstairs? They'll be back from lunch break soon. Just wondering?"

Kraft straightened up. Looking at Dash rather than Danny, he said, "Got a copy of that letter? And perhaps a first name for this Callahan fellow?"

"Yes and no. I'll text Mae and have her pull up my file and forward it to you. Is that okay? As for a first name, nothing in the letter."

"Only the letter for now." Kraft looked around, shaking his head. "I'll call the coroner and get Mr. Callahan removed. He turned to Danny, "No, won't shut your work down but contain it to upstairs for the next day or so." He pulled out his phone and began making calls.

Dash texted Mae and Owen. Holding Kraft's card in one hand, he typed in the address so Mae could send the transcribed letter.

Mike and Ryan walked into the living room. They surveyed the scene. "Dasher, anything you want us to do?" Mike asked.

"You took care of the car, right?"

"Yeah, he's going to call you with a price to bring it up to snuff or if you want to junk it," Mike said. "When are we going home? I mean, should we be helping Danny, or do you have more for us to do?" Mike peeked around his uncle. "What's going on?"

"Found a body, so nothing new. Let's see what you can finish in the yard. I'm hoping we can head out of here soon. Personally, I'm bushed and want to go home and collapse."

"Roger that. Read you loud and clear," Ryan said. He pulled Mike out the door. "Let's finish what Dash hoped to accomplish today. I wouldn't mind getting home well before dark."

Dash moved to Kraft's side. "What happens next? Do I get to go home, or will I be spending the day and night here in Cleveland?"

"Nah, you can go home as soon as the coroner picks up the body. Don't worry. The coroner is sending someone. He should arrive soon. I'm taking a few photos and I'll bag what little evidence there is. Could I ask that you write out a statement when you get home and email it to me? And anything else you think pertinent. Anything that might help us get a positive I.D." He looked around. "What a mess! Who knew that little old lady was a murderer?"

"Well, she wasn't always a little old lady. That's the problem. And, yes, I'll gather what we learned, not much, but at least you will have a base to build on."

They turned as they heard the thump and bang of the cast iron tub being maneuvered down the stairs. Instead of offering to help, they moved aside allowing Danny and his men to step into the living room. The tub was set down as the men took a breather.

"What's the decision? Do we keep working?" Danny asked.

Dash shook his head. "I'm wiped and not from working."

One of the crew laughed, "As usual, sir. Poor example of leadership." Since most of the crew were ex-military and none of them officers, Dash often found himself the butt of their well-intentioned jokes. The ex-sergeant turned to Danny. "I'm tired but from working. Let's knock off and head home. Dash can fire up the barbeque and feed us some of his famous hamburgers. What about it, Colonel?"

"Do it. I'll lock up here after the coroner leaves and you guys come over," he checked his watch, "about six. That okay?"

"Roger that. See you then, Dash." Danny turned to his team. "Okay, men, bend and lift with your legs." As they exited, Danny said over his shoulder, "Better have plenty of beer."

Dash leaned against the wall. "Mae is going to kill me. Better let her know she won't be having a quiet evening."

The renovation men no sooner exited than the coroner's man arrived. It was just a few minutes to collect the remains and other evidence.

Dash did a walk-through and locked up. Bidding Kraft goodbye with a hardy thanks, more for the hot dogs than anything else, he shouted for Mike and Ryan. "We're heading home, guys. Mike, you drive, okay?"

CHAPTER TWENTY-ONE

Two days later, Dash found himself pulling into Maud's driveway for what felt like the thousandth time. As he exited his truck, he automatically glanced across the street to Leon's house. He expected to see the truant sitting somewhere on the porch waiting for his arrival, but today he saw no one.

He bounded up the stairs to Maud's house and stopped short. Out of the corner of his eye he spotted Leon, curled up on the old rocking glider.

"Leon, my boy, don't tell me it's another free day from school."

The young boy pulled himself up, pushing off the dirty blanket he had used for warmth. "No, Mister, today I really am feeling poorly. Ma said I could stay home but I got bored sitting over there by myself. I was hoping you'd show up and bingo, bango, here you are."

"Ah, the power of positive thinking," Dash said as he unlocked the door. "Well, come on, get inside. There's a dampness about the air this morning. No wonder you're cold. Let's see if we can find something better than that old rag to keep you warm. If nothing else, I have work blankets in the truck that you can use."

Leon dragged himself inside to collapse on the nearest chair in the dining room. He let out a long sad sigh. "Mister, can I tell you something? I think I'm going to miss you coming here. Are you going to sell the place?"

"Don't know the answer for that yet, Leon. How about a cup of tea to warm you through and through?"

He watched closely as Leon barely nodded, staring into space. While he made the tea, Dash remembered his childhood, full of laughter, kids running from one house to another. Hell, the McCafferty's had a houseful. He was never alone, left to fend for himself. He needed to have a talk with Etta Rae. Twelve was still too young to be on one's own for the whole day. He smacked himself in the head when he remembered the cookies and a surprise for Leon in his truck.

"Wait a minute. I'll be right back. Got something for you," Dash said.

When he returned, he had his hands full: blankets, cookies, and a bag full of books. He motioned for Leon to follow him into Maud's old bedroom. Dash dropped the blankets onto the bed and handed the cookies to his young companion.

"Sit yourself down. I have a present for you."

Leon pulled the blanket over and rearranged everything so he had a pillow and cover.

Dash sat down on the bed's edge, handing the bag full of books to Leon. "Here, look through these. I'll get the tea, turn on the heat, and we can discuss the books, which ones you like and which you have already read."

He smiled as Leon's face lit up like a Christmas tree. He left the boy sorting through the twenty books.

Dash returned with two cups of tea and several packets of sugar and creamers.

"Wow, these are great, Mister. Can I borrow them? I've read these two," he said pushing Sachar's *Holes* and Paulsen's *Hatchet* toward Dash. "They are really good."

Pulling a chair over, Dash pushed the books back at Leon. "Listen, kid, if you like them, keep them. And whatever else tickles your fancy. The only caveat is that you promise me to go to school every day. No more playing hooky, okay?"

"Really! I can keep them! All of them? You must be really rich, Mister," Leon said, cradling the books. "And yes, sir, I'll go to school every day, even when there's no school."

They ate and drank and talked about the books. Dash's smile grew as Leon held each book and wondered at its tale.

"Well, Leon, I hate to end this party, but I need to get over to Lemmich's house to talk to Zeke's mom, I mean stepmom. What can you, oh fountain of neighborhood knowledge, tell me about her?"

Dash chuckled as Leon threw his head back, rolling his eyes.

"First, I would say to keep your belt buckled!"

This caught Dash by surprise as he wondered about this twelve-year-old, "What do you know about keeping one's belt buckled?"

"I'm pretty sure old lady Lemmich tries to get every man separated from his pants. I think that's how she earns the rent money, or at least that's what I overhead my ma say to Mrs. Brady a bit ago." He put his book down. "Between me and you, Mister, old lady Lemmich, well, she's no looker unless you like them big and mean."

Dash stared at the boy, remembering Zeke saying his stepma could give Dash a run for his money.

"Okay, first rule, don't unbuckle my pants. Is there a second or third rule?"

Leon squirmed around, settling himself into the bed and blanket. "Of course, there is. Second, if you do lose your pants, hold onto your wallet. Rumor is men and their money is soon parted when Mrs. L is around. Got that?"

Dash nodded.

"Rule number three, if she gets mad, she gets violent, so run like hell. Leave those pants and wallet behind. Even you won't stand a chance if she starts swinging."

Second warning about her size and boxing prowess. Dash smiled, thinking he couldn't wait to meet this paragon of femineity. *Wait until I tell Mae!*

Dash pulled himself up. "Leon, I'm going over there now. Since it's going to take a bit to heat this place, take the books back to your cozy bedroom and read the day away. I guess

I should add if I don't reappear in an hour, call 911 to send out a search party for me."

Leon nodded but he was fully into the tales of Poe. "Got it, home, cozy, hour, police." He looked up for an instance, "Best of luck to you, Mister. And thanks again for the books."

CHAPTER TWENTY-TWO

Dash knocked on the side door to the Lemmich house. Now is the time for all good men to meet their nemesis.

The door opened a few inches. A woman's face partially appeared.

"Hi, I'm Dash Hammond. I inherited the house from Maud Grealis, around the corner. Could I ask you a few questions?" He smiled his best smile.

He heard the chain slide and watched the door open wide. There stood a woman that his mother might describe as 'big boned.' *Amazon* was Dash's first thought. She reached out and pulled him inside as if he were a ragdoll. He suddenly felt like Zeke, out of his weight class.

He collected himself and studied the woman before him. She was tall, not six feet, but close. Her ample body was covered in the most diaphanous material Dash had seen since his first honeymoon decades ago. All her virtues and vices were on display. Her pendulous breasts strained the chartreuse material. Long bottle-blonde hair contrasted with her puffy red eyes which were accented with enough liner and mascara for three women. Her face told the story of a hard life lived even harder. If she were twenty years younger and a hundred pounds lighter, she might be a looker, but only if you were shortsighted.

He glanced around the room. Turquoise! The walls, the cabinets, the molding, all a bright turquoise. He looked at the floor, surprised it wasn't the same garish color. His stomach lurched at the combination of colors before him.

Lemmich leaned provocatively against the stove and smiled. "I'm sorry. I thought you were a friend calling earlier than expected."

Dash swallowed hard and lied. "If I were that friend, I'd definitely be early." He shook his head to realign his thoughts. He told himself, *back on mission; be pleasant but not overly friendly.* "I'm sorry to interrupt. I won't be long, just a few questions about Maud."

She arched her brows. "We've got time. Coffee? I just made a pot." She moved over to a stove covered with leftover scraps from last year's meals. The coffee was in an old dingy percolator.

"Thank you. That would be good." Dash said, determined not to eat or drink anything in this kitchen. Ptomaine hot spot for sure. He glanced around the room and spotted a large black crockpot sitting on a small rolling cart in the corner. Maud's? He wondered how he could work that into the conversation. Does one compliment the cook on her cookware? Instead, he surreptitiously pulled out his camera and snapped a photo while his hostess was shuffling mugs around, peering into each one determining which had the least amount of dust in it.

She reached above the stove and pulled down a bottle of Jack Daniel's.

"A little pick-me-up?"

"Sure." Dash watched her pour a little coffee and a lot of Jack. Pretty early in the day for that much of a pick-me-up, but the alcohol would kill whatever germs were lurking in the mug.

Handing him a cup, she raised hers. "Here's to the beginning of a great friendship." Her eyes scrutinized his body, stopping below his belt. She raised her eyes and smiled coyly. She again leaned seductively against the counter.

Dash felt as if he was being undressed. He touched his belt buckle, still fastened. Rule number one covered.

They both drank. Dash sipped cautiously as he asked, "Mrs. Lemmich, do you have time for a few questions?"

"It's Lorna to you, handsome, not Mrs. Lemmich. That piece of shit left me years ago. He forgot to take his worthless son with him, so I have him for at least a few more months. I told him when he turns eighteen, he's out the door."

Dash frowned at the description of Zeke but held his tongue. Information, he needed information.

Lorna straightened up, smoothing the gown over her body.

He wondered at the holding power of the material.

"Then I'll have the house to myself, all day, all night." Smiling she asked, "Will you be moving into Maud's house? Joining the neighborhood?"

He noticed her eyes strayed to his crotch, again. He shivered. All he could mutter, more to himself than Lorna, was, "All day and all night, you say."

Dash cleared his throat and moved around the kitchen, careful to avoid corners. His mama didn't raise any fools. "How well did you know Maud?"

She followed him around. "Not very well. She would wave at me if I passed her house. Zeke, that's the stepson, knew her better. He did odd jobs around her place."

"When did you last see her? We believe she died sometime on March 18th, which was a Saturday." He motioned with his hand hoping to get her to think, answer, stop staring at him. "I ran into your son the other night and he thought you may have gone over to check on her that morning."

He watched her eyes darken. She moved her mouth around before she said, "Maybe. I'm not sure. What day did you say?" She walked over to the calendar hanging on the wall, tapping the day in question with her bright red nail. Running her tongue over her lips, she turned to him, smiling coquettishly.

"Refresh your coffee. Let me think about it, Mr. Hammond or can I call you Dash?"

Dash smiled but didn't answer. He thought '*How about calling me gone!*

She winked at him and said, "We have at least a half an hour before my friend shows up. Anything else I can do for you? And you're welcome to stay when he gets here. Guaranteed fun."

A knock on the door interrupted the conversation. A smallish man timidly opened the door. He thrust forth a bouquet of flowers, asking "Is my baby girl at home?"

Dash jumped and set his cup down on the counter. "Your friend is early, like I said he'd be. Thanks for the coffee. We'll catch up soon." He moved past the new visitor, almost knocking him over. The man was skinny, short and wore glasses with thick lenses. Dash steadied him, apologizing for his swift exit. Would hate to crush him before 'baby girl' had her way with him.

The door slammed as Dash fled. He shivered as he jogged back to Maud's house. He stopped to lean against the tree, doubled over in laughter. He hadn't been that unsettled since, well, he must have been thirteen. His first job cutting lawns. He chuckled over his young self, walking up to the door to collect his fee, only to be greeted by the lady of the house standing there in her birthday suit. A certain part of him wanted to accept the invitation in, but he just shouted 'complimentary' and dragged his mower home, smiling all the way.

He heard a banging on a glass window and turned to see Leon waving a book from his window. A second later, the window opened, and the boy shouted, "Thanks again, Mister."

Sitting in his truck, he texted Kraft, telling him about the crock pot. Promising to call him the next day, he backed out of the driveway.

Dash chuckled all the way home. He wished he had photos, so he had visual evidence to show Mae. She always accused him of exaggerating. *Well, Maevis*, he thought, *not this time*.

CHAPTER TWENTY-THREE

Dash's favorite time of the day was post-dinner when everyone would just nibble on the remains of the relish tray and tell of the day's events. His mother insisted the family should sit and talk about this, that, or anything. Dash honed his storytelling skills making up adventures for his family. His father was the only one who cast an unbelieving scowl at his youngest son.

With that in mind, Dash accepted whatever T.J. told him and the rest of the family no matter how outlandish it seemed.

When it was Dash's turn to relate the day's experience, he wasted no time in telling an exaggerated tale of the giant Mrs. L. Both Mae and Owen shook their heads at this nonsense.

Just as Dash was putting the cherry on top of his unbelievable story, his phone rang. He glanced at the caller I.D. and read 'Etta Ray.' Leon? Dash stood, held up a finger and moved away from the table.

"Leon, what's going on?" he asked. Then he shook his head slightly. "Hold on, slow down." Dash frowned and listened.

Leon talked so fast enough Dash could barely understand him. "Mister, that sommabitch mother of Zeke's finally did it. She beat the crap out of him. I found him outside, bleeding all over the sidewalk. I dragged him into my house but he don't want to go to the Urgi Care on Twenty-Fifth. I decided to call you. You'll take care of everything. That's right, ain't it, Mister?" Leon sniffed, close to crying.

"Calm down, take a breath. How much blood?" He glanced at Mae who moved so she could hear Leon's answer.

Dash listened, then said, "Ice packs on Zeke's face. If he loses consciousness, call 911 and then me. I'm on my way. I'm bringing my wife who's a doctor."

He looked at Mae. "Doc, bag, now." He turned to his father. "Owen, can you stay with T.J. until we get back? Don't think it will be long but …"

As Mae scrambled for her medicine bag, Dash bounded up the stairs to retrieve his weapon from the safe. Tucking it into the back of his pants, he stopped long enough to kiss his son. "T.J., we have to go to Cleveland right now. A young man's hurt and we're going to take care of him. Listen to Gramps and we'll call as soon as we arrive."

He left his father and son sitting at the table, eyes and mouths open wide.

Dash and Mae found Leon standing by his open front door. He led them into the dining room where Zeke sat, an ice pack covering his face.

"Zeke, this is my wife, Doctor Maevis Summers. She's going to examine you. If she decides you should go to the hospital, that's what we will do. No arguing, okay?"

The battered young man nodded slowly. He removed the ice pack so Mae could see the extent of his injuries. Lorna had used the full force of her fists to mash his face in. Welts formed around his eyes as tears ran down his cheeks. His lips were bloodied and swollen.

Dash knelt next to him. "Zeke, did she body punch you? Use anything beside her fists?"

Zeke pointed to his chest and stomach.

Mae gently removed his shirt. His chest was a mottled canvas of black and blue. "Leon, bring me some fresh towels and a bowl of warmish water. You did the right thing getting him inside."

Leon shuffled his feet. "I just did what Mister would have done. He said to take care of your friends and neighbors. I'll be right back with the towels. Ma ain't gonna be pleased with all this blood."

"Don't worry. I'll buy her new towels and you, my man, will be rewarded for this." Dash turned to Mae. "As soon as possible, I'd like to ask Zeke a few questions. Toying with calling the police and/or going over there and beating the crap out of good ol' Lorna. See how she likes that."

Mae turned to her husband. "Don't even think about leaving this house without me."

Before she could finish her threat, the owner of the house, Etta Rae Patton, walked into the dining room carrying bags from Mickey D's. "What the hell is going on here?"

Dash stepped forward, leading her from the dining room into the kitchen. "I can explain everything, well, not everything, but most of it. Leon, help me out here."

Etta Rae listened, and nodded, and listened some more. "Got most of it. What happens now? Zeke looks like he needs to be in the hospital."

Mae entered the kitchen, nodding her head. "Definitely agree with you. Dash, the boy needs X-rays, probably a CT scan. I can't determine from an external exam if anything inside is damaged. We need to call an ambulance and the police. That woman cannot get away with this."

Dash pulled out his phone. "I'm calling Kraft now. I'll have him meet me at Zeke's. You call for an ambulance and I'll meet you at the hospital after Kraft and I talk with Lorna." He held up a finger signaling that Kraft had answered. He moved into another room to talk with him. He glanced back to watch his wife as she dialed 9-1-1.

Dash jogged down the street and around the corner. Kraft was on his way with a search warrant for the Lemmich house. Dash was now convinced Lorna had stolen the crock pot from Maud and, if tonight was an example of her exerting her power, she was his candidate for homicide or manslaughter where Maud was concerned. What else did she have belonging to this distant cousin of his mother's, one who he was growing fonder of each day? Poor little thing, pushed around by the brute Lorna.

Rather than waiting for Kraft, Dash bounded up the porch stairs, yelling for Lorna to open up. He glanced over his shoulder as a black and blue pulled up spilling Rainbeaux and Lachman out. Kraft arrived in an unmarked car.

The men assembled on the porch. Rainbeaux pounded on the door, which swung open. They peered into the darkened house. Dash reached around and flicked on the lights.

Sprawled on the sofa was Lorna, an empty bottle of Jack Daniel in her hand. Groggily she tried to sit up. She spotted Dash and said, "Hey handsome. Back for fun with your baby girl."

Kraft looked at Dash, who frowned.

"Get up, Mrs. Lemmich. We need to talk," the detective said. He pulled out his badge and the search warrant. Explaining all this turned out to be a challenge since Lorna was only interested in refreshing her drink. She pulled herself off the sofa and wove her way to the kitchen, muttering about having more Jack around.

Dash muttered to Kraft, "She buys it by the case." Then he followed her, yelling, "Lorna, why the hell did you beat the crap out of Zeke? The kid is harmless and now he's enroute to the hospital. What the hell is wrong with you?"

He observed her sway a bit, trying to focus. She watched through her blurry eyes as Lachman walked over to the rolling cart and studied the crock pot.

"Hey, whatcha doing? Get out of my kitchen. You have no right to poke around. Maud gave that to me the last time I saw her. It's mine right as rain." She picked up the empty bottle of Jack, holding it like a weapon.

Dash approached her, putting his hands out, trying to calm her down. "No need to get excited. The police have a warrant, so they get to look around. See, I don't believe Maud gave you the pot. And it's not nice to lie to me, Lorna."

Suddenly Lorna charged at him. She waved the empty bottle in his face spewing expletives left and right as he backed toward the living room.

"Lorna, put down the bottle. Don't make me hit you. My mother said that wasn't allowed." Dash back pedaled as fast as he could without turning to run.

Kraft wisely moved out of her way. He yelled for Rainbeaux who was searching for stolen goods in the upstairs bedrooms.

Dash held up his hands again, still trying to talk her down but she was having none of it.

They moved into the living room. Dash caught his boot in the torn carpet. Before he could get his balance, she punched him in the face, cutting him right below the eye. The blow knocked him back onto the sofa. He yelled, "What the fuck!" He tried to stand but the room was titling, so he dropped back onto the cushions.

Kraft and Lachman stood still, frozen in their places. Indecision all over their faces. An observer might say they were looking for a place to hide.

The front door flew open, and Dash watched his wife and Leon storm into the house. The look on Mae's face scared him and that was with only one eye open. He saw Mae glance at him and then step forward to Lorna.

"Did you hit him? You bitch." she said more calmly than he expected. Dash knew that tone and suddenly he almost pitied Lorna. Mae took another step.

Dash started to rise but fell back. "Maevis, watch out. She's one helluva beast." Leon huddled next to Dash, using him as cover.

"You wanna bet on that, soldier boy," Mae said, bouncing on her toes.

The big woman waved the bottle toward the doctor. "You want some, cutie pie?" And she moved forward with a smirk on her face and menace in her eyes. She got ready to backhand Mae when the doctor shifted her balance and threw a roundhouse kick to Lorna's chin sending her flying backwards, down, and out. Doc 1, Lorna 0.

"You killed her! You killed Godzilla! Wait 'til I tell Zeke." Leon jumped up and down.

Dash leaned slightly forward and waved a hand toward his wife. "Gentlemen, may I present my wife, the Irish warrior Queen. She's one of the two redheads that I see." Then to his wife, he said, "Damn, wish I had two good eyes. Damn, but that was the sexiest thing I've ever seen."

Mae leaned over Lorna to study her handiwork. She turned to Dash, "I do believe I've broken her jaw and possibly my foot but that will teach her to pick on my poor soldier boy." She looked around at the policemen standing with their mouths open. "Gentlemen, anyone going to arrest her for assaulting her stepson and my husband? Cuffs? Read her rights? Call an ambulance? Any of that sound familiar or is it just what they do on TV?" She clapped her hands. "Anyone want to do *something?* Leon, towels, ice, you know the drill." She limped over to the sofa. She studied her husband's swollen eye and the cut now slowly bleeding down his cheek.

Kraft introduced himself then moved to stand over the prone body. "Very impressive Doctor Hammond. Are you always this fierce?"

Mae shrugged. "That's Doctor Summers, and only when I have to defend what's mine. I heard about her glances at him this afternoon. Think she's going to lure him into something nasty, does she?"

"Whoa there, Doctor. Stop talking now. We're going to call this self-defense, *not* a fit of jealousy." Kraft shook his head. He rolled Lorna to her side and cuffed her, jumping back as she regained consciousness.

Lorna moaned and struggled to sit up. After realizing she was cuffed, she tried to scream but only muffled expletives escaped her broken jaw. She glared at Dash and Mae.

Rainbeaux joined the party carrying an old-fashioned black vinyl purse also known as a handbag.

"Detective, this is Maud's. I remember it being on her dining room table. Inside is her wallet with the driver's license, Medicare card and some jewelry. Bet Maud didn't *give* this to her. If there was any money in it, that's all gone now."

Leon crossed to inspect the purse. "He's right. This is Miss Grealis'. I'd know it anywhere."

Dash leaned his head on Mae's shoulder, "That answers that question." He sighed. "Mae, can we go home now? Everything is swirling around, and I want to go to sleep."

"A trip to the hospital is on your agenda. Sorry, I know how you hate that but I'm afraid you have another concussion, and we need to get it checked." Mae kissed his forehead.

Kraft stepped over to them. "I've got an ambulance on its way for Lorna. Wanna hitch a ride?"

Dash waved him off. "No, I'm going home. Mae, can you drive the truck, or do I need to call Sam and complete my humiliation? I can only imagine what he'll say – me being hit by a girl."

Kraft leaned in. "First, I wouldn't call Lorna a 'girl' and secondly, why didn't you punch her first? Self-defense and all."

Muttering, Dash said, "My mother said never hit a girl. Can't do it. Not right."

Mae reached behind him and pulled Dash's gun out of his belt. "What about shooting her? Not to kill but to slow her down."

"Subsection of rule number one: don't hit a girl. Shooting must be part of that." He put his head back. "Just going to nod off here for a minute. If I have to, I can sleep at Maud's tonight. Or right here." He put his finger in front of his mouth, "Shhh …"

CHAPTER TWENTY-FOUR

Dash opened his eyes. Who the hell was knocking at this hour of the night? Then he heard Sam's voice.

"Excuse me, is my brother … Sorry, I see him," Sam said as he walked over to the sofa. Crouching down in front of Dash, he removed the ice pack from his brother's eye. "Nice shiner you got there, bro." He turned to Mae, who sat rubbing her foot, "And a good evening to you dear sister-in-law. That a little swollen?"

Dash took a deep breath. "Sammy, what are you doing here? I was thinking of calling you, but pretty sure I didn't."

Sam stood. "Dad called me since he knew I was in Cleveland having dinner with a friend. He told me a bit about what happened and how you two rushed off to save the world, or at least Maud's neighborhood. Really think you'd get tired of all that."

"Still doesn't explain why you're here now," Dash said.

"Oh, Mae texted Dad that things had gone south so, of course, he texted me to find you. Said to look for an ambulance and cop cars. Easy peasy. I just look for the flashing lights." Sam shook his head and sighed.

Dash waved his hand about. "Hey, Kraft, come meet my brother."

"Can I ask a question? Anyone can answer. What the hell happened here that my relatives are the only ones injured?" Sam asked.

Kraft shook his finger, "No, no, you've got that wrong." He pointed toward Lorna who sat leaning on the wall, hands behind her back. "That is one Lorna Lemmich, heavyweight champion of the neighborhood. She beat the crap out of her stepson and then moved onto your brother. He says he can't hit a 'girl'." Kraft used air quotes to show what he thought of that maxim. "Your mommy told him not to. Apparently, his wife's mother had no such rule."

Dash waved his hand again, asking to speak. "Close but not exactly accurate. In another step or two, I would have defended myself instead of having Mae come to my rescue. She kicked the shit out of good old Lorna. My fine Irish warrior, though it's possible she broke her delicate tootsie while doing it." He shook his head slowly and then kissed Mae's hand.

Sam scratched his ear, covering his mouth so the others couldn't see the broad grin on his face. "Can I take the wounded warriors home now or do you need statements?"

Kraft motioned, "Take them. Get them out of my hair. Hammond, or should I be specific, Dash, I'll be in touch tomorrow. Lorna gets a free ride to the hospital and then to jail. Statements from you and the field goal kicker wife by noon tomorrow. Go home and get some rest." He chuckled, "Dream the dreams of the almost hero."

Both Dash and Mae groaned at that. Sam assisted Mae to his SUV, while Dash and Leon trailed behind.

Dash stopped. "Hey, what about my truck? Shouldn't just leave it here. I'm sure I can drive. Well, pretty sure. Well, maybe."

Sam turned to his brother, "Got that covered. Mike and Ryan should be here by now. They'll take the truck home. We have a family contingency plan that goes into effect the minute you leave Lakota County. Always on alert for one of your disasters, so, bro, relax."

"And to think I once saved your life. If only I could go back in time, you'd be wishing for a contingency plan of your own," Dash muttered to Leon as he walked to Sam's SUV.

Leon sprinted away, telling Dash he wanted to get home and report on the world's greatest kick ever.

"Home, Samuel," Dash said while Mae directed, "Lakota General, Sheriff, and step on it."

CHAPTER TWENTY-FIVE

A phone was ringing somewhere. Dash was almost certain of that but where? He shifted his body; every tiny move reminded him of last night. He reached over Mae to the bedtable where the phone was dancing around.

"Hello," he croaked, trying to find a clock. It felt like it was still the middle of night, the time Sam finally dropped them off at their house. Grandpa and T.J. were asleep upstairs so the wounded couple could sleep downstairs avoiding further injury as they climbed the stairs.

"Good morning, sunshine. How's the savior of Marlowe Street doing this bright sunny day?" Kraft asked.

Dash grimaced. "Spit it out, Kraft. My mother never said anything about not punching detectives."

Chuckling, Kraft continued, "Sorry to wake you so early, well, for those of us who were up most of the night anyway. I was certain you wanted to know Lorna is tucked safely away, mouth wired shut at my request. Her stepson was released from the hospital into the care of one John Mullins who will take care of the kid until the court decides what's to be done. He's almost eighteen, the kid not Mullins. You'll be happy to know that the neighborhood has rallied around him, again the kid, but also Mullins for being such a stellar fellar to take care of the kid."

Dash sat up in bed. "Are you drunk or just punch drunk? And what time is it? Can't find a clock." He heard Kraft sigh loudly and then burp. *Definitely drunk,* thought Dash. "Listen, Kraft, old buddy, go home, get some sleep and we'll have a nice long talk later today. I have a two o'clock appointment with the eye doctor, so I'll call you after that. Nighty night, Detective."

He felt Mae stir. She asked, "What time is it? I have a few patients to see today. God, I ache all over. Not so sure I haven't thrown out my hip, my back, my whole body."

"Being a hero is hard work, babe. Why don't you call off today? We can stay home and watch T.V. in our underwear or, better yet, nothing at all, and guzzle beer to our hearts' content. Doesn't that sound lovely?"

Before Mae could answer, the bedroom door flew open and T.J. stood there, a frown on his face and his hands on his hips. "There you are. I thought you left me too. Here," he said as he handed his father a note. "Grandpa woke me up and said he had to see Tom who's sick. Told me to give this to you."

Dash pulled himself up and turned on the light. He struggled to read the note without his glasses. "Can the old man write any smaller?" He jostled Mae. "Can you read this?"

Mae sighed, one of those sighs that starts in your broken foot and slowly travels north. "Give." She adjusted the note so the light shone on it. "Says here that Tom called. Said he felt poorly and asked Owen to come." She groaned as she threw off the covers. "Get a move on it. We need to find out what's going on." She grimaced as she stood. "Stupid Lorna!"

Dash glanced at T.J. who was staring at his father's eye.

"What happened to you?"

Mae answered. "He got hit by a girl! What do you think of that, T.J.?"

"Daddy, did you hit her back? Give *her* a black eye?"

"No, T.J., I didn't. A man isn't supposed to hit a woman, or in your case, a boy shouldn't hit a girl."

"Humph. Dumbest thing I ever heard. If a girl hits me, I'm gonna whomp her good," T. J. responded. "Are we ever going to eat?"

Again, Mae groaned, "Not if your father has his way. He wants to stay in bed and guzzle beer all day."

Dash shook his head. "Talk about the wrong side of the bed." He pushed the covers aside. "I'll be in and out of the bathroom in a minute. Then Mae, you take a nice long shower to wake up your good side. I remember there being one. I'll take care of T.J."

And so starts my day, thought Dash, as he looked longingly at the bed.

Dash and T.J. walked slowly down the hospital corridor searching for room 427, Father Tom's room.

He glanced down the hall and saw his brother exit a room. "Sam, what's going on? Is Tom in there and where the hell is Owen? He's not answering his phone."

Sam walked slowly toward them, shaking his head. "Tom is throwing a helluva fit saying he is being kept against his will. Interesting to watch since he can hardly breath, but he's threatening to call an attorney and wants me to arrest any number of doctors for unlawful detention."

"So, Tom is doing just fine. How'd he end up here if he isn't sick? And again, any sign of our father?"

"I called Ruthie who picked Owen up and took him to her house for some TLC. And Tom *is* sick, a bit of bronchitis or just a bad cold. Had a tough time breathing last night so the nurse at Lakeview called an ambulance," Sam answered.

T.J. tugged at his uncle's pants. "Uncle Sammy, if a girl hit you, wouldn't you hit her back?"

Sam crouched down. "Unfortunately, I'm a sheriff so I can't go around hitting girls, or boys for that matter. I just arrest them." Standing, he turned to his brother, "I'm guessing this has to do with your rainbow eye."

"I'm not going to discuss it, my eye that is. Enough jawing, let's see the current miscreant." Dash started for the door when he saw his favorite nurse's aide approaching the room.

"Hey Sarge, what are you doing here?" he asked.

She stopped and shook her head. "Hammond, another Hammond." Getting a good look at Dash, she asked, "What happened to you now? Looking for a bed in your uncle's room?"

"Nah, just checking on him. What are you doing here? Isn't the fifth floor where you usually terrorize the patients? I recall you doing that to me."

"Well, that old man is kicking up a fuss about staying here. Understand he's a priest so he's about to have a come-to-Jesus meeting. And I'm the big Black Jesus. He'll settle down and behave, just like you did once you understand the rules." She pushed the door open.

Dash turned to his brother. "This won't be pretty."

Dash entered Room 427. "Tom, are you dying? Should I start on a eulogy, cause I ain't got nothing to do all day. I'm not allowed to sit around just drinking beer, which was my plan."

Tom waved at Dash. "Do it, write that eulogy. If this stupid cold doesn't kill me, that damn nurse will." He made the sign of the cross and folded his hands in prayer. "Dash, I have something to tell you …"

Sarge interrupted him. "Out now, the patient needs his rest. Scram."

Saluting Sarge, Dash closed the door. Bookstore, the next the stop, then pick up Mae from her office and home to bed!

While T.J. poured over all the new books in the children's section, Dash sat on the one comfy chair in the store, scrolling through his phone messages. Then it rang.

"Leon, how are you, buddy? Can't believe you still have a voice. Is there anyone in the neighborhood that hasn't heard about the scene at Lorna's?"

"Hey, Mister, you won't believe where I am and what I am doing! Guess, go ahead and guess. You won't get it in a million years."

"I bet I get it in one. You're at Zeke's house with a detective from Robbery. You're helping him find more of Maud's stuff, right?"

"Aw, who told you? Ain't fair!" Leon complained.

"Leon, Leon, one of the lessons you need to learn early in life is that life is not fair, not even close. And I cheated. I got an email from Detective Hardy telling me he was taking you and Mrs. Brady for a quick look-around. He's building a case again Lorna of the wired mouth." Dash looked up to see his son holding a half a dozen books, a question on his face. Dash gave him a thumbs up, what the hell, a reward for being abandoned by his parents last night. Back to Leon, he said, "Listen, I can't make it in today but tomorrow for sure I'll be there to check on Zeke and catch up with you. What time do you get out of school? We'll do a late lunch or early dinner, maybe we'll do a carryout and see if Zeke is hungry."

"Hey Mister, I can skip school if you want."

"Leon, remember the books and our bargain. School first, then food."

Dash looked at T.J. who was frowning. The little boy asked his dad, "Can I come to lunch with you? I want to meet Leon."

Avoiding answering his son's question, Dash said to Leon, "Later, kiddo. If you see Zeke, tell him I'll talk to him tomorrow. Is he doing okay?"

He could almost see Leon shrugging.

"Yeah, Mister, okay for a kid who's black and blue and sore all over. What do *you* think? See you tomorrow then," Leon said.

CHAPTER TWENTY-SIX

After his eye appointment, Dash tiptoed into his house. It was as quiet as the proverbial tomb. When he left for the optometrist's, Mae and T.J. were curled up in bed. Mae's foot was propped up on several pillows and T.J. was showing her all his new books. After a few minutes they both fell sound asleep.

After letting the dogs out for a quick run, Dash grabbed a beer. He moved into the front room to review all the boards. He studied the timelines and news clippings. What did it all mean? Now they have Callahan's body. And the missing crock pot. What exactly did that settle? Where's the missing child? What to do with the house?

He glanced at the recliner. Very tempting to just sit down, drink beer and turn on the television. Instead, he moved to his office.

Dash sat at his desk re-reading Maud's letter for the umpteenth time. He was torn between burning the whole thing or picking up the phone to harass Father Pat, Maud's best friend. Where the hell were the names of any relatives left in Ireland? Surely there were one or two grand-nieces or nephews.

'*Always waiting for the knock on the door. Our past invading our present.*' Maud wrote those words and believed them. Decided to use them as an excuse to get rid of Callahan. Wonder if she killed the Callahan that started all this. She said she didn't, but could you believe her? '*Cleansing of the clans,*' another turn of phrase that stuck with him. Wars had been fought for that reason. So why *not* choose him, the soldier, the man who wanted to save the world, right the wrongs?

He sighed and leaned back in his chair. Well, dear Cousin Maud, maybe when he was younger; now he didn't give a shit about the world out there. He couldn't save it. All he could do was hope the whole f'ng planet didn't blow up before his children had a chance to enjoy whatever would pass for life in the coming years.

Realizing he was about to sink into a deep funk, he closed his eyes and tried to think happy thoughts: Mae, T.J., and the new babe, Delia Rose, due in a short while. Wonder what she'll look like, behave like – more Maevis than Dashiell, or vice versa. Either way, she'd be a handful if he remembered his own childhood shared with Mae and his cousin Billy. He couldn't wait to hold her. The only thing better than the new car smell was a new baby smell.

He nearly drifted off when he heard the knock on his front door. He shook himself. Who could that be? Anyone who knew them always went around to the backdoor. Crap, someone selling something.

He put on his 'get off my steps' face and walked to the front door, yanking it open. A woman stood there, the map of Ireland on her face. His heart started beating a little faster. Could this be the missing daughter? She found him rather than the other way around.

"Good morning. Are ye Dashiell Hammond?" The voice had the Irish lilt to it. Right off the plane if he had to guess. She was older, or so she looked, than Dash, not by much, but enough. Her eyes were a bit glazed over and she swayed just a bit.

"And you are? What do you want?" Dash asked testily.

"Aye, you're himself alright. A regular gobshite related to the original gobshite, one Maud Grealis." The woman slipped her hand into the pocket of her trench coat.

Dash stiffened. Was he about to be gunned down on his own doorstep? Where was Charlie Dog when he needed backup?

The woman pulled out a warrant card and shoved it in his face. Eileen Varner, Garda Siochana, Detective Inspector, Dublin, Ireland.

After verifying the face on the photo matched the face on the woman, Dash said, "A bit off your patch, aren't you? Take a wrong turn at Liverpool, did you?"

The woman's face darkened, and her eyes narrowed. She muttered again, "Gobshite. What happened to youse eye? Some soldier."

Dash held up his hands in truce. "So sorry, me mam, as you would say, would skin me alive for such manners." He swung the door open wide. "Please come in. From the look on your face, I'd say the skies weren't all that friendly. Have a seat." And he motioned toward the sofa.

Detective Inspector Eileen Varner collapsed, kicking off her shoes. She reached down to rub her swollen feet. "Apologies. I thought walking the beat was hard but not as hard as sitting for eight hours fearing you're going to meet your Maker in the blue waters below." After a few more rubs, she asked, "Aren't you curious why I'm here?"

Dash shrugged. "Not really. You said the magic name. Don't know why you bothered to come all this way. She's dead, you're late by several weeks."

"Like I said, gobshite." She licked her lips, a signal to Dash that she needed something liquid to quench her thirst.

Dash said, "A cup of tea or something stronger?"

"Maybe not such a thick gobshite after all. Got any Jameson or Guinness?"

Laughing, Dash said, "Really fond of that word, are you? Got both."

That set the Detective Inspector to laughing. She threw her head back and howled. "Jameson, and don't be shy. What do people call you, colonel or mister? Got to call you something."

"Dash will be fine. Back in a second."

He returned quickly with the bottle of Jameson and a glass into which he poured a generous amount. Maud's idea of a good host—ply your guests with plenty of liquor.

One sip and Varner visibly relaxed. "I needed that. Can't drink on a plane; can't eat either. Don't like anything that moves – car, lorry, plane, ship, those are the worst." She worked her way out of her trench coat. She wore a now-rumpled, simple white blouse and black slacks.

Dash sat on the edge of the recliner and watched Varner gulp rather than sip the very expensive whiskey.

"I hate to interrupt your drinking, but can I ask why you are here. Here as in my house, Ohio, the United States. I just told you Maud is dead so whatever you were going to ask her is now a moot question."

Varner waved her hand about, dismissing what Dash just said. "No, no, no questions for Maud. A few for you. Understand you inherited it all, all of her possessions. I knew she was dead before I got on the plane. Never wanted to meet her. Heard she was a regular terror." She swallowed the rest of her drink. "No, Finn told me she was dead. Figured it was a good time to come over." She held out her glass, motioning toward the bottle.

Dash complied with another generous pour. "Finn told you. Would that be Father Finn Flannery, the genealogist?"

"One and the same. He also is a research assistant to many authors who write about the families of Ireland." She leaned forward and looked around, glancing at all the whiteboards. She swallowed the Jameson. "Where the devil is my satchel? I've got all my papers in there." She put the glass out, indicating she needed a refill. "Shite, if I lost it, years of research down the loo."

Dash reached for the glass and poured another, thinking she must have a hollow leg. "How did you get to my house? Take a taxi, or what passes for one in Clover Pointe? Think you could have left it in that. Suitcase?" He was about to hand her the glass, but he got no answer. He looked in her direction. She was out cold, mouth open, a loud snore erupting.

He retrieved the glass before it could tip over. Glancing at the inert figure, he said, "Make yourself at home, why don't you!"

Dash retreated to the kitchen with the almost-empty bottle, pulling the pocket doors shut so he didn't have to listen to

Varner's snoring while he prepared chicken and veggies for grilling. Mae and T.J. would wake eventually and dinner was his responsibility, one he loved.

Dash turned as the back door opened and in walked his father, shaking his head and carrying what could be the missing satchel.

"Where'd you find that?" he asked his father who ignored the question, just setting the satchel on the table.

"Dash, my boy, wait 'til you hear what Finn told Tom and I'm here to tell you. We're going …"

Leaning against the counter, Dash held up his hand to stop his father. Adopting the Irish brogue of his mother, he said, "Faith and begorrah. Is it a foul-mouthed leprechaun that is about to visit ourselves? And one who drinks Jameson like it was water from the River Liffey?" He nodded toward the bottle on the counter and then towards the closed doors.

He reached for the briefcase and began to pull out the contents.

His father objected. "What are you doing? You can't go through other people's stuff without permission or a warrant."

"You can if said owner called you a 'gobshite' several times, drank all your Jameson, and passed out on the couch."

Owen straightened up, planting a frown on his face. "What?" He nodded toward the bottle on the counter and stepped closer to sniff his son's breath. "Drinking this early in the day? And what are you looking for? Do you know?"

Dash shook his head. "No idea but she said the magic name 'Maud Grealis' so I'm hoping to find something to tie the two together. Hoping for a leg up on the old gal."

"Old? Gal? I thought Finn said he was sending a detective to help us."

T.J. came down the stairs and walked over to the pocket doors, sliding one open a bit. He turned to his father, "Who's the old lady snoring on our sofa?"

Dash put a finger over his lips. "Shhh! Don't wake her up. Please." He watched his wife hobble down the stairs. She sat down on the second to bottom step.

Mae pointed to the nearly empty bottle on the counter. "Please tell me you haven't taken to drinking at this hour of the day."

He rolled his eyes at the second question in minutes about his drinking. Thinking maybe I should start, but instead he pointed toward the front room. "I haven't, but our guest is on a different clock than ours, and very possibly a different planet. Give me a second to get the chicken on the grill and I'll try to explain the very little I know."

When Dash returned to the kitchen, he found Mae and Owen shifting through the papers from the briefcase. "Find anything interesting?"

"Define interesting," said Mae. "From what I can gather, more family history though in book form than genealogical charts. Did you say who the owner is?"

With a bang, the pocket doors slid open. "Detective Inspector Eileen Varner, Garda, from the Dublin Castle station," she said flashing her warrant card. She walked unsteadily over to Dash. "Okay, gobshite, explain why yis think yis can go through my papers?"

Dash pulled himself up to every inch of his six-four, put on his military face and called up his military voice. Using his right hand, he pointed at her. "I think I can do it because I *can*. This is *my* house; you drank all *my* booze and you keep calling *me* names. So, Detective Inspector, sit your arse down and tell me just what you're doing here and just *what* you think I'm going to do for you."

Varner looked around the table, pulling out a chair. "Himself's a bit tetchy for such a big laddy. Some American hospitality." She sat down, changing her demeanor into one of a long-suffering woman. "Don't suppose you have any food to spare a poor old lady, do ya?" Getting no response, she added, "I talk better when I've a full stomach and a wet tongue." She nodded toward the Jameson bottle.

When Dash didn't answer, Owen walked over to the stove. "A cup of coffee is on the menu now."

Silence filled the room as the coffee brewed. The aroma did nothing to soothe the inhabitants of the kitchen.

Owen set a cup in front of Varner. "Cream, sugar?"

"Yes, thank you, sir." Varner said as she surveyed the adults, all scowling at her.

T.J. tugged at his father's pants, motioning for him to bend down. He whispered, "Is she here to take all my Irish money?"

"She's not taking anything from anyone, but let's not mention that, okay, kiddo." His son nodded.

Dash turned to his guest. "I'm grilling chicken and vegetables. Would that suffice as dinner for you, or should I search for something else?"

Eileen squinted at him and, for a moment, he thought she was going to call him something worse than gobshite. Instead, she said, "Chicken on the barbee would be fine. Sorry about falling asleep. I'm really messed up timewise." She took another sip of her coffee and stared off into space. "Ya know I've never been out of Ireland before, not even to the north. I'm more than a bit off my patch. Should have brought one of me grandkids. They know how to do everything. Feeling really old, gobshite."

She suddenly put her hand over her mouth.

Dash rushed across the room to open the door to the half-bath. "Please, please, be my guest."

As he closed the door, he turned to his family. "I'm think I'm going to like this old leprechaun."

CHAPTER TWENTY-SEVEN

The next morning as the family gathered around the table for breakfast, a very pale Garda slowly made her way to the table. She gently sat down and timidly said, "Thank you for getting my suitcase from that place. And bed was what I needed. I owe you an apology for last night. Not used to being away from mine. Yis can kick me out at any time."

T.J. started giggling. "You talk funny but it's kinda pretty."

"Ah, the wee bairn. You only have the one?" she asked Dash who figured she was trying to be polite after last night's fiasco.

He wasn't having any of it. He said curtly, "Yes. Would you like some oatmeal or toast? I could scramble an egg or two, but that's about it for now."

"Too kind. Oatmeal it is and some tea." She turned to Mae. "I owe you thanks as well for that little pill you gave me. Made my dreams sweet. A doctor, is you?"

Dash held up his hand. "Love the small talk, Varner, but I need the answer to a question before we have a love fest here. You never answered this last night. Why are you here? Here. Now. Since Maud is dead."

Varner's shoulders slumped as she said, "I'm Maud's niece, her older brother Pete's daughter. The oldest brother joined the priesthood and the younger brother, Michael, died unwed and of a broken heart. Me Gran told me that she gave Maud the family jewelry to use if she needed money while running from Ireland. As the oldest daughter, I'd like them back so I can give them to my granddaughter when she marries this July. That's why I'm here, for the jewelry."

Dash looked puzzled. "But we didn't find any jewelry and we scoured that house, top to bottom and even in the floors."

Mae touched her husband's hand. "Wait, when we were at Lorna's, the Black cop said he found Maud's purse with her wallet and papers and a little jewelry." She turned to Varner. "Sorry but we were preoccupied and didn't think to ask to see it or what exactly he found."

Dash chewed on his bottom lip. "I'm afraid, but it's possible the jewelry is now evidence in at least a robbery/burglary and even a murder/manslaughter. I'll text Detective Kraft to see if he can enlighten us about status and contents. You know the drill, D.I."

Varner reached for the oatmeal Dash had set before her. She drew in a breath to inhale the sweet smell of cinnamon on the cereal. "Seems like Finn forgot to tell us the whole story. He just said she had died, nothing about robbery, murder, and such." As she ate, her demeanor slowly changed from hung-over guest to Detective Garda. "I'll finish this, make myself decent and then let's go visit this Kraft fellow."

As he bussed the table and rinsed the dishes, Dash turned to his family, "You have a good day at the sheriff's house with Auntie Re and their sweet granddaughter, little Rissa. I understand we're to join you for dinner at Marie's tonight, right?"

"Got it in one. We'll see you then. Try not to strangle Varner." Mae kissed his cheek and T.J.

Dash stood on the back porch finishing his cup of coffee. He breathed in the fresh morning air and watched his dogs race around the yard. A beautiful day, he thought, another one where I'm not tilling my garden. Maybe if he and Varner got moving, he could be home in time to do a bit of yard work before the family get-together. As he waited for his guest, he texted Kraft asking for a meeting to examine the jewelry. He mentioned Varner as an interested and related party. A meeting was set for two in the afternoon. He turned as Varner stepped outside, ready to hit the road.

Dash helped Varner climb into his truck. The look on her face made him wonder if sitting up so high would give her another upset stomach. "Are you all right? Don't want you feeling sickly once I start. Should I get a bag or a towel or motion sickness pills?"

Varner swallowed hard. "I don't suppose I could wash down those pills with some good Irish whisky, could I? That always seems to help."

Shaking his head, Dash answered, "No, no whisky, good or rotten this early in the morning. It's none of my business, but do you drink like this back home?"

"Oh no, me husband Jimmy would have me head. He's been sober for ten years now and I only sneak a drink when well out of his sight. I figured the ocean was big enough he couldn't smell it on my breath. You'll not say anything to him, will ye?"

Dash drew his fingers across his lips. "Sealed. Now I'm going to get those pills and some water. We need to get moving. Lots to do."

After making sure, Varner was medicated and the interior of his truck was safe from harm, he played the tour guide as they drove into Cleveland, pointing out areas that Eileen might find interesting as many were where the Irish settled when they first arrived here. The Cleveland skyline glistened as the sun rose higher in the very blue sky.

Marlowe street was quiet, unlike the last time Dash was there. He pulled into Maud's driveway and walked around to the passenger side and opened the door, giving Varner a helping hand as she stepped down, quite a drop for her.

"Well, D.I., this is Maud's house. From what we were able to learn this is where she moved shortly after landing in the United States. Never sure why Cleveland and not a bigger city like New York, Boston, or Chicago. There were a fair amount of Irish living here. Can't understand it since I got the feeling she was avoiding anyone who might recognize her."

Varner turned to him. "A feeling? Why would she be hiding?"

"I gathered she was wanted as a witness, even a suspect, in the murder of Jimmy Callahan. Got that from the news clippings she saved. When we get back to my house, I'll pull all that out and you can see where my feelings come from."

Snorting, Varner said, "She didn't murder Callahan, though I will say from what me da told me, she was at the top of the list for a good bit. And Declan Rooney, his biggest sin was deserting his wife and kids for Maud. No, Callahan's own wife Moira stabbed him. She admitted to being tired of his wandering eyes and hands. Guess he wanted Maud and Rooney also wanted Maud. Popular old gal, my aunt."

Dash laughed out loud. "It was probably her charming personality." He started up the porch steps. "Come on, not much to see but you're here now. Take pictures if you'd like. I've brought in a team to bring it up to snuff, modernize the bathrooms and kitchens. The place is pretty torn up, but we can walk around. I'll try to answer any questions so fire away," Dash said as he led Varner up the front steps.

He heard his name being called and turned to see Leon waving. "Come on over, Leon. Want you to meet someone."

Leon didn't have to be asked twice. He jumped off his porch and dashed across the street.

"Detective Inspector Varner, I want you to meet Leon Patton, one of Maud's friends and my helper." Dash watched Leon's face light up. "Leon, D.I. Varner is Maud's niece, straight from Ireland. She's here to visit a bit, sorry she missed Maud." He looked pointedly at Varner hoping she would get the message to mind her Irish tongue.

After opening the door, the trio entered, and Leon took the lead in explaining the house to Varner. Dash did interrupt to explain where Maud was found; he wanted the D.I. to get a sense of why manslaughter/murder might be under consideration.

Dash watched as the D.I. inspected what there was left of Maud's possessions. She turned up the mattress and peered into the corners of the closet. A big smile broke out on her face when she saw the photo shrine of Maud's holy trinity: the pope, the Kennedy brothers, and Major Dashiell Hammond.

"I'm surprised she didn't have one of Daniel O'Connell or any of the uprising. Me da crossed himself every time he passed the photos hanging on our walls. That was our catechism as well as the ones the good sisters and fathers taught us in school."

She asked Leon where he went to school, what his favorite subject was, and subtly slipped in a question or two about her aunt's life here in Cleveland.

Leon did not disappoint Dash in retelling of Maud's good deeds to the kids in the neighborhood. He especially emphasized the storytelling and the reading of books which made Varner and Dash smile. Leon's portrait of Maud was one of kindness and charity. He left out the boxing of ears and the tyrannical rule of the street.

"Hey, Mister, you want to go next door to see Zeke. He'll make you feel better about your black eye. He's black and blue all over. Says he feels miserable cause he can't go to school looking like that and he only has a few weeks left before he graduates. Then he wants to run as far from here as possible and I don't mean joining the circus, the Army so you should talk to him or at least that's what I think."

"Take a breath, Leon. And, yes, we'll visit him now if D.I. Varner is finished here," he said turning to the Garda. "Not much else to see. Zeke is the young man whose stepmother is accused of stealing from Maud, helping her on her way to salvation and beating up her stepson and me while she was at it." He said to Leon, "Lead on, my man. Let's cheer up Zeke."

Leon was only too happy to be the point man, heading out the door and guiding Dash and Varner next door to John Mullins' house. He politely knocked on the front door, which was answered promptly by John himself.

Mullins wasn't a tall man but very sturdy. A pleasant face and a firm handshake. He wore plain but durable work clothes with an embroidered patch proclaiming his name and his employer, Cuyahoga Electric. He ushered the visitors in, taking Dash aside for a quick word.

"We need to have a good long talk about Zeke and his future. I don't know all the ins and outs of social welfare, but we've already had a visit from one of the workers. Thinking they want to make sure poor Zeke didn't land in the fire after being in the frying pan. Pretty sure I convinced her he was safe with us, at least for now."

Dash nodded. "You're right about Zeke's future. It's only a few weeks, maybe a month, before he is declared independent in the eyes of the law. He'll need a job and a place to live unless his father owns the house where he and Lorna lived. Let me talk to Zeke and then you and I will have a good sit-down." He was about to turn away but stopped. "We also need to talk about the medical expenses. I have a very close friend who is a family lawyer. I'll call her and see what she can do for Zeke and us."

The front room was now the sick room. Tray tables with bottles of medicine and tubes of salve were scattered throughout. In spite of all this, the room had the scent of lemon furniture polish, not illness.

Zeke was holding court. He lay on the sofa, wrapped in blankets, another TV tray by his side covered with snacks and drinks. His face was still a mottled mess of black, blue, purple and a sickly green which clashed with the oversized red and yellow plaid shirt he obviously borrowed from Mullins.

"Mister Hammond, I never got to thank you and your wife for helping me the other night. I wasn't thinking straight at all, too much pain and blood. Not good with blood."

"I'd say you look good, but I'd be lying. You look better than you did, like I did two nights ago. I'll never underestimate what you tell me again. Should have believed what you said about Lorna's temper and fire power." Dash took a seat across from the sofa. "Any word from the doctor on your injuries, recovery?"

Mullins stepped into the conversation. "He's got an appointment at the end of the week for a follow-up. Obviously, he's sore but we're making sure he gets up every two hours and walks around, does some mild exercises. He could go to school but what good would all the stares do him."

Mrs. Mullins entered the room with a tray full of cookies and slices of cake. She set these in front of Varner and turned to her husband. "John, there's coffee and tea and soft drinks in the kitchen. Why don't you make yourself useful and ask the guests what they'd like?"

After more small talk, Dash got to the crux of the matter. "Zeke, I know you're graduating in a month or so. Any thoughts about what you want to do after that?"

Zeke sat up straighter. "I don't know for sure. Thinking it would be best if I got out of town, but I don't have anywhere to go. My dad's remarried and his new wife doesn't want me around my little half-brother and sister. Leaning toward joining the Army. You made a success of that, didn't you?"

Dash sipped his tea. "Whole different ballgame for me. I went through ROTC at Ohio State and was a second looey when I moved on a basc. And hate to point this out since I'm sitting here with a big black eye, but I was bigger, stronger than you are. No, kid, the Army is not for you right now. What about college?"

Mullins chimed in. "I've been talking to him about apprenticing with me. He can stay here, sleep in my boy Chris' room while he's serving in the Corps. I'll help him get started on a career for life. Back me up on this, Hammond."

"That's a wonderful idea. You'll never be unemployed with a skill like that. Zeke, I'd think long and hard before I turned down such an offer. And I'd be happy to help with room and board until you can pitch in here." He nodded his head. "This might give you an idea of a good family life, show you it's not all evil stepmothers."

Dash glanced at his watch. "Hate to break this up but Varner and I have a meeting downtown with the detectives. John, one last word with you, in private."

The two men moved to the kitchen.

"What do you know about Leon's father?"

"That there isn't one. Etta Ray moved here when the boy was a toddler. At first she was a stay-at-home mama. Never talked about her life before Marlowe Street. Her accent tells me she's from either Southern Ohio or West Virginia. Why are you asking?"

Dash shrugged. "As my brother would say, I'm trying to save everyone on Marlowe Street. I just worry about a young boy all alone all hours of the day and night."

"Don't worry. You were right about those of us who live here. We do watch out for our neighbors. There are many adult eyes on that young boy when he's out of the house roaming the neighborhood. What we don't know is what he's up to when he's inside, alone." Mullins shrugged. "Basically, Leon is a good kid."

"Even good kids can get into trouble because they don't know enough to stay out of it. I have so many pieces on my plate, but I don't intend to abandon him. I'll give Etta Ray a call and see if there is anything, short of adopting him, I can do to help." He extended his hand. "Like I said, give a call if anything comes up for either Zeke or Leon."

Dash and Varner took their leave to head.

CHAPTER TWENTY-EIGHT

A text to Kraft brought the detective down to the lobby. On the elevator ride up to the third floor, Kraft said, "Dash, I need to tell you something, but don't shoot the messenger. Lemmich is asking that Mae be charged with assault and battery." The detective watched as Dash's eyes grew black with anger. "I've alerted Mae." He held up his hand as Dash pulled out his phone. "Not so fast, cowboy. Before I could put my phone down, it rang and I found myself talking to 'The' William McCafferty, legal eagle of Ohio. He's coming to town tomorrow to 'sort out this bullshit.' I take it you know him."

"Best friend, first cousin, old playmate, roommate at OSU, best man at several of my weddings, so yes, I guess I can honestly say that Mae and I know him." He turned his head slightly. "Batton down the hatches and hide Lorna. If my ginger-headed cousin arrives with steam coming out of his ears, there will be fireworks all around. I'd almost like to be here, but I have many other things to do."

As the elevator doors opened, Kraft said to Dash, "One being writing a statement about what transpired at Lemmich's that night. Whatever you can remember, and no fiction allowed."

Dash just smiled. "I apologize. I meant to do that after I got home. Bit of a headache and then I just forgot. I'll have it for you later today unless you'd like to lend me a laptop."

Kraft shook his head. "Let's get this over with and then we'll think about the statement. Need one from Dr. Summers as well."

Once in the homicide bullpen, Dash pulled over a couple of chairs so he and Varner could sit while Kraft shuffled through all the stacks on his desk. Phones were ringing left and right. Chattering filled the background.

"Got a few cases going?" Dash asked.

"Sadly, yes. Wish they were all as cut and dried as the two you handed me." Kraft turned to Varner. "Has he brought you up to snuff about Maud's death? Did you say you were her niece?"

Varner raised a hand slightly. "Correct, Detective, but I'm not here about her death but about the jewelry you found when himself was getting punch by 'Godzilla' which can't, for the love of God, be her real name." She glanced at Dash. "I doubt himself gave me all the story. Tightlipped that gobshite."

Dash rolled his eyes. "Varner, one more gobshite and you're walking back to Clover Pointe or I just might stick you on a plane back to Ireland."

Kraft looked from one to the other, deciding not to get into that discussion. Instead he asked, "Let's find Detective Hardy of the Robbery Unit. He's down the hall and he'll be happy to hear from both of you."

With that the trio moved down the hall and found Detective Hardy at his desk crouched over some photos.

Introductions were made. Dash asked Hardy if any more items were found when he last searched the Lemmich home.

"Only a few bits, not worth the effort. Here's the list of what we do have as evidence. Not sure the prosecutor will want to go to trial over this. Doesn't amount to much," he said as he handed the list to Dash.

Varner peered over Dash's shoulder and pointed to the jewelry items. "If it will make a difference I have photos of the jewels and the appraisal my Gran had done, well, now it's probably sixty or seventy years ago." She rifled through her bag, found a large manila envelope, and pulled out several sheets of paper. These were handed to Hardy.

Dash and Kraft moved to stand behind the detective so they could read over his shoulder. Dash whistled, "Seventy years ago that was a lot of money. Probably should have them reevaluated for probate. Surprised Maud never pawned them *or* mailed them back to her mother."

"Probably afraid they'd get lost in the mail. Gran never talked much about Maud after the Callahan episode. She only told me about the jewels a few months before she died. I promised her I would bring them back to the family, whenever I got the chance. I was young with wee bairns, never even thought about crossing the pond. Me da wrote to Maud but never said if she answered. She didn't come home for her own mam's funeral."

Dash shook his head, "Gobshite, for sure." He smiled at Varner whose eyes narrowed, causing him to wonder if only those born on auld sod had the right to use that word. He decided not to find out.

Hardy asked if he could make copies of the papers. "If you want to see the jewels to verify they match what your Gran told you, I'd be happy to take you to the evidence room. As you know you can look but can't touch."

Dash said, "Hey Hardy, shouldn't you have them appraised so the current value could be added to the theft charges? As Maud's heir, I'd be happy to pay for it, like I said, I'll need an appraisal for the estate. Kill two birds with one stone. Your call."

As they walked down to the evidence room, Dash stopped Kraft. "One moment please. What's going on the skeleton we're calling Callahan? Where do we stand on that? I haven't told Varner about that aspect yet. Hard to believe but I'm leery of talking about it with her. She is the niece after all though I suspect she doesn't hold her aunt in high regard."

"While they check the evidence, why don't we adjourn to the cafeteria and have a quiet discussion about Callahan?"

After informing Hardy and Varner of the new plan, Dash and Kraft headed to the refreshment center. They each grabbed a beverage and found an empty corner.

"Here's the deal, Dash. The medical examiner wants a DNA sample from one of this Callahan's relatives. For all he knows, these bones belong to someone else."

Dash laughed, "Does he think Maud was like the little old ladies in *Arsenic and Old Lace*? Bumping off people willy-nilly. I mean we have her confession; doesn't that count?"

"Yes, but only if the victim *is* Callahan. I've put in a call to the police in the hometown that you listed as his. Haven't heard back yet. Don't supposed this D.I. could help with that?"

"All we can do is ask," Dash said as he nodded toward Varner and Hardy as they walked over to the table. "Anything to drink, folks? Kraft is paying, so be extravagant." He stood to pull out a chair for Varner.

"I doubt they have what I'm craving but a spot of tea wouldn't be wasted," Varner said to Kraft. She turned to Dash. "Those are the family jewels, so to speak. Beautiful. Detective Hardy is going to talk to the decision makers and hopefully I'll be able to carry them home with me."

Dash put his elbows on the table to hold his head in his hands. "Eileen, there is something you need to know about Maud."

"Eileen is it now? Bad news? Out with it then."

So, Varner learned of the murderous Maud and the dead Callahan.

CHAPTER TWENTY-NINE

D.I. Eileen Varner sat silently after Dash finished his spiel. She leaned back in her chair and pursed her lips. After a few minutes she motioned for Kraft to join her and Dash.

"Is what himself says about my Auntie Maud true? That she was a cold-blooded murderer? Not sure I trust the Army chappie. I heard he had a brain injury. So, Detective Kraft of the Cleveland Homicide Department, is it true?" She skewered Kraft with a narrowed eyed look.

Kraft shrugged, holding his hands out. "Ma'am, I only know what Hammond told me. He did send me a copy of her confession so I have to give some credence to that. Our biggest problem is that we are not sure the bones we found are Callahan's. I've a call into the police department or Garda over there to see if we can get DNA to match."

Hearing that, Varner stood almost knocking over the chair. "Gentlemen, let's see if my Jimmy can help. He still has friends throughout the Garda. Anyone have a phone I can use? Need to charge mine. Any idea of the time over there? Can't remember how many hours they are ahead, and I'd hate to wake himself up. Grumpy old man."

Kraft led the way back to homicide and opened the door to the captain's office. "This is empty. Hammond, give her your phone. The hoops I have to jump through to get authorization for an international call is ridiculous."

Hammond dutifully handed Varner his phone. "I'll stay here until you get through, just in case you need help dialing."

Varner scoffed at that. She pulled out her notebook with instructions on how to 'phone home' provided by her granddaughter. After punching in the number, she said, "Ah, my Jimmy. No, no, not an emergency but wait 'til you hear this." She paused and then glanced at Dash. "Yes, yes, he's a gobshite like I thought but he's likeable one." She waved Dash out of the room.

Ten minutes passed before she opened the office door and walked over to Dash handing him the phone.

She sighed a very big sigh and pulled out a chair next to Kraft's desk. "My Jimmy is brilliant. He knows who to call so he'll check with them to see about the Callahan DNA. We figure one or the other of the family must have been nicked at one time or another. He'll check to see if one of them has gone missing." She handed Dash his phone. "I've told Jimmy to call you, Detective, when he learns something."

Dash pushed the papers on the desk aside and perched himself on the corner. "What's next? If the bones do belong to Callahan, and since Maud is dead as well, will that case be closed? The bones returned to his family if they so desire?"

"I'll tell you what has been discussed, but, again, not the final word. The district attorney wants nothing to do with this. Case closed as far as he is concerned. He'll write it up and file it away. If it's not Kevin Callahan, the search to find out whose bones we have will begin, but very low on the totem pole." He glanced at Varner and added, "Low priority to be sure" She nodded. "To be honest, right now, the D.A. is more interested in prosecuting Lemmich for burglary, plus assault and battery. He's building a case in the hopes he can convince her to plead guilty and opt for room and board on the county. I certainly hope that hot-shot cousin of yours doesn't throw a wrench into this. And, just out of curiosity's sake, why is he involved anyway?"

"Ah, Billy of the white hat, horse, and knighthood. He's always seen himself as Mae's personal protector."

Kraft laughed out loud. "If he had seen her the other night, he'd think differently."

"No, to Billy she will always be the little girl next door, the one with the drunken bully for a father and a sickly mother.

The three of us were playmates since the play pen. I don't have enough time to tell it all, but trust me, when Mae even whimpers, Billy is at the door or on the phone."

He stood up to stretch his back. "As I was saying, no worries on that front. If I know my cousin, and I do, he'll stomp in here, talk to Lorna who will then confess to everything including the torso murders of yesteryear and volunteer for life imprisonment." He crossed his arms. "Okay, tell me what's next on the agenda. What do you need from me or my family? I've got a to-do list that is longer than my arm and I'd like to start crossing items off."

Kraft threw a pencil across his desk. "Why should you be the only one marking things off?" He pulled a battered legal pad over and turned pages until he found the one with cross-outs and circled items covering the sheet.

He took a sip of his very cold coffee. "First, we'll close the Grealis/Callahan murder case. Get 'dem bones back to 'dem relatives. Then, we'll need to settle the Lemmich robbery/battery/manslaughter issues. Here's hoping you're right about that golden boy cousin of yours."

Dash slowly shook his head. "Trust me, it will be a thing of beauty. Seriously, anything else you need from me?" He glanced at his watch. "Varner and I need to head back to Clover Pointe."

Kraft laughed, saying "From your tongue to God's ears." He closed his pad. "Get thee to a computer and write out your statement, then compose your wife's and you might as well type out Leon's while you are at it. I'll hand these into the county prosecutor and he can decide whether you get the Pulitzer prize for fiction or non-fiction. Now, scat." He stood and extended his hand to Varner. "D.I., it has been a pleasure. As soon as I hear from your Jimmy, I'll let you know. Thank you for helping out. Enjoy Cleveland."

"My pleasure, sir. Give him 24 hours and, if you don't hear from him by then, call the gobshite here."

"Gobshite, it is," Kraft said with a chuckle.

As Dash and Varner walked to the car, he stopped and turned to Varner.

"Eileen, me lassie, there is one more thing this gobshite hasn't told you yet. And it could be, as we say here in the good old U.S. of A., a game changer. Keep in mind that I have one brain injury and would like to keep it at that so don't go punching or hitting me."

Varner leaned against a car, crossing her arms. "Well, if yis don't start talking, I may have to stomp on those large feet of yours. Say your piece. How bad can it be? One murderer in the family sets a new record. Speak."

Dash made the sign of the cross and stepped back. "You know I inherited all of Maud's belongings." He held up his hand. "And that jewelry is yours. I will not stop you from taking it. That being said, there is someone who might feel otherwise."

"And who might this person be?"

"Maud's daughter."

"Her what? And yis didn't think this was important enough to tell me when I first arrived. Well, you fooking idjit, where the devil is she?"

"I don't know."

Varner made a slow circle around Dash. "You lost her?"

"Never *had* her; still don't. Listen, I'll tell you the story on the drive home and when we get to my house, I'll let you read her letter." He took a step towards his truck, muttering "Thank God the Garda isn't allowed to carry weapons."

On the ride home, Dash didn't take his eyes off the road as he told Varner the contents of Maud's letter. He could feel the anger heating up in the passenger seat.

"Why didn't she say anything? And you're saying that Declan Rooney, the man buried beside her as Sean Kelly, is the father. Just because he died didn't mean she should abandon her child."

Dash snorted. "That's a ripe sentiment coming from the land of atrocities against unwed mothers whose babes were torn from their hands. Those rules, sentiments were ingrained in her. The shame of being unwed. The struggle to raise the child on her own. I just hope the girl was raised in a warm and loving family."

Varner wiggled around in her seat. "Always ready to hit the nail on the head, ain't yis? And yis not heard from this agency? How long yis going to wait and what are yis going to do?"

Dash finally turned to her and shrugged. "This here gobshite has no answer to any of those questions. I'll be a good guardian of Maud's estate until it becomes obvious that the daughter cannot be found. And then I'll flip a coin. Heads I keep it all and tails I give it all away."

CHAPTER THIRTY

Back at the homestead, Dash took care of the dogs and then pulled out all the whiteboards still covered with Father Tom's notes about the case. "Study this while I get my files for you to read. I can copy anything you want or email it to Dublin. Your wish is my command."

Varner put on her glasses. She studied the boards, making notes as she went along.

"That Finn fella owes me some explanations. Why did he tell this Father Tom things that he didn't tell me?" She yelled to Dash as he routed around in his office.

He walked out, phone to his ear. After nodding several times, he ended the call. "Eileen, me lassie …"

She hung her head. "Now what? I suppose Declan has risen from the dead to say he did the killing to save the reputation of his beloved."

"No, but that would be very cool if he did. No, that was my father on the phone inviting you to dine with him, Ruthie Malloy, and Father Tom. It would be retirement home food as Tom is under the weather and confined to his room, but it is a very nice place and the food is top notch. Then you and Tom can curse Finn's name together since Finn *never told us about you*. I'll pack up all this stuff and Tom can wear your ear out explaining it."

"Sounds good. I'd like to spend time with your father and this good priest. I take it yis da knew Maud better than you?"

"My mother was the supposed cousin Maud sought out when she arrived here. Now that I think of it, Maggie McCafferty would be the one for you to meet. She was my mother's best friend and the one I asked for help in searching for Maud's daughter. Maggie lives in Kentucky with her daughter who is a nun. Would you want to talk to her? I'll arrange a phone call for you unless you want to visit them, in which case you're on your own. I've a babe on the way and preparations to make."

When he saw the look on Varner's face, he explained about the surrogate and the expected baby.

Eileen walked over to the large window facing the front of the house. She studied the stained-glass border. Without turning to face Dash, she said, "Yes, yes. I'd like to dine with Owen and Tom and this Ruthie and also talk to Maggie McCafferty. What time is dinner? I'm getting hungry. Those cookies at that neighbor's house didn't do the trick."

Dash headed toward the kitchen, tossing back to Eileen. "Let me get us some cold chicken and fruit to snack on. I apologize for not thinking of your stomach when I am very aware of my empty one. The rest of the Hammond family is dining at my brother Sam's house. My little one is spending the night there so I'll get a chance to see him."

Dash's phone rang again. This time it was an invitation for Eileen to spend the night at Ruthie's and the next day with Owen as he returned to Cleveland to work on Maud's estate. She accepted. Dash contained his glee at having the house to himself and Mae tonight.

"Back to work then. I do need to get home to my Jimmy sooner rather than later. This is much more complicated than I ever thought." She returned to the whiteboards. "Bring me a bit of fruit and a glass of whisky, okay?"

"I'll see if we have any left. You do remember having more than a bit of a drop last night. Clear head tonight, Eileen, clear head."

CHAPTER THIRTY-ONE

The next morning at JoJo's diner, Dash looked through his emails, jotting down notes for the day. He was scooping a generous forkful of hashbrowns when his brother Sam slid into the booth.

"Morning, Samuel, what brings you to JoJo's at this time? A little late for your breakfast or is this an early lunch?"

Sam signaled the waitress and requested a large black coffee. He was silent until the coffee arrived.

"Just how much do you know about this Eileen Varner? Did you vet her like you do everyone else?" Sam asked.

Dash threw down his napkin. "You're about to spoil my breakfast, aren't you? What gives? And to answer your question, no, I didn't do any research on her. She caught me on a bad day and I was off my game. Tell me, oh learned brother, what do you know that I also should?"

Shrugging, Sam said, "I don't know anything. I am surprised that you, the most paranoid person I know, didn't think to run a background check on her. And I'm saying this cause Dad called me last night. He got bad vibes from her. Said she was asking odd questions."

"And he called you and not me? Know why?"

"Said he figured you and Mae were doing what you two do best and he didn't want to disturb you, having the house all to yourselves. Oh, by the way, that son of yours is quite the entertainer. Had Marie and me laughing all night."

Dash sighed. "Well, last night, having the house all to ourselves as you pointed out, we finished painting the baby's room, arranged all the furniture and supplies. And, then yes, we fell into bed but never got around to doing anything but snoring." He moved his scrambled eggs around on the plate. "Bad vibes? What kind of odd questions?"

Sam shrugged again.

Both men turned as they heard the sound of little feet running towards them.

"Daddy, guess what? Rissa and me are going to live with you today." T.J. announced.

A breathless Mae caught up to them. "Sorry, they are overexcited." She turned to Sam. "Marie is on her way to Toledo. Claire went into the hospital this morning. A complication was all I got before she tore off."

Sam slid out of the booth. "I'd better find out what's going on. Rissa, give Grandpa a kiss and behave yourself or Dasher will swat your butt."

Once that side of the booth was empty, the two children slid in and sat staring at Dash expectantly.

"I'm sorry, honey, but I can't take the kids. I have a full line-up of patients. Will this ruin your day?" Mae asked.

"Never. I don't have anything scheduled that can't be cancelled." He stood up and kissed his wife. "Give me your keys since you have the kiddie seats. Take my truck and try not to scratch it. I'll see you when I see you."

Mae kissed T.J. and blew a kiss at Rissa. "Behave yourselves." She scurried down the aisle waving at various folks.

Dash motioned for Gloria, his favorite waitress. When she arrived, he said, "Gloria, I have two starving children here. How about an order of say, a g-zillion, pancakes, sliced banana on the side and milk with lids on?" He looked at the kids who were bouncing up and down at the prospect of pancakes.

Gloria said, "Might I suggest sugar-free syrup?"

"Oh you wise woman. Good call and when they've finished, how about a damp towel or two?"

While the children ate, Dash texted everyone on his to-do list to reschedule all the meetings.

At home, Dash got the dogs out and told the kids to chase them around. His hope was that both the dogs and the kids would wear each other out and he might have some quiet time. After a half hour of frenzied running, he brought everyone inside. The kids were given a fairly sophisticated puzzle to work on in T.J.'s room while Dash sat at the kitchen table ready to make the important phone call to Ireland.

He scrolled through his call history and found the number Varner had dialed when at the police station. He hesitated a moment and then punched it in.

After three rings, a woman answered.

"May I please speak with Jimmy Varner?" Dash asked.

"Who? Oh, himself's not here. Can I ask who's calling?"

"Only if you tell me who you are, ma'am."

"Fionnuala Rooney, and you sir."

"The dumbest man on earth. Thank you." Dash rang off.

He leaned back in his chair. *Rooney! Bound to be a relation to Declan. But does that mean Eileen Varner isn't Maud's niece? And why wouldn't she just say she was in touch with the Rooneys?*

He pulled out an old address book from his Army days. Turning the pages, he found the name of an Irish soldier who had worked with Dash on several intelligence operations. Hoping the number still worked, he punched it in.

When Captain Sullivan answered, Dash settled in for a nice long conversation with an old comrade only to be interrupted.

"Daddy, Daddy," T.J. shouted.

Dash moved to the bottom of the staircase. "Daddy, Pansy Pup's eating the puzzle pieces."

"Sully, have to go. Domestic crisis here. I look forward to hearing from you. As I said sooner rather than later. Thanks."

CHAPTER THIRTY-TWO

Dash paced the hallway outside of the interview room wondering where his cousin Billy was. McCafferty had two days to prepare for this visit so where the hell was he. Dash glanced at Detective Kraft who smirked and pointed to his watch. The assistant county prosecutor, Michelle Radcliffe, stood silently, studying Lorna Lemmich who sat in the overheated interview room waiting to hear what troubles would be placed on her plate.

A hallway door slammed open and William 'Billy the Kid' McCafferty strolled in like it was a Sunday afternoon in the park.

"Where have you been? You asked me to be here and then you're not," Dash said as his cousin approached. He was about to make introductions but Billy stopped to check out the occupants of the interview room.

"Hell, is that her?" Billy squinted. "I do believe there's shaving cream behind the public defender's ear. It'll be like taking candy from a baby." He winked at Radcliffe and pulled open the door.

Dash could only mutter, "Sorry, sorry."

Kraft sidled next to him, saying "This better be good, Hammond, or your head is on a platter."

They both watched Billy hurry into the room, tossing his briefcase onto the table. After taking a deep breath, Billy held out his hand to the young defense counselor. "William McCafferty, here on behalf of Doctor Maevis Summers who is being accused by Lorna Lemmich of assaulting her." He turned to Lorna and asked, "Is that true? You, in the orange jumpsuit, are suing my client?"

Dash slowly banged his forehead on the window. "Don't make me come in there, Billy. Act like a professional, you twit."

Billy addressed the young public defender. "I'm here to interview your client and hopefully convince her that she should just forget about filing the assault charge or suing my client for damages. I'm not acting for the prosecutor's office, though I could since I have a lot of experience on that side of the table. Had a helluva conviction rate by the time I left. But I digress." Billy gave them his best Steve McQueen smile.

Dash folded his arms, turned, and leaned against the window. "No shit, William. Digress my ass."

Billy turned to the window and winked as if he heard his cousin's words. He opened the briefcase and pulled out a file. He shuffled through the papers and then tossed the file onto to table. "Wrong one. This one lists the robbery/burglary charges against you. Looks like you carried quite a bit out of Grealis' house." He nodded toward Lorna, then pulled out another file, again skimming the papers. He sighed. "Sorry, this one is about you assaulting Dash Hammond, you know, the tall, some say good-looking, guy whose wife defended his honor by kicking your jaw. Man, that musta hurt, but you need to be grateful Hammond has this gentlemanly code. Never hit a woman. He definitely shouldn't even hit a man; he's former military, deadly, no sorry, special forces, assassin squad." He returned to rummage through the briefcase.

The public defender leaned forward to see how many more folders McCafferty had in there.

"Ah, here's another one. Nope, this is the charges against you for beating up your stepson, Zeke Lemmich." He shook his head at Lorna, "Not a good move, I mean, really not a good move. And this was before you got hit in the jaw so no claiming diminished responsibility."

One more dive into the briefcase, he pulled out a bright blue file. "This is it. Forgot I put the papers in the blue folder. Busy, busy." He spread several papers around the table. "I made copies for you, Lorna, and you, I'm sorry, what did you say your name is?"

"Sidney Shiprek, I'm new with the Public Defender's office, sir."

"Well, then, Mr. Shiprek, or may I call you Sidney, these are copies of the statements by Detective Kraft and Officer Rainbeaux. They witnessed this whole sorry affair. If you haven't already read them closely, please take a minute now. You will see that they do not support Lorna's version of the story. In fact they downright contradict your client. You did get copies of these, didn't you? I would hate to think the county prosecutor's office was negligent."

Dash looked sideways to see Ms. Radcliffe's reaction. She turned to him, daggers shooting from her eyes. She asked, "Does he know what he's doing?"

Shrugging, Dash answered, "I'm told he does. A little unorthodox, a little theatrical since he wanted to go on the stage before he decided to be a lawyer." *Please Billy get to the point and get out of there.*

Billy folded his hands. "Mrs. Lemmich, Lorna, if I may, well, when I got the call from Dr. Summers, I sent a team of my investigators up to Cleveland to find out just who is this lady who thinks she can accuse a very reputable doctor of harming another human being."

He sighed. "Well, in just twelve hours we learned that you, Lorna Lemmich, are *not* a reputable person."

Lorna pulled herself up, grabbed the tablet and pen from her counselor's hand. She wrote: What???

"Oh, reputable vs. disreputable. You, Lorna, are not what can be termed a reputable person. As far as we can determine, you have no visible means of support unless you count whatever funds the five to ten men who visit you daily leave on your table." He tilted his head and leaned forward. "This is just me, but it looks like you are either dealing drugs or sex. I have statements from your neighbors who all tell of the various men at various hours. All circumstantial but I wouldn't count on them for character references. Again, that will only become relevant if we go to trial.

"Why don't you take a second and review the statements, Lorna? If I were sitting in the chair next to you, I would suggest you forget about this nonsense with Doctor Summers and concentrate on all the other charges heading your way. I know right now you're being held on burglary/robbery charges, and, I must say, stealing from a little old lady is just not done by good people. You stole her black purse that contained all the important papers in her life. No way would she give these to you so I wouldn't even try to convince anyone of that. But you see the other folders before you. Charges after charges that the county attorney is considering." Again he leaned in. "Now I can't speak for her, but if I could, I'd throw the book at you. Maybe try to include manslaughter since Maud was found dead. Might be circumstantial but every little crumb adds to the building of the loaf."

Billy glanced back and forth from Lorna to Sidney. "Shall I give you a few minutes to contemplate all this? Seriously, drop all this nonsense against Dr. Summers. You have bigger fish to fry." He pushed back his chair, asking "Coffee, anyone?" And then he left the room.

Dash moved to meet him. "What are you playing at?"

Billy pushed past him to stand next to Michelle Radcliffe. "Counselor, how did I do? Hopefully, I got them where you wanted them."

Radcliffe moved her head side to side. "Unorthodox for sure but we'll see if it's effective. I'm tempted to send you back in to impress upon her the untenable position she is in. Got her cold on the burglary/robbery. It's the assault on her stepson; I'm pushing this up the ladder into felonious assault. That will send her away for a decent stretch."

The door opened. Shiprek motioned McCafferty to his side. "Mrs. Lemmich has decided to drop all efforts regarding Doctor Summers. You convinced her she should concentrate on the other charges leveled against her."

"Let me hear it from her lips or in her case, I'll need a written note from her for my files," Radcliffe said.

Dash trailed after the two lawyers but they closed the door before he could enter. He resumed his place at the two-way window.

Billy set a legal pad down in front of Lorna. "Shall I dictate what you need to say or should Shiprek, or you could use your own words? I'll just make sure they're the right words. Then we'll have this typed up. You can sign with your attorney as a witness. Then, it's you and Prosecutor Radcliffe." He leaned over the table. "Between you and me, she looks a bit mean and mighty competent. Seriously consider any deal she offers. You get to court with her and mincemeat comes to mind, as well as a very long prison sentence."

Dash and Kraft watched as all color drained from Lorna's face and they thought Shiprek might faint.

It was going to take a bit for the statement to be typed so Radcliffe decided to get her ball rolling.

Dash, Kraft, and Billy stood watching. Lorna looked worse for the wear. Her armpits were almost dripping with sweat and her breathing became measured as the prosecutor sat down.

Lorna grabbed her attorney's pad and pen again. She scribbled furiously then shoved the pad toward Radcliffe who read it.

"Are you sure? You haven't even heard if I have a deal and what it is," Radcliffe said as Shiprek pulled the pad toward him so he could see what Lorna had written.

Dash asked Billy, "What do you think she's written?"

Billy shrugged. "Damned if I know but both the attorneys looked a bit shocked. I bet Lorna just wants to get the hell out of that room so she can breathe again." He turned to Kraft and asked, "Do you guys turn up the heat to literally sweat the 'guest of the city'?"

Kraft shook his head. "No. We do play fair. Most of the time the guilty sweat because they're guilty unless they are a sociopath or psychopath. Lorna's neither; just lazy, greedy, and stupid."

Dash smiled. "Really Detective? So she's not on your Christmas card list?"

They turned back to the window when Radcliffe asked Lorna if she even wanted to know what was being considered. Shiprek nodded. "She may not, but I do. Only seems right for me to advise her about whatever you're offering. I mean that is my job."

Lorna grabbed the legal pad and the pen. She scribbled furiously then slid it over to Radcliffe who let out a howl. The county attorney stood, walked to the window, and plastered the pad on the two-way window.

Dash, Billy, and Kraft leaned forward to read the message:

"Mr. McCafferty, would you be my attorney?"

CHAPTER THIRTY-THREE

Dash sat on the back porch staring at the starry night. He breathed in the cool air and reminded himself that he was safe, he was home, and his beautiful family was asleep in their beds. Soon he would be holding a beautiful baby girl. A lucky man, indeed.

He turned his head when he heard the back door open, wondering who was bold enough to disturb his peace. Owen, of course.

"Well, son," Owen emphasized. "Do you believe her?" He took a chair and sighed.

"There's a movie quote floating through my brain right now. Something along the lines of 'who would say that if it wasn't so?' Maud sure brought a lot of strange baggage with her." Dash stood and turned to face his father. "And, Dad, what is there to gain? I mean Maud was fairly well off, but not rich, rich. The necklace, even with the new appraisal, has more sentimental value than dollar."

He stood up to lean against a post. "What I don't understand, even now, is why she thought posing as the niece was better than the truth? I do feel sorry for her, Jimmy. Not only does he have to deal with cancer, but his wife is a few ideas short of a good one."

Owen patted the chair next to him and changed the subject. "Thanks for letting me put the little ones to bed. A real treat for me and hopefully for them."

"And a bigger treat for me. I'm hoping tomorrow is a better day for Mae. I don't mind having the kids another day, but

I do have some things that need doing. Two little ones poking their fingers into everything isn't going to help." Dash peered around the end of the porch, looking at the lit window of his workshop in the garage. "I guess they're still at it. Told Varner there wasn't anything new in all those shoeboxes. Mae and I combed through them when we first brought them home. It's my bedtime and theirs. Owen, go over there and drag Ruthie out. Maybe Varner will follow."

Owen got up to do as his son asked. "About Varner, what's next on your agenda? Should I tell Ruthie she has a new roommate for life?"

Dash shuddered. "God, no. Like I told Eileen, nothing is going to be settled, final, until we find Maud's daughter or Maud's grandchildren. As far as I'm concerned, I'm just the caretaker until then. And I'm adamant about this, I'm willing to wait, search for a year. After that, I might just put it all into a trust fund for twenty years. I'll compile a list of all who might get a share, Rooneys included."

He moved away from the railing and looked longingly at the door. "Tomorrow I will talk to the Robbery detective to see if I can get the jewelry and stuff released. Then I will buy a ticket for Eileen on the first plane back to Ireland. She can take the necklace and I'll face the daughter if she ever turns up. And as for Callahan's bones, I'm ready to give them a decent burial near his murderer Maud and nemesis Rooney." He brushed his hands together. "Enough is enough. The daughter, who will learn of a whole set of relatives in Ireland ..."

"Relatives, what relatives?" Owen asked.

"The Rooneys, that's who. This Finnoula is Declan's granddaughter and Jimmy Varner is a nephew of Declan. Hell, if mom was a distant cousin of Maud's, Finnoula and Jimmy are a damned site closer on the Rooney side." He stood up. "I'm going to bed. You and those crazy women have five minutes to clear the area or I'll sic Charlie Dog on you."

Owen stood. "Let's go in. I'm getting chilly and I'm tired. Don't know what Ruthie has in mind. She has boundless energy, that woman. Glad she's taken over Varner."

"Tomorrow is another day, that's for sure." Chuckling, Dash said, "And to think Varner thought up the whole niece thing while on the plane. Talk about rushing in with no plan."

This time Owen laughed. "It's a good thing she caught you on an off day, isn't it? One little black eye, and you stop thinking."

CHAPTER THIRTY-FOUR

The next morning Dash dragged the old suitcase into the front room where Owen, Ruthie, and Eileen sat. The sun poured through the window, sending rays of color from the stained-glass border.

"Ladies and gentlemen of the jury, you have before you exhibit A, a suitcase belonging to the late Moira McCreevy a.k.a. Declan Rooney." He lifted the case onto the card table in the center of the room. "Gather round and I'll tell you a fairytale of Declan fleeing Ireland, oh so many years ago."

Owen raised his hand. "I remember you saying, when we found what is now exhibit A, that you suspected Declan of disguising himself as a woman when he left but what has changed?"

Dash nodded. "Nothing. I've been giving this whole 'let's do a Bonnie and Clyde and run from the scene of the crime' scenario a lot of thought. Eileen tells us that, although both Maud and Declan were interested parties in the death of Callahan, both were dismissed when the wife fessed up to the crime. So, my friends, why did they run? Did they have to run? If I understand the situation correctly—and that is a big if because of the limited information at hand—why run? Why leave their families, their lives, and head across the ocean, knowing full well that they would never return?"

Ruthie stood up. "I'm pretty sure we're going to need some libation to figure all this out or listen to this. No offense intended, Dash my dear, you're a lovely speaker."

Owen and Eileen followed Ruthie into the kitchen, rooting around for snacks to go with the drinks, grabbing the bottle of bourbon from the night before.

Dash stood patiently, wondering why he did this to himself. There were more pressing chores waiting than walking through Declan's run for the border.

When his audience returned and settled into their chairs, Dash resumed his Q & A. "First question that springs to my mind, is why leave? My conclusion, and you can come to your own, is that Declan was a villain at heart."

Owen interrupted. "How did you arrive at that?"

"Look at this suitcase and its contents. Was this thrown together in a flurry of activity heading for the coast? And why the disguise? Why not leave as Declan Rooney?"

Ruthie reached for a handful of pretzels and answered, "You think this was planned? Declan was going to flee Ireland and didn't want anyone to know that he had left or where he was heading. Where's his passport? Did you find that?"

"No, but to your point, where did *he* find someone to make him a false passport? Could it have been done so quickly when he determined it was time to get out of Dodge, or in this case, Duleek, County Meath. But let's start with the basics. I stand before you, a man, what would you do to disguise me as a woman?"

A voice from the edge of the room, Mae said, "I'd chop you off at the knees. A six-four woman would attract attention for sure, especially back in the fifties." Mae stood at the base of the stairs looking better than she had even earlier in the day, a few spots of color in her cheeks.

"Ah, my lovely, how are you feeling? I must say you look fetching all wrapped up in that fuzzy robe. Come join us." Dash said as he led Mae to the recliner. He took an ever-present blanket and covered his wife, gently kissing her cheek.

Owen chimed in. "I can think of a few more parts that should be chopped off if we're turning you into a woman." He laughed out loud at his own joke.

"Dad, Declan didn't intend to run naked through the airport so his private parts can remain intact *and* private. But there are other signs of gender." He tilted his head, much like a professor standing in front of his class.

Eileen raised her hand, solidifying the classroom atmosphere. "A beard, an Adam's apple, lots of hair where women don't usually have hair."

"Gloves, he'd have to wear gloves in case he had hairy hands. Do you think he waxed them? Was waxing a thing back then?" Ruthie asked, looking at her fellow jurors.

"Makeup in the fifties was heavier than the current stuff we use. So if Declan got a close shave, or he wasn't so hairy, or his beard so dark, he could slather on a good bit of pancake. Earrings, clip-ons, to cover his large ear lobes. We assume he wore a wig, right?" Mae got into the spirit of the game, motioning for pretzels to nosh on.

Not to be outdone, Owen said, "His Adam's apple. Wear a scarf around his neck. Shoes would be a problem. Doubt he wore heels."

Dash pulled out a pair of shoes from the suitcase. "You're right. Since these are several sizes larger than everything else in Maud's closet, and being in the suitcase a big hint, I'd say Declan wore these. Low heels, so much more comfortable for walking." He then held up a dress in front of him. "What do you think? The getaway outfit?"

Mae said, "The colors aren't right for you. Needs to be bluer to match your eyes."

Dash scowled at her. "We're not dressing me, Mae. Keep up."

"Whoa, whoa. We've got him dressed for success but why the disguise? You said he didn't want anyone to know he's left the country but everyone knew Maud had gone to America. Her trip could have been planned for some time," Ruthie added to the discussion and added pretzels to her mouth. She chewed contemplatively.

T.J. came into the room to sit on his mother's lap. "Why are you holding a dress Daddy? Is it Halloween? Cause I think you would make a better monster than a lady?'

Dash rolled up the dress and tossed it onto the floor. He up-ended the suitcase dropping its contents next to the dress. He turned the suitcase so his audience could see the silky fabric that lined it. "Look closely." And he walked around the room holding Exhibit A so each member of the jury could examine it closely.

T.J., with his very young eyes, raised his hand. "Daddy, there are rips in the fabric. Did you do that on purpose?"

Owen jumped up. "To hide his passport, the one identifying him as Rooney."

Mae almost stood up but stopped short so T.J. didn't slide off her lap. "He hid money in the suitcase. His getaway money. The money ..." And she clamped her mouth shut before she inadvertently told Eileen about the money in the floor.

T.J. yelled, "Mommy, don't tell."

Ruthie and Eileen looked at each other. It was Ruthie who asked sweetly, "Dash, my dear wonderful friend, what is it that Mae isn't supposed to tell? What, darling, are you, and Owen, hiding from us?"

Dash put the suitcase back on the table, gathering the clothes to stuff back in it. He moved his mouth around, stared at the ceiling, glared at his wife and child, and looked at his father hoping for a rescue. He finally decided he'd have to use his quick wit to answer. He shrugged a bit and said, "Nothing, my sweet Ruthie, longtime friend and confidant. T.J. found some Irish notes while playing in one of the bedrooms. Irish notes, probably worth nothing in today's world, but most likely part of the getaway money, either Maud's or Declan's. I promised T.J. he could have the money to use as a down-payment on a pony. And, yes Eileen, I didn't declare that currency. So sue me!" He kept his crossed fingers out of sight.

Eileen took a swig from the bottle of bourbon she had commandeered. "Unless you tell me he found a fortune, I say let the wee bairn have the money. Every child should have a pony." She hiccupped.

There was a palpable sigh of relief from the Hammond family. T.J. snuggled back into his mommy's arms, figuring he shouldn't say anything about the other dollars he found. He had inherited a good bit of his father's cunning. So he just sat there smiling at the thought of a new pony.

Eileen said, "You began by calling Declan a villain. I would hate to tell my Jimmy that his uncle, so revered by him, was truly a villain. Do you have any proof? And I remind you that my Jimmy would suffer terribly if you do have."

Dash looked around for a free chair, and finding none, walked to the kitchen and dragged one back. He sat down, nodded slowly. "All I have is speculation and mirky conclusions drawn from a life-time of watching people, tracking people, and studying people. This is what I have: Declan Rooney didn't run impulsively. He had this all planned. What exactly was he running from? I'd say his wife, his children, his life in Ireland. It is a known fact he was in love (and this again is speculation through distanced observation) with Maud. We know from family gossip that she planned to leave, well, if I'm honest, she was encouraged to leave for any number of reasons. The main one I'm willing to say is that she was causing all kinds of trouble with the male population immediately surrounding her. The Callahan killed by his wife and Declan, who should have remained by his family's side, not getting involved with Maud."

"Why a villain? That sounds so much more ominous than just a runaway husband," Ruthie added.

Turning to Eileen, Dash asked, "How much do you or your Jimmy really know about Declan's life before he headed for America? Have you investigated his past? I call him a villain because he prepared to leave, not just scarper on a moment's notice. And he disguised himself so he wouldn't be easily tracked. Again, more speculation, is that dear old Declan should have used that Irish money, if it was his, to pay off the shylock who held his betting slips. Then maybe he wouldn't have had to run."

Owen spoke up. "So you're thinking this Declan was, what do they call them over there, a chancer? And he ran because of a debt. Wouldn't those holding his slips go after his family? I'm pretty sure that's how they do it over here."

Eileen downed the rest of the bourbon and stood. "I'd swear up a storm if the little one would cover his ears. Here I am, Garda fraud division. When I get back, I'm going to drag out all the old files and see exactly what Declan up was up to." She wagged a finger. "Mind you, I won't be telling my Jimmy if I find out his idol is a true villain, but I will let Finnoula know. Family records should be truthful, don't yis think?" She swayed a bit and collapsed in her chair, closing her eyes.

Dash let out a howl. He pointed at the recumbent figure slowly sliding off the chair. "And we have now come full circle, Detective Inspector Eileen Varner of the Dublin Gardai."

Ruthie said, "Should we do something? I mean her plane is leaving at six tonight. Should she travel while intoxicated?"

The answer was a resounding 'yes.'

CHAPTER THIRTY-FIVE

Six o'clock couldn't come soon enough for Dash. He decided to let Eileen sleep for a bit, so he stole the blanket from Mae and tucked it around his guest. T.J. brought a pillow to slide under her head. Then everyone tiptoed out of the room.

When it was time to leave for the airport, Dash handed over the waking of Eileen to Ruthie. Eileen was given a packet of pills put together by Mae to make the Atlantic crossing easier for both this passenger and all the others on the flight.

Dash, Owen, and Ruthie accompanied Eileen to the airport. Dash because he wanted to make sure she got on the plane. Owen and Ruthie because they were fond of this little Irishwoman.

Before she went through security, there was the round of hugs and promises to stay connected. As soon as the new babe arrived, Dash would send photos to her.

"I have to tell yis that this has been grand. You are such sweet folks to treat this old hag like she's a queen. If you ever get to Ireland, you'll have a home away from home. And please say yis will visit. Not sure if my Jimmy will recover enough to travel and I would love for him to meet you. But you'll have to promise not to tell him how much I enjoyed your whiskey," Eileen said as she gathered her satchel which now contained the so-called family heirloom jewels.

Dash said, "D.I. Eileen Varner of the Dublin Garda, it has been an experience I won't soon forget. I'll let you know about my babe Delia's arrival. If Maud and Declan's daughter ever turns up, I'm sure she will want to meet the Rooney clan."

"Ah, and I'll want to meet her. I'm working on my own family history which is how I found Finn Flaherty. Wouldn't it be sumthing if you turn up on the tree!"

Dash bent down a bit, afraid to ask the question. "What family tree would that be?"

"Why, the Flynn family. I'm a Flynn just like your mam. I'm from the Dublin Flynns and your mam, the Galway Flynns. As yis knows, you could spit in Dublin and hit Galway." She kissed Dash's cheek one more time and headed for the security check. She waved, shouting "Goodbye, cousin."

A very pale Dash gestured weakly while his father and Ruthie stood with their mouths open.

"Tell me she just said that to mess with me, right, Owen?" Dash looked around. "Where's the bar? Ruthie, you're driving." He tossed her the keys.

After one drink, Dash decided they should head home. He wasn't being very responsible to his wife and child, and to all the myriad pies he had his fingers in. There was a lot of preparations yet to finish for the Memorial Day picnic and formal remembrance program. And he was sure his bookstore partner, Annie, was ready to have his head if he didn't review all the papers she handed him yesterday. He could almost hear her tearing him a new one about his lack of involvement in the store.

The trio traversed the parking lot, weaving in and out of the rows, since no one thought to record the exact spot they parked. Dash stopped short causing Owen to crash into him. "Dad, watch where you're going."

"Me, you're the one who stopped short. It's your phone, isn't it? You're just like all the kids nowadays. Can't take your eyes off it."

Dash stood still, reading the text he just opened. "Find Me, Inc., did what they were supposed to do. They found Maud's daughter. Confirmation via DNA match. This woman wants to meet us as soon as possible." He turned to look toward the skies watching the planes take off. "Should I see if Eileen has left yet or just wait?"

Owen and Ruthie gathered around Dash, reading his phone for themselves. Ruthie spoke first. "No, let her go. If this daughter wants to meet any more of her relatives, she'll have the money to do so. I'm thinking you're going to give her all the money, right?"

Scowling, Dash asked, "Why would you think that?"

His father answered for Ruthie. "Because that's what Maud would want and I thought you said you would do."

"Options open," Dash said as he punched his key fob and looked to see if any vehicle near him flashed its lights. "Over there." And he strode off with a new purpose.

CHAPTER THIRTY-SIX

Dash paced nervously around the conference room of Find Me, Inc. He tugged at his tie while facing the windows and turned to his father, "If this daughter is anything like her mother, I might just jump."

"Don't be stupid. Push *her* out instead," Owen said and then added, "I'm not sure why we're so nervous. She's just a woman after all."

"That's what they said about Lucretia Borgia." Dash straightened his tie for the umpteenth time.

They both jumped as the door opened and watched a smallish woman enter. She had a very fair complexion made paler since her hair was a rich deep auburn. The red highlights were streaked with strands of silver. She was slender, with very straight posture. She moved gracefully to the opposite side of the table and stood.

Dash's first thought was *prim and proper, a far cry from Maud, but she has the look of Declan about her.*

Following her were two men. They were tallish, not Dash's six-four but close to Owen's six feet. It was obvious they were brothers. Same square face, dark brown eyes and black hair with gray highlights. They moved in step, stopped to flank the woman.

Miss Elrod motioned for them to sit, and she began the introductions. "Obviously, since there is only one other woman at the table, she is Maud Grealis' daughter, Mary Isabella Carducci. To her left is her brother, Carl Carducci, and to her right is her brother, Sal Carducci."

The gentlemen nodded across the table at the Hammonds.

"Now," Miss Elrod proceeded, gesturing to the opposite side of the table. "This is Sheriff Owen Hammond. He is the executor of Miss Grealis' will. Seated next to him is his son, Dash Hammond." She smiled at everyone. "Sheriff, would you like to begin?"

Before Owen could speak, Mary Isabella raised her hand. "If I may, please?" Everyone nodded so she began. "First, thank you for meeting with me today, but as I told Miss Elrod on the phone, I'm *not* Maud's daughter, DNA test results aside. So if you have something else to do or somewhere else to be, you can leave." She stood to indicate that she did have something else to do and somewhere else to be.

Dash rose immediately. "Ma'am, please take your seat for just a few minutes. I have some questions. The first being, why are you so sure you're *not* Maud's daughter? Why throw out scientific evidence to the contrary?"

Mary Isabella sat down, folding her hands on the table. She smiled broadly and kindly at Dash as if he were a recalcitrant student.

Dash turned to Miss Elrod and said, "I don't suppose you have a ruler in your desk. You might want to get it, for I'm thinking Ms. Mary Isabella Carducci is about to smack my hands. She has the look of a schoolteacher about her. I'd even hazard a guess that she is a nun or was a nun."

The Carducci brothers started laughing, nodding in agreement. "Spot on, Hammond, spot on."

Mary Isabella turned to scowl at her brothers, then straightened herself up as much as she could. She glared at Dash. "Good guess, Mr. Hammond. I take it you have, shall we say, first-hand experience at getting your hands slapped by your teachers."

"Yes, ma'am." He laid his hands out on the table. "I have the scars to prove it."

Owen sighed, muttering, "He was a trial as a child and continues to be one today."

Mary Isabella leaned across the table to stare intently at Dash.

He ran his lips over his teeth, sure he had a piece of his breakfast stuck there. He sat back in his chair.

Chuckling, Mary Isabella said, "My turn. You were in the Army, weren't you? Served in Iraq and I'll hazard a guess Afghanistan as well?"

Dash nodded.

"You take a nice picture, sir. And Maud was mighty proud of you." She leaned back in her chair and laughed loudly. Then she walked around the table to Dash. She pulled him up and gave him a big hug, murmuring, "Thank God, you made it home in one piece."

Dash towered over her and drew in a deep breath when she grabbed him. Suddenly he felt lost, awash in the sweet perfume she was wearing. He took another deep breath, wanting to hug her back but his good sense prevailed. When she released him, he stumbled back into his chair.

"Bravo, Miss Carducci. I don't believe I've ever seen anyone leave my son speechless." Owen began clapping. Then he said, "The picture in Maud's house. You *knew* Maud?"

"And that's why I know she's not my mother. She would have told me." She walked nonchalantly back to her seat and sat down, grinning from ear to ear. She looked across at Dash who sat with his mouth open, staring at this little lady. "I prayed and prayed for your safe return. That's how I met Ms. Grealis. In church, lighting candles. We started talking and she told me all about you, her favorite relative. I was half in love with you. Tales of heroism and adventure. You had quite the career."

Dumbfounded, Dash slumped in his chair. "Son of a bitch! Oops, sorry ma'am. I did not see that coming." He shook his head, "Nun? Correct?"

She smiled, "Nailed it, soldier. Actually, a former nun and teacher. I left all that to take care of my parents when they got sick. My brothers and sisters-in-law have growing families that need them. It was the least I could do. My parents were very good to me, very loving."

Miss Elrod sat with her mouth open. She got up and walked over to the side table and brought back a pitcher of water and glasses.

Owen poured himself a glass, then passed the glasses and pitcher around. He stood, inviting the others to join him. "A toast to Miss Mary Isabella Carducci. It is not often that someone gets the best of my son. I only wish his mother and his wife were here to see this." He raised his glass. "To Miss Mary Isabella, one of a kind."

Dash frowned and mumbled, "I really think this calls for some good Irish whisky, not water."

"Sit down, son. Our business isn't finished."

Everyone sat down and released a collective sigh.

Dash said, "Shall we begin again, Miss Carducci? You've met Maud, or Miss Grealis as you call her, but since she didn't tell you who she was, you're convinced she isn't your mother. All scientific evidence aside. Correct?"

"I know it sounds dumb, but if I had given up my daughter and then encountered her, I certainly would tell her who I was."

Her brother Sal put his hand on hers. "Listen, Izzy, we've been over this. She would have no idea who you were. The last time she saw you, you were a newborn. You've changed more than a bit since then." He turned to the Hammonds. "Sorry, but we've been arguing about this since Miss Elrod called and announced that Maud Grealis is Izzy's mom." He nodded toward his sister. "Stubborn as the day is long."

Dash raised his hand. "Sorry, but as for Maud not recognizing Izzy, if I may call you that ..." He tapped the binder sitting on the table. "In here is a photo of your father, Declan Rooney. I spotted the resemblance the minute you walked in. I'm surprised Maud didn't *faint* when she saw you. Declan's face, back from the dead."

He slid the green binder across the table. "This is the research we did on Maud and Declan Rooney while searching for you. My retired uncle is hot and heavy into all the genealogy websites. He has a friend in Ireland who provided him with most of this information."

Izzy opened the binder to see the newspaper photo of Declan staring at her. Sal leaned over one side while Cal leaned on the other. Both brothers looked at the photo and then at their sister.

"Good God, he's right." Cal said. "Izzy, you're the spitting image of your father." He looked at Dash. "I take it this Grealis woman and Rooney here were involved, but not married."

"Simply put, yes. But read the binder to get a full picture. When we found Maud dead …"

Izzy looked up. "How did she die? When? Where?"

Owen rubbed the side of his face. He murmured to Dash, "Nice going, son." He then turned to Izzy. "Maud died at home of a heart attack and/or old age this past March. At that time we didn't know she had a daughter or we would have notified you. Long story short, we discovered she had a daughter. We searched, or more accurately, Find Me, Inc., searched and here we are."

Sal asked, "If I may be so crass, but since you're the executor, I can assume there is an estate. Of any value? Is this why you searched for Izzy?"

Owen nodded. "The estate is being readied for probate by Maud's attorneys. Unfortunately, there is no mention of a daughter in Maud's will. Right now, the bulk goes to Dash. Now that we've found the daughter, I've asked them to see what Miss Carducci's inheritance rights are." He held up his hand to stop the inevitable question. "Right now, the estate is heading toward a quarter of a mil. There are taxes and fees that will be deducted but a nice sum by anyone's standard." He took a card from his wallet and slid it across the table to Sal. "These are Maud's attorneys. I suggest you meet with them asap."

Dash sat quietly waiting for the inevitable question.

Cal looked across the table at Dash. "Were you and Maud close?"

"Frankly, no. Other than a few times when I was a child and she pinched my cheeks, I only saw her once as an adult when I was on leave. It was at a St. Patrick's Day party at her church. There was quite a bit of Irish whisky involved. We sang a few songs, and 'poof' I was gone as fast as I appeared." He looked to the ceiling to gather his thoughts. "When we opened her lock box at the bank, we discovered that Maud had written a letter to me in which, among other things, she revealed she had a daughter. She tasked me with finding her." He looked across the table at Izzy. "There is a message I'm to give you, but not now, in private."

He glanced around the table. Curiosity about this new puzzle piece replacing the interest in the estate.

"Why did you have to search for Izzy? Didn't this Maud just tell you who she was?" Sal asked, wrinkling his brow. "Seems a bit fishy to me. A lot of unanswered questions here. As a deputy sheriff, I'm all atwitter to find the answers."

Dash shrugged, finding it interesting that the brothers were concerned but Izzy just sat paging through the binder. "I'll just say this: Maud gave no hint she knew where her daughter was, who she had become. Didn't even give me a birthdate. Nothing, nada." He threw his hands up, "Maud was a complicated woman. A woman of her times and she should be viewed through that lens. A Catholic Irish woman, alone, pregnant. If you don't know what that meant in the 1950's and 60's, I suggest you read some Irish history. I can recommend a few books that will shed considerable light on the subject."

Silence descended on the room.

Dash glanced around to study each of the Carduccis. He let out the interior breath he had been holding since learning of the daughter. It looks like Izzy had a good childhood with loving parents and very protective brothers. Maud was right in giving her up for adoption. The Carduccis provided much of what she could not.

He stood. "I don't know about the rest of you but I'm thirsty and not for water. And a good burger wouldn't go amiss. There's a very good burger and brewski joint two blocks from here. I suggest we adjourn there to continue this conversation, which is just the first of many, I'm sure."

He turned to Miss Elrod. "Thank you for all this. I'll be in touch." He gestured toward the door. Everyone filed out following Dash's lead.

When they arrived at Johnnie's Burgers and Brews, Dash settled his father and the brothers in one booth. His announcement that this was on him brought the comment from Carl, "And so it should be. You and all your shekels from Maud."

Izzy put out her hand. "Sal, the car keys please, and then you guys can drink all you want. I'll be the designated driver."

Dash guided Izzy to another booth. "Alone at last. Order whatever you like. As your brother pointed out, I got all the dosh and you got nottin', sister."

Izzy laughed. "I honestly don't know what to say. If only … If only I had known that Maud was my mother, how different those years would have been. Any speculation as to why she, if she recognized me like you think she did, she didn't come forward."

"Ma'am, the feminine mind is the biggest mystery to me. I've known my wife since we were in diapers. She's the girl next door. And 99% of the time I get it wrong. Sometimes I think she changes her mind just to confuse me. My Maevis is one helluva woman."

The waiter brought their drinks, beer for Dash and coke for Izzy.

After taking a sip, Dash said, "Only a guess, but she might have been embarrassed by giving you up, though I'm sure it was the right decision. She was fairly new to the U.S. and wouldn't have known much about how to navigate whatever resources there were for a single mom."

Izzy pulled the binder over. "I skimmed this and saw the date my father died. He passed before I was born. Did he know about me? What do you think?"

"It's possible. From the letter Maud wrote, she indicated that she had several miscarriages before carrying you to full term. She thought it ironic."

"Can I see the letter? Or, if not, would you please tell me what's in it? And why can't I see it?"

Dash looked to the ceiling and then at Izzy. "Maud revealed several things in the letter that … and I'm not sure how to say this, but you might wait until you've reconciled the whole Maud as your mother thing."

The waiter brought their burgers. He set the veggie burger in front of Izzy, and the burger with extra onions in front of Dash. Before he could ask if they needed anything, Izzy blurted out. "She killed someone, didn't she? Or did she run a brothel? You can tell me. She was *my* mother after all."

Dash glanced at the waiter whose mouth dropped open. "Don't mind her. The asylum granted her an afternoon off. I'll be taking her back right after we eat." He turned to Izzy, saying in a sugary sweet tone, "Come now, darling, eat up. You know this is the best meal you'll have all week."

She smiled. "You're just lucky I don't take after my mother. I could kill you with that knife before you swallowed a bite."

The waiter reached for the knives and backed away, nodding at Dash.

"Back to the letter, Mr. Hammond. What's in it? Do I look so fragile?"

Dash laughed. "Hell no. But I didn't know that before today. Well, actually before two minutes ago." He wiped his hands on the napkin and reached inside his suit coat pocket. He pulled out a copy of the letter and handed it to her. He then proceeded to chomp down on the burger while watching Izzy read the letter.

He waited for the reaction to her learning of the murder of Callahan. Izzy read through the letter twice and then tossed it aside.

"Finder of lost things … that's you. And I guess that makes me a lost 'thing.'" Tears began to well up in her eyes. "Yes, it's a good thing she gave me up. Sounds like my father was the most important person in her life. If he had lived, she might not have even paid any attention to me."

She signaled for the waiter. "Bring me a large whisky."

Dash shook his head. "No, don't. Thank you." The waiter backed away again with a confused look on his face.

They finished their burgers in silence. Dash watched Izzy's face as one emotion replaced another.

"Okay, Miss Mary Isabella Carducci, are you ready to talk business? We have a sizable amount of money sitting on the table. I'm sure you're entitled to some, maybe all, of it. Let's negotiate now and finalize later."

CHAPTER THIRTY-SEVEN

Dash sat on the glider sofa on the back porch. He gently rocked it, smiling down at Mae whose head rested on his lap.

"So there you have it. Izzy and I came to an agreement about the estate. The bulk will go into a fund, trust or otherwise, for the students at St. Pat's. We're not just looking at the education aspect but also if they need basic necessities, like shoes, winter coats, etc. You get the idea."

He shifted his seat and continued. "After lunch, the Carduccis followed us over to Maud's house. Danny and the gang were working so introductions were made. I handed the keys to Izzy. Leon ran across the street and I informed her that Leon was part of her inheritance, stressing her job was to make sure he went to school every day. That sparked the teacher gene in her so she was all over him. We were going to visit the gravesite, but it started to rain. I invited the whole street out to Clover Pointe for the Memorial Day picnic. Anything to boost attendance."

He smiled down at Mae.

"Is she in love with you?" Mae asked, looking up.

"I suppose so. I seem to have that effect on women. Not sure why. Though it might be my brilliant blue eyes, rugged good looks, sharp wit, or that hint of danger I exude …"

Mae sat up, cocked her head, and sniffed. "Exude like the scent of onions after you've had too many on your burger. No, I think you're on the wrong track. All that stuff is okay but what really gets women is your humility. 'Humble Hambone,' that's what we called you in high school."

Dash scoffed, "Yeah, when you weren't calling me something obscene." He sighed. "Did I tell you I've set up a series of meetings with Owen, the Carduccis and Maud's lawyers. The sooner we get this through probate, the better. I think Izzy and I are on the right path with the money. She taught there and understands their needs. The rest Izzy and I will split, after we deduct the cost of the house from her split."

"Does this include that hundred grand, pal? Have you rolled that into the estate or is it sitting in your sock drawer?"

"Seriously, what do *you* think?"

Mae leaned back, looking out over the backyard where T.J. and the dogs were rolling around in the mud. "It's already in the pot, isn't it? I mean, Owen is the executor and you won't do anything to smudge his good name, even if it means the children and I go barefoot."

"With all the shoes you have in the closet, half of Clover Pointe could be shod. Yes, my darling, I factored in all that when I made my decision. Owen's name and reputation are very important to him and so I must do the right and honorable thing. Besides, I can always rob Izzy later if I have to," he said grinning. He glanced at T.J. and the dogs layering mud upon mud. "I'd better save him. One of these days he's going to meet a dog he doesn't know and will get his little butt bit. Wait 'til I tell him that Leon is coming here Saturday. He'll be thrilled to meet the great Leon, savior of Marlowe Street."

Mae snuggled closer. "Personally I can't wait to meet this Izzy character. We can compare notes on why we both love you."

Dash pushed her away. "You say the daftest things." He yelled to T.J. and the dogs. "Let's get cleaned up. I understand we're watching a movie tonight. Ten hut, double time troops. You grab the kid and throw him in the tub and I'll wash the dogs off outside. Throw all his clothes in the washer and I'll get it going. See you upstairs."

After washing the dogs, Dash took his muddy clothes and tossed them in the washer. He showered downstairs, making sure he also brushed his teeth and gargled away the onion. Let's see what Mae thought now! Wearing only a towel wrapped around his waist, Dash made his way into the bedroom. "Where's T.J.? Here I was ready to watch *Cars* for the umpteenth time.."

"Little guy practically fell asleep in the tub. We're doing the movie tomorrow night. Suits me better." Mae snuggled back into the pillows. "Drop that towel, you sexy thing, and show me what you got."

Always one to follow orders, Dash did as he was told.

CHAPTER THIRTY-EIGHT

Dash leaned against a tree watching the picnickers ebb and flow. He paid special attention to his son and his new best friend, Leon the Great from Marlowe Street. A muzzled Charlie Dog lay at Dash's feet, looking very sad, wearing a vest declaring him to be a support animal, not the guard dog he was.

The Memorial Day picnic was in full swing.

"Hey, Hammond. You look mighty serious for a guy at a picnic," Detective Kraft said as he and a beautiful woman walked up to Dash.

Dash looked from the rumpled detective to the woman who wore a pristine white tee shirt and matching shorts. Not a speck of dirt or mud on them.

"Are you always on guard? You keep looking like you're afraid of an imminent attack from any side," Kraft chuckled.

"Old habits die hard. Truth be told I'm not all that comfortable with crowds, even here in my hometown. All someone has to do is set off a firecracker, and you'll see how fast this old soldier can duck and run." He stuck out his hand to shake Kraft's. "I didn't know you were coming. A nice surprise," he said, nodding a hello to the lady. "An introduction would be nice. I don't want to put my foot in my mouth with any number of assumptions."

"Assume away, but this is my wife." Kraft turned to her and continued. "Darling, this is the man I've been telling you about. Carol, Dash Hammond. Dash, my long-suffering wife, Carol."

Kraft sidled up to Dash and joined in watching the picnickers.

Dash nodded in the direction of T.J. and Leon. "I'm keeping my eye on those two over there. The small one wearing the Army tee shirt belongs to me and ..."

"Is that Leon? How'd he get out here?"

"Just wait." Dash pointed to his right. "Three o'clock. That's my wife, as you know, and the lady with her is none other than Maud Grealis' daughter, Mary Isabella Carducci. She prefers Izzy and is taking over Maud's house. As you know, Leon comes with it."

The trio turned to greet Mae and Izzy.

Izzy reached out to Dash. "Thank you so much for letting me go through Maud's things. I'm taking one box for now but will relieve you of the rest after the house on Marlowe Street is habitable." Izzy's gaze followed everyone else's. "Oh, how are Leon and T.J. getting along?"

Just as she finished the sentence the two miscreants came tearing over to them.

T. J. huffed and puffed, leaning over and pulling on his shorts just like he'd seen the out-of-breath basketball players do. Leon stood behind him with a shy smile on his face.

"Daddy, I've been thinking." T.J. motioned for his father to bend down. Dash squatted down in front of his son.

"You thinking is good for you and trouble for me. Spill it son, what's bouncing around in your little head?"

"Well, as you know, I'm getting a little sister and I don't have anything to say about it. Well, you have a big brother, right?"

"Yes, Uncle Sammy."

"So, Daddy, I'm thinking that I could use a big brother like you have. And I think Leon would be the best big brother ever. And if he can be my brother, you won't even have to get me a pony or anything. Leon won't be any trouble. He likes to read, too."

Dash glanced at Leon who just shrugged. "T.J., that's a pretty big decision. Don't you think Leon's mother might object?"

T.J. shook his head. "Nah, she's never home. I bet she wouldn't even miss him. And I sure could use him."

Dash stood up and said, "T.J., *I'm* thinking we're going to table this until tomorrow when we can discuss all the ramifications."

The look on T.J.'s face revealed what he thought of this. He turned to Leon, "When he says discuss, that means no." He shifted from foot to foot and then stuck out his hand. "We need more money."

"Get a job. What happened to what I gave you?"

Leon spoke up. "Mister, I still have some money. I'm going to buy my mom a vase I saw in one of the booths. T.J. won a bunch of stuff. It's in a bag over at Mr. Johnson's booth. I don't need any more money, sir. You've been very generous, letting me get all those books from your bookstore."

Dash looked at his son. "You hear that, T.J.? Leon knows how to save money and even how to say 'thank you.'"

T.J. gave his dad the stinkeye and then frowned at Leon. Grabbing his hand, he said, "Let's go." He yelled bye over his shoulder.

The adults watched the kids run away.

Mae said, "Five will get you ten he's back with another proposition. Remember we're not trading the baby for Leon." She crossed her arms over her chest waiting for her husband's reply.

"No, his next proposition will be that he moves in with Leon and asks me to provide a subsidy for his food and clothes. My son is very aware of his comforts." Dash turned to Kraft. "You have any kids?"

Carol spoke up. "You think you have trouble. Try having triplets, all boys, about a year older than your T.J. We should get them together and they can take over the world while we sit quietly watching the grass grow."

"Triplets! Dear God, no wonder you work such long hours," Dash said to Kraft.

His wife said, "Yes, I noticed that."

"Where are they now? Not running wild, are they? I have only so many men patrolling the place."

Kraft spoke up, "Nah, we chained them up in the basement" Then he said, "Actually my mother-in-law has them. She only had girls and thinks these renegades are cute. We'll see what she says tonight unless she calls and begs us to come home early."

Dash changed the subject by announcing he was hungry. "I'll get the kids and we'll fill their bellies. I've reserved a table near the hall."

He reached for Charlie's leash. "Up boy, we're going to follow Huck Finn and his little brother to minimize the damage. Lunch should distract them. Ladies, Kraft, shall we?"

"Do you really need the support dog? Or is it just a ploy for sympathy?" Kraft asked.

Mae jumped in. "Yes, he does need support, from a dog or anything that helps him through events like this. He loves his fellow townspeople, but one by one, not in large crowds. But duty calls so he comes and smiles." She raised her voice and stood at attention. "Duty! Above all! The brotherhood and all that ..."

Dash turned to Mae, saying sharply, "Don't. Not now, not ever. Until you ..." He didn't finish the sentence since a couple of young teens called to him. They held up a football, yelling, "Two o'clock, Coach, remember you promised."

"Coach? I heard you played a bit in college but you're coaching now. Hey, why didn't you turn pro?" Kraft asked.

"You'll not understand this but I didn't want to get killed by those gigantic defensive men," Dash said.

"So, let me get this straight. Instead of *possibly* getting killed in pro football, you signed up for the Army where you *probably* could get killed. Defies logic."

Mae held up her hand. "There were many decisions in his life that defy logic, and a lot of extenuating circumstances.

Sometime when you have nothing, and I mean *nothing* to do, we can sit down and I'll bore you with the details."

Kraft laughed. "Fair enough. Now let's get some chow. Hey, what did your son mean about getting a little sister? Adoption in your future?"

"No, we have a surrogate named Sue who is about to pop, two weeks at the most. You'll need to talk to the doctor here to understand all this surrogacy entails. But I'm about to be the proud papa of, I hope and pray, a very healthy baby girl," Dash said.

Dash gathered the group and guided them to a table with a reserved sign on it. Under a tree, the shade welcomed the adults. Dash sat at the head of the table, Charlie Dog at his feet. Leon jockeyed for a spot next to his hero, Dash.

After taking off Charlie's muzzle, Dash pulled out a water dish and bottle from his backpack so he could refresh the dog. Ruffling his dog's fur, he asked Charlie if he wanted a burger or some chicken tenders.

Dash took orders from everyone, then he and Kraft went over to the food truck and gathered everything. It took several trips back and forth to get the food and drinks. Once everyone had a plate in front of them, the men sat down to eat.

"This is quite good," said Carol. "Do you have special recipes? Definite step up from what one usually gets at these affairs."

Leon tugged at Dash's shirt sleeve. "Mister, I want to thank you for letting me come out. This picnic is a lot of fun. I especially enjoyed seeing the ambulance and police car. And I even got to climb on the fire engine. T.J. asked a lot of questions but the fireman didn't seem to mind."

"Yeah, we thought it was a good idea – a chance for kids to get up close with these men and women. You get a better sense of what these folks do."

He turned to T.J. "I've been thinking about what you said and I have a compromise. How about if Leon comes out a few times this summer and spends a bit of time with us? Only if his mom says okay. What do you think?"

T.J. jumped up. "That's great. Is it okay with you, Leon?"

Leon's eyes almost popped out of his head. "Great. Yes, I'm sure my ma won't mind."

T.J. scooted over and then patted the seat next to him. "Sit here and we can plan all the things we're going to do."

Leon obliged after asking Dash if he could change seats.

Dash looked at Mae who subtlety shook her head. She mouthed 'softie.' He ignored her and started telling Kraft about the fund-raising aspect of the picnic and all the veteran charities it helped support.

The adults chit-chatted for the next hour while T.J. and Leon squirmed eager to get back to the games.

Glancing at his watch, Dash announced it was time for him to put on his football cap. The ladies decided to remain behind but Kraft, T.J. and Leon decided to follow.

Dash's role was that of referee. He decided not to embarrass himself by joining the younger men running and pulling out flags. He said in an aside to Kraft, "It's been a good while since I did all that twisting and turning. Mae would kill me if I got hurt. God forbid I should twist an ankle or break a leg. That homicide would be the easiest of your career."

The game was in full swing when Dash felt his phone vibrating. He pulled it out of his pocket and glanced at the screen: Billy Mac. 'Now what' drifted through Dash's mind. He blew the whistle and indicated a referee's time out. He trotted over to the sideline and punched the button to accept the call.

"Okay, Billy, my love, what are you doing interrupting me during a football game?"

Dash's face fell when he heard Billy say, "Don't blame the messenger. Sue's water broke and it might behoove you and Mae to get your fine asses down here."

"Is Elena phoning Mae now, or do I have time?"

"What do you think?"

Dash rang off and motioned for the teams to gather round. He told them of his emergency. Slumped shoulders all around. Then the good wishes began.

Dash trotted off the field, gathering Kraft, T.J., and Leon. He explained the situation to them.

"I have a good mind to just finish the game and Delia Rose can just wait. I don't want to begin this relationship with her calling the shots. Sets a bad example."

T.J. tugged at his father's pants, pulling him down to eye level. "Daddy, you can't do that to that baby. She doesn't know how to walk or read. What will she do? And you know Mommy will be upset if you don't get her." He put his nose right up to Dash's. "Daddy, you have me to play with but Mommy has no one. If we don't get this baby, she'll continue fussing with us. Do you want that?"

"Hell, no. Let's find Grandpa and get this show on the road."

CHAPTER THIRTY-NINE

The house was eerily quiet after all the earlier fuss over the newest member of the Hammond family. Dash stood in the living room and surveyed the mess: wrapping paper everywhere, ribbon on top of that, baby gifts (unnecessary since he was the totally efficient dad who brought in supplies of everything the baby would need until high school) and dirty dishes on every conceivable surface.

A movement caught his eye and he realized Mae was standing at the kitchen sink gazing out the window.

"Hey, sweetheart, I thought you were going to get some sleep. Why aren't you upstairs tucked into bed?" he asked.

When she turned he saw the tears in her eyes. He opened his arms and she crossed to him, wrapping herself tightly around him.

"Dash, I'm scared, I'm terrified. What if …"

He kissed the top of her head. "What if …what if Delia *doesn't* die like Gracie? Delia is as strong as a linebacker. She will outlive us for sure." He held his wife at arm's length. "You're overtired, and all this …" he swept his arm over the remains of the party, "isn't helping. I must apologize for the way my family ignored my plea for a few days of quiet to help us settle in."

"They're just as happy as we are about the baby. I'll be fine. I just need to take a few deep breaths every time Delia closes her eyes."

The back door opened quietly. Billy Mac and his wife Elena started to creep in, but stopped when they saw Dash and Mae.

"Why aren't you two sleeping? I mean I was on my best quiet behavior so you guys could relax a bit." Billy glanced around. "Mind if I ask where the baby is? I mean there was a baby here several hours ago."

Dash smiled. "Delia is fast asleep in her bassinet in the front bedroom. T.J. is asleep on the bed. I just got up and found Mae here."

"So let me get this straight. You left a newborn babe under the care of a four-year-old. I obviously missed that chapter in my parenting manuals," Billy said.

"Nothing ..." Before Dash could finish, they heard a baby yowl and the door to the front bedroom flung open.

T.J. marched out, hands held high. "I didn't touch her. She just woke up screaming."

Mae pulled free from Dash so she could run to the baby. Elena followed.

"Aren't you going?" asked Billy.

"No, Mae needs time with Delia. She's having a few issues now that we actually have the babe in our arms."

"If you don't want her, I get first dibs," Billy said.

T.J. had flopped down in one of the kitchen chairs. "I'm starving. Do we have any cake left?"

Dash joined him at the table while Billy moved to open the fridge. Leaning in, Billy reported on the contents. "We have tuna salad, egg salad, three different types of pasta salad, one could be macaroni salad, a garden salad."

"Ah, my sister the salad queen provided well. I don't suppose my sister-in-law, the real cook in the family, brought over any lasagna or spaghetti with meat balls?"

T. J. said, "I'll have cake."

Both Dash and Billy said, "No."

"Is there any cold chicken? I bet he'll eat a drumstick or chicken finger if any are left," Dash said as he smiled at his son.

"Coming right up," Cousin Billy said and proceeded to produce two well-filled plates.

Dash looked around. "If I wasn't so hungry, I'd start on cleanup. Hey, T. J., would you like to make some money? If you help Uncle Billy, I'll pay you ten bucks."

"And what does Uncle Billy get for all his hard work?" Billy asked.

"The undying gratitude of your poor penniless cousin."

Mae, carrying Delia, and Elena joined them.

"Miss Delia is changed, sweet-smelling, but hungry. So, we're going to feed her. After you eat T.J., would you like to hold her?" Mae asked.

T.J. shook his head. "No way, her head might fall off. And if she bites you, she'll take your finger. Jaws like a snapping turtle."

All the adults looked at him in amazement.

"Did you just make that up or did someone tell you that?" asked Dash.

"Grampa. He told me not to mess with the baby."

Dash put his head in his hands, praying silently to the patron saint of patience. He looked at T.J. saying, "We'll talk about all that after you clean the kitchen."

Elena asked Mae if she would like her to take the gifts upstairs as part of the clearing up effort. Mae nodded as she fed the bottle to Delia.

Dash cleaned his plate and offered to hold the baby so Mae could get some sustenance. They later moved to the sofa to cuddle with Delia.

"Listen, Maevis, Delia is ready for another nap. How about we retire to the front bedroom where you can curl up next to me? The baby will be by our side, and you can fall asleep knowing I'll keep my eye on her. What do you think? Can you finally relax?"

Mae nodded. "I'm about to fall over now so I must be getting close to a relaxed state. Pretty sure if I'm in your arms, all will be well."

Dash told Billy of the new plan. Billy suggested they put in one of the tapes of Dash's old college football games, adding that these always put him to sleep.

Mae settled Delia in her bassinet and then settled herself on the bed with Dash by her side.

"We are going to be alright, aren't we?" she whispered to her husband.

"Absolutely, guaranteed. Now close those green eyes. I'll do a play by play."

The couple snuggled together. Dash had one eye on the baby now sleeping. He pressed the remote and his first Ohio State game sprung to life on the screen. He looked down at Mae who was also sleeping. His eyes drifted back to the screen just in time to see a very young #87 score his first touchdown. He smiled at the memory, just another thing to share with his curly-haired daughter. Yes, everything would be just fine.

About The Author

Elaine Munsch, a native of Cleveland, Ohio, has divided her adult life between that state and Kentucky. She graduated from Nazareth College of Kentucky located outside of Bardstown, and close to her maternal grandfather's home in Balltown. She attended The Ohio State University doing work for a Masters in English Literature. In 1972, she embarked on her life-long passion, that of bookselling. In 1995, she moved from Cleveland to Louisville to open the first Barnes & Noble in Kentucky. She set up a mystery reading group, taught classes in the mystery genre for the Veritas Society and joined the local chapter of Sisters in Crime.

With Susan Bell, she co-edited Mystery with a Splash of Bourbon, an anthology of bourbon-related crime stories for the chapter.

She writes the Dash Hammond series set on the shores of Lake Erie. OLD SINS is the seventh book in this series.

Acknowledgments

First, I must give thanks to my Sisters in Crime critique group: Susan Bell, Leanne Edelen, Pam Hirschler, Miki Reilly-Howe and Sherry Youngquist. Their advice made this a better book.

Secondly, my wonderful circle of friends and readers: Theresa Berry, Wanda Brooks, Mary Kay Quigley Branton and, of course, long-time friend, researcher and encourager, Laura Barda Thomas.

Thirdly, thank you to Sarah Glenn and Gwen Mayo for taking on another of my Dash books.

Fourthly, a nod to all my cousins who support me at all my signings. What a fun group.

Finally, I must again thank my daughter, Kristin, who may just shake her head at my imaginings but always has my back.